Once Found:

The Pocket Watch Chronicles

By
Ceci Giltenan

This is a work of fiction. The characters, incidents, locations and dialogues in this book are of the author's imagination and are not to be construed as real. Any resemblance to actual events or persons, living or dead, is completely coincidental. Any actual locations mentioned in this book are used fictitiously.

No part of this book may be reproduced or transmitted in any form or by any means, electronic or mechanical, including photocopying, recording, or by any information storage and retrieval system, without permission in writing from the author.

Duncurra LLC

www.duncurra.com

Copyright 2016 by Ceci Giltenan

ISBN-10:1-942623-37-2

ISBN-13:978-1-942623-37-3

Cover Art by Earthly Charms

Produced in the USA

Praise for Ceci Giltenan

"Few authors touch hearts so deeply."
- *Sue-Ellen Welfonder, USA Today Bestselling Author*

"Fine historical romance writing at its best."
- *Suzan Tisdale, Bestselling Author of Scottish Romance*

"Ceci Giltenan continues to leave me spellbound weaving her trail of exceptional books that are absolutely magnificent the ones that stay with you long after you have read it."
- *Barbara, Tartan Book Reviews*

"Ceci Giltenan tells beautiful stories with strong characters and an intriguing storylines"
- *Lily Baldwin, Bestselling Author of Scottish Romance*

Other Books by Ceci Giltenan

The Fated Heart Series

(Available as digital, paperback and audio books)

Highland Revenge, Book 1

Highland Echoes, Book 2

Highland Angels, Book 3

The Duncurra Series

(Available as digital, paperback and audio books)

Highland Solution, Book 1

Highland Courage, Book 2

Highland Intrigue Book 3

The Pocket Watch Chronicles

(Available as digital, paperback and audio books)

The Pocket Watch

The Midwife

Once Found

Coming Soon:

The Christmas Present
The Choice

Dedication

To Natalie Vincent, my dearest friend. I have so much to thank you for.

Thank you for being another mother to my children. For making pasta and reindeer food with them. For being there when I couldn't be. For kicking their arses occasionally when needed and for loving them as only a mother can.

Thank you for Christmas dinners and birthday dinners and just-because-you-made-extra dinners. Thank you for decorations and silly hats and traditions.

Thank you for your help with this book and for allowing me to name Gabriel's mother Natalie in your honor.

But most of all, thank you for your steadfast love, faith, and eternal friendship.

And, as always, to my beloved Eamon, the heart of my heart..

Acknowledgements

The devil is in the details, and I like to get them right as often as I can.

I owe a huge thank you to my friend and colleague, Dr. Brian Murphy, MD, MPH, FIDSA, who not only helped make sure the emergency medical details were accurate, but also explained the residency matching process.

Many thanks to my dear friend, Paul Vincent, my expert on all things related to EMS. Thank you also for your years of service as a Fire Commissioner and volunteer firefighter.

Another big thank you goes to my cousin Gerald Bowen, who helped me understand certain police procedures. Also, thank you for your years of service as both a police officer and a US Marine.

And finally, a sincere thank you to Mostafa Alami of the New York City Cab Company, who provided information on how luggage left in a cab would normally be handled.

Glossary

Bairn	(BAIRn) A baby
Canonical hours	The medieval day was ordered by these times rather than clock times: Vigil, Matins, Lauds, Prime, Terce, Sext, None, Vespers, Compline
Carraigile	(Kah rah GEEL) the name of the fictional MacKenzie stronghold
none	(rhymes with bone) Literally the ninth hour, about 3 in the afternoon
sweetling	An endearment

Note to the reader

The snowstorm described in this novel really did occur in February 2006. It is referred to as the Blizzard of 2006, and it dumped a record amount of snow on Manhattan from the evening of the 11th to the evening of the 12th. For a while, the storm was so intense that it thundered. As I mention in the book, no one died as a result of this storm.

That said, while the snowstorm is real, as far as I know, there wasn't a major accident on I-495 during the storm. Also, the hospital portrayed, New York University Hospital Center (referred to as NYUHC) is completely fictitious. It is not intended to represent any actual New York City hospital. Why didn't I set it at a real hospital? I needed a twenty-first century hospital in Manhattan that treated both adults and children, and in most major cities, pediatric care is now provided in dedicated pediatric facilities.

I could have given Gabe some other specialty, but look at him. Doesn't he look like he should be a pediatrician?

Love is our true destiny. We do not find the meaning of life by ourselves alone—we find it with another.

~ Tomas Merton

Chapter 1

Gabriel Soldani had worked twelve-hour shifts for seven straight nights, and he'd had big plans today.

Sleep.

Maybe get a pizza in the evening and watch a little of the winter Olympics. Then sleep some more.

He had accomplished part of his primary objective. After getting back to his apartment late that morning, he fell into bed and slept the afternoon away. He'd only been awake long enough to shower and flip on the television when Dr. Sweeny, the chief of pediatrics, called.

"I'm sorry to interrupt your Saturday night plans. Call your date and give her my apologies, but this nor'easter looks like it's going to be a bad one. I want extra staff tonight. I'd like you to back up the ER."

"My date? The only date I have is with the Swedish women's Olympic hockey team. They'll get over it."

His boss chuckled. "I should introduce you to my niece."

Gabe rolled his eyes. "You'll need to get in line behind my mother if you want to set me up on a date."

"Is Mama Soldani anxious for grandchildren?"

"That's putting it mildly."

"Well, I guess it's a good thing you don't have a date anyway. She'd be pissed at having to spend a snowy Saturday night alone."

"No doubt. But there's always makeup sex."

"Don't let Mama Soldani hear you say that."

"Not in this lifetime."

His boss laughed. "When do you think you can get here?"

"Give me about forty-five minutes."

"Christ, Gabe, you only live ten minutes away and that's walking."

"I need to pick something up on the way."

He guessed his mother's desire to feed people had rubbed off on him because the "something" he needed to pick up was a stack of pizzas for the staff, from his favorite hole in the wall. Although his mother would have managed to whip up a lasagna or baked ziti instead of buying pizza. Still, he'd had his heart set on pizza, and food from outside the hospital was always greeted with elation. Tonight was no different.

In spite of Dr. Sweeny's worries, it was unusually quiet. There hadn't been a major influx of pediatric patients and when Gabe arrived, Davis, the pediatrician scheduled to work, had things well in hand. Gabe kicked back in the lounge with a slice and watched a little of the Olympic coverage anyway.

However, a few hours later, all hell broke loose. There was a huge pile-up on the 495. Thankfully, no seriously injured kids had been brought in so far, so Gabe pitched in to help with other victims as ambulances arrived.

An emergency medical technician hopped out of an ambulance and started giving report while unloading a stretcher. The patient was strapped to a backboard and wearing a rigid cervical collar. "Hey, Doc, crazy night. We have an unresponsive female in her late twenties with a presumed head injury. She has some swelling on the back of her head but no severe, gross trauma. Her vital signs are stable, pupils equal and reactive to light. She's banged up— bruised and minor lacerations. Most of the blood is from a small laceration above her left eye and it's already stopped bleeding. It looks like she might have a broken left arm and maybe some broken ribs. We stabilized her spine. I started a twenty gauge in her right forearm and hung lactated Ringers."

Gabe frowned. "She's completely unresponsive?"

"Yup, even to painful stimulus. She's a three on the Glasgow coma scale."

He started giving orders as they rolled her to an exam room. "Shelly, start another line and send blood for a CBC and chem panel. Get a tox screen and blood alcohol too. And let's get a Foley in." He asked the EMT, "Was she driving?"

"No, she was in the back passenger side of a cab. The impact was to the rear driver's side. She was wearing a seatbelt. "

Gabe grabbed an ophthalmoscope from the wall and double-checked her pupillary responses before assessing her optic fundi for signs of increased intracranial pressure. He took a step back so she could be moved from the ambulance stretcher to the hospital gurney and looked at her, taking in her appearance for the first time. "Jesus Christ. Get Chuck in here."

"What's the matter, Gabe?" asked one of the nurses.

"If he's free, I'd rather not treat her. I know her. Her name is Elizabeth Quinn. Dr. Elizabeth Quinn. She's an old girlfriend."

~ * ~

It was midmorning before things finally quieted down and Gabe could take a break. He sat alone in the lounge, drinking a bad cup of coffee and thinking about Elizabeth. Of course, he hadn't been able to get her off his mind from the moment he'd recognized her. Hell, it had taken several years to stop thinking about her after the last time he saw her: the day they graduated.

The door opened and his friend, Chuck, Dr. Charles Zaminisky, walked in. Gabe really didn't want to talk about this, but it was too much to hope that Chuck would let it drop.

"So, an old girlfriend."

"Yup."

"Did you say you knew her from medical school?"

"Yup."

"According to her driver's license, she just turned twenty-eight last week."

"Yup."

"You're five years older."

"Yup."

"Damn it, Gabe, could you say something more than 'yup'? How could you have dated her in medical school? Was she an undergrad?"

Gabe sighed. "No, she was in my class. She wasn't your typical med student. For that matter, she's not your typical anything. She was one of those genius kids who sailed through high school and college in record time. She was eighteen when we started med school, but no one knew how young she was for ages."

"How the hell is that possible? Teenagers are...well, teenagers."

"She didn't look like a teenager. You saw her. She's only about five three, but she's always had curves." Luscious, womanly curves that Gabe had adored. "She's looked pretty much like that for the last ten years. Plus, she didn't dress like a teenager. I don't think I ever saw her in jeans until after I started dating her. She always wore sharp, business-like clothes."

"Yeah but, *like*, an eighteen-year-old girl, in *like* medical school? How could you *like*, not know...*like*?" Chuck gave his best imitation of a particularly annoying teenager.

"She didn't act young, either. In class or clinical environments, she was the picture of confidence. Not in the cocky, competitive way. She was smart and quiet. She never volunteered anything, but if she was asked a question, she always knew the answer. I mean *always*. I never saw anyone trip her up. All in all, she transmitted a no-nonsense, I'm-going-places-stay-out-of-my-way kind of vibe. And most people did stay out of her way."

"When did you find out how old she was?"

"That bomb didn't drop until the end of our second year. She was in my clinical rotation group. Rotations were over, and we decided to go out to a local bar to celebrate. We'd done it before, but Elizabeth had always begged off. We were determined not to let her that night. We kept insisting, and she kept trying to say no. George Reed, a total dick, finally said: 'If the princess can't pull the stick out of her ass long enough to have a drink with us, to hell with her.'"

"A little harsh."

"Yeah. She turned several shades of red, looking uncharacteristically vulnerable, and said 'I'm not twenty-one, so they won't let me in the bar.' Then she just turned and walked away."

"Why'd she keep it such a secret?"

"I think she didn't want the attention. She just wanted to keep her head down and become a doctor. She didn't want to be Doogie Howser."

"I can see someone wanting to do that. And I'll bet the dick called her Doogie from that moment on."

"Princess Doogie, actually."

"Why princess?"

"As it turns out, George had asked her out earlier in the year, and she'd declined. It couldn't have been because she was young and he was a dick, so he decided because she drove a '96 Audi A4 and wore nice clothes, she thought she was too good for him."

"It sounds like she *was* too good for him, but then again, she was probably too good for *you*."

"Thanks."

"Don't mention it. But she dated you anyway?"

"Yeah. To this day, I think she is one of the most attractive women I've ever met. I finally got the courage to ask her out and she said yes. And she kept saying yes. It turns out, I was her first boyfriend."

"Wow. I don't think I've ever been anyone's first."

"It does make things different. At least it did for me. I fell head over heels."

"What happened?"

"You know how important family is to me. I talked about my family all of the time. She always appeared interested and asked questions. I took her to visit one weekend. She seemed to really enjoy it, and they liked her."

"And her family?"

"That was the problem. Every time her family came up in conversation, she sidestepped it. The only thing I really knew was that her parents lived in Baltimore and she was an only child."

"Was she ashamed of them?"

"I think she was ashamed of me. They came for graduation. Two parents, four grandparents. Whereas, my whole big Italian family was there. She was the valedictorian, so she was on the dais with the VIPs. We didn't meet up until afterward, but I'd learned who she really was by then. Turns out, she *was* a princess. At least the closest thing to it in America. The whispers began circulating before the ceremony started."

"Who is she?"

"Alastair Matheson's granddaughter."

"Alastair Matheson as in Matheson & Matheson, one of the largest law firms in the country?"

"Yup. Her mother is Charlotte Matheson Quinn, the other half of Matheson & Matheson. But it doesn't stop there—she's in the medical aristocracy, too. Her other grandfather is Dr. Giles Quinn, a pioneer in cardiac surgery."

"*Damn*. So her dad is James Quinn?"

"Yup, another key opinion leader in thoracic surgery."

"How the hell did she keep that quiet?"

"The same way she kept her age quiet: she just didn't tell anyone. Jesus, the administration didn't even know. They were falling all over themselves when they realized it that day. She finally introduced me after the ceremony at the reception."

"What were they like?"

"Polite and cold. Her father asked about my residency. He clearly wasn't impressed with my answer. After a few minutes of small talk, they said they had to be going."

"What did she do?"

"She asked me to wait for her and walked them to the door, where they appeared to have a very heated discussion. Then she came back, said she had to go with them, but that she wanted to see me later. By the time we met up that evening, I was pretty pissed. I could understand her not telling the whole school, but not telling me? I broke up with her. We were doing our residencies in different cities anyway. It wouldn't have worked."

"Did she give you any reasons for keeping it from you?"

"Yeah, she had all kinds of reasons, but nothing shatters the illusion of love like discovering your lover has kept her whole life hidden from you."

"I'm sorry, man."

"Well, she wasn't the first girl I'd loved and lost, but hopefully she'll be the last."

"You haven't been serious about anyone since then?"

"Nope. But not for lack of effort on my mother's part." Gabe drained his coffee cup before asking, "So, how is Elizabeth?"

"You know I shouldn't tell you anything."

"You know I can just look in the computer. I ordered the initial tests." His friend frowned at him. "Chuck, I'm worried about her. Give me something."

Chuck sighed. "Well, there's nothing really to tell. Her labs are all fine. Some of the toxicology won't be back until tomorrow, but her blood alcohol is zero and urine was negative for drugs of abuse. The x-rays of the chest, arms, and pelvis revealed a simple fracture of the left ulna and uncomplicated fractures of her eighth and ninth ribs on the right side. No pneumothorax. The results of the head and neck CTs weren't back when we transferred her to ICU. At that time, there were still no signs of increased intracranial pressure. Her vital signs were stable, she seemed to have normal deep tendon reflexes bilaterally, and negative Babinski. The neuro assessment was basically normal…except that she was still completely unresponsive."

"Has anyone contacted her family?"

"She has an Ohio license. The police ran it, but she has no registered next-of-kin or emergency contact. Do her parents still live in Baltimore?"

"I suspect so. I think her dad is on staff at Hopkins."

"I'll let the police know and they can go through their channels. I'll also go call the ICU and let them know who she is…and by that, I mean who her *family* is."

Chuck left, and Gabe's thoughts turned back to Elizabeth and the night they broke up. She had left a message on his machine. "Hey, Gabe, give me a call when you get this or just come over. It doesn't matter what time it is. Or if you want me to, I'll come to your place. Okay, I'll see you later."

He had gone to her apartment. She lived alone, and he had nosy roommates. When she opened the door, she had smiled, looking both relieved and genuinely pleased to see him.

"Come in, Dr. Soldani."

He hadn't been in the mood. He strode in past her. "Cut the shit, Elizabeth."

That had wiped the smile off her face. She motioned to the couch. "Have a seat. Can I get you something to drink?"

"Well, aren't you the lovely hostess, but no, I don't want a drink and I don't feel like sitting down."

Hurt had flashed across her face, but she masked it quickly. Clearly, she had a lot of practice hiding things. "I'm sorry, Gabe."

"You're sorry? For what? That I found out the truth? All the times when I asked about your family, you didn't feel the need to tell me who they were? I don't understand what the

Ceci Giltenan

big secret was about anyway."

"You don't? Really? It was bad enough when everyone found out how old I was. What do you think it would have been like if they knew my mother and grandfather own a multibillion-dollar law firm, and my father and his father are celebrated surgeons? No one would ever have taken me seriously again. They would have assumed I'd gotten where I am because of *connections*. Christ almighty, did you see the way the VIPs acted around them today?"

"I'm your boyfriend, Elizabeth. We're lovers, and you didn't think you could trust me with that information?

"It isn't that. I just wanted to keep that part of my life separate as long as I could."

"I repeat: we're lovers. You know everything about me. How could you keep something this big from me? Were you afraid I'd ask to meet them? Were you afraid I'd embarrass you?"

"No, Gabe. I was afraid *they'd* embarrass me. And they did."

"Oh, I could tell. You left with them."

"I didn't want to, but they're my parents. What was I supposed to do?"

"You were supposed to be honest with me about who you were before the entire university knew."

"I never dreamed they'd show up."

"What the hell, Elizabeth? You were graduating from med school. You were the freaking valedictorian for the love of God."

"You don't understand—"

"No, I don't."

"Gabe, please listen. My family isn't like yours."

"Clearly."

"But that's why I didn't tell you—or anyone. As long as nobody knew, I was ordinary, just like everyone else. When people know, they change."

"You thought it would change the way I feel about

you?"

"It seems to have."

"Not being honest with me is what changed the way I feel about you."

"I never lied to you."

"I suppose you didn't. You just kept your entire identity hidden."

"My family is not my identity. I am who I am, the person you know."

He had ignored that statement. How could someone's family not be a major part of their identity? "How long did you plan to keep it a secret? Maybe you intended to spring it on me on our wedding day?"

She had just stood there and stared. Looking back on it now, he realized she'd looked exactly as she had the night she told them she wasn't twenty-one: young and vulnerable. And he'd been too much of a self-righteous prick to notice. Instead of trying to understand her, he'd said, "Right. Well, we're going off to different residencies anyway. I suppose this was destined to end. I'm heading back to New Jersey tonight. Have a nice life, Elizabeth."

Chapter 2

Elsie stepped into the great hall at Castle Macrae and stood just inside the door, letting the joy of the celebration wash over her. The feast was over, but that didn't matter. This is what she loved the most: the merriment, the high spirits, and, most especially, the music and dancing.

Her friend Adaira, one of the serving maids at the castle, spied her instantly and hurried toward her. "Elsie, where've ye been? Ye missed the feast."

"Effemy went into labor right after the midnight Mass. Aunt Dolina and I were with her all night. She only had the bairn, a lad, about an hour ago."

"They are both well then?"

"Aye, they are. Effemy's tired as ye might expect, but the babe's a big, sturdy lad. Aunt Dolina teased that he ought to be splitting wood by next week."

"Dolina didn't come with ye?"

"Nay, she's too tired and went home to bed. But I didn't want to miss the celebration."

"Well come on then, we need to find partners. Some new minstrels arrived a few days ago and they're particularly talented."

It took little coaxing. Elsie wanted nothing more than to dance. And dance she did. Her feet flew through the familiar patterns as she spun from one partner to the next, giving in to the enchantment of the music.

Several hours later, Elsie was nearly spent. Still, even though the clan would feast and celebrate for eleven more nights, she wasn't ready to leave the music behind. She took a tankard of ale and sat on the floor, resting her back against the wall, just soaking it all in.

Before long, a young man with brown hair, gray eyes, and a shy smile crouched next to her. She recognized him as one of the *particularly talented* minstrels who had been playing earlier.

"Do ye mind if I sit here with ye?"

"Nay, it's fine."

He sat next to her. "My name's Geordie."

"I'm Elsie. Ye and yer friends were wonderful."

"Thank ye."

"I love music."

His smile broadened. "I do too. But what I love most is seeing the pleasure people take from music. When the tune leaves my fingers and reaches the hearts of those listening, it gives me joy. When it stirs their feet and they dance, becoming one with the melody, we are connected in an extraordinary way. It feeds my soul."

She stared at him. He had just put words to everything she felt about music but could never describe. "Aye, it's just so for me. I mean, I can't make music but dancing, letting the music flow through me…there is nothing else like it."

"I have to confess, I've watched ye dancing all night. I've barely been able to take my eyes off ye. Ye're lovely, and when ye dance…I don't think I've ever seen anything more beautiful. I dreaded the last note of every song because it severed that momentary connection between us."

Elsie had never heard such honeyed words, and his sincerity took her breath.

He caressed her cheek with his fingertips. "So beautiful. If only…"

She felt heat rising in her cheeks and an odd fluttering in her belly. "If only what?" Her voice sounded breathy.

He smiled sadly. "'Tis nothing."

Elsie glanced around. The night's celebration was

winding down. "I—I suppose I should be going home. It's late."

"Will ye be here again tomorrow?"

She nodded. "Aye, I will."

He stood and offered her a hand. "I'll look forward to it."

She took his hand, allowing him to help her stand. "So will I. I always do."

"Until tomorrow then." He kissed the back of the hand he still held before letting her go.

She nodded, her blush growing deeper. "Until tomorrow."

She started to walk away, but he stopped her. "Elsie, I was just thinking, we won't be playing until after the feast. Will ye sit with me?"

"Sit with ye?"

"Aye. During the feast."

She smiled. "Aye, I'd like that. I'll look for ye."

~ * ~

Elsie didn't have to wait until the feast to see Geordie again. He was at the St. Stephen's day Mass the next morning. When their eyes met, he smiled broadly and worked his way through the gathered worshipers to stand at her side.

That simple act filled her with warmth.

No words were exchanged other than those required by the liturgy. Still, just as she had experienced a connection to him through the music and dancing the night before, she felt a closeness that was hard to describe.

She had gone to Mass with people her whole life. This was the first time she truly felt a bond with someone while she worshipped.

As they walked out of Mass together, he took her hand in his. Again, she was flooded with warmth.

"Do ye have any work to do before the feast begins

later? I mean are ye free for a while?"

"Aye. I mean, nay, I've no work that needs doing. I'm...free."

"I'm new here. I thought maybe ye'd walk with me. Show me the village."

"I'd be happy to." She cringed a little. She hoped she didn't sound too enthusiastic. He might think her wanton.

His smile was warm and she saw no hint of disapproval. "Good."

They walked through the village, chatting about nothing and everything. She told him she was an orphan and lived with her aunt. "Well, she's not really my aunt, but I call her Aunt Dolina."

He told her about the minstrels he had met there. "Robin and Paul are really great. And Paul's wife has a lovely voice. They asked me to play with them. We just seem to fit well together. I've never had so much fun."

Before long, it was time for the feast to start. They found a spot together at one of the trestle tables. They ate and talked and laughed—Elsie had never enjoyed a feast more.

He disappeared to join the musicians when the feast was over. Just as she had the previous evening, Elsie allowed herself to be lost in music and dancing. And just as he had the previous evening, Geordie sought her out when he was through playing.

Over the next days, she spent more and more time with Geordie. Her heart leapt every time she saw him, and his face spread into the broad, warm smile she was coming to adore.

"Mind yerself there, Elsie," Aunt Dolina told her just before the Feast of Epiphany.

"What do ye mean?"

"That lad's a minstrel. He is full of sweet words and romantic ideas. He has to be to earn a living. But soon enough, he'll be on to the next lass in the next clan, and he'll leave ye with a broken heart. Just make certain he leaves ye with nothing else, ye ken?"

She knew Aunt Dolina was right. Elsie should probably be more careful and guard her heart. He was a minstrel. He was destined to leave. But when she was with him, all thoughts of holding back her heart fled.

When the celebration of Epiphany was winding down, they sat together in a dark corner of the hall in the wee hours of the morning. She was curled up against his side with his arm around her shoulders.

He kissed the top of her head. "Elsie, ye are so lovely. Ye have such a sweet nature and a lively spirit. Ye're ever on my mind. I've never felt like this about anyone. I fear I'm falling in love with ye."

She looked up at him. "I've never felt this way either. But if it's love, why is it something to fear?"

"Ah, lass…" He brushed a wisp of hair from her cheek and then slid his fingers behind her neck, lowering his head to kiss her. He drew back after a moment. "So beautiful," he whispered as if in awe. Leaning down, he planted a soft kiss on one eyelid and then the other. His lips continued their tentative, tender journey. He planted kisses along her temple to her ear. He nibbled her earlobe before nuzzling her neck.

She giggled, causing him to chuckle richly. "Ye're entirely delicious." His lips returned to hers. He caught her lower lip between his teeth and sucked it gently into his mouth.

She opened her mouth, allowing him to deepen the kiss. He slid his hand into her hair, capturing it in his fist and tugging lightly to tip her head back and grant him greater access. When he finally pulled away, they were both breathless.

"I've wanted to do that since the first night I saw ye, lass." He pulled her close, resting his cheek on the top of her head.

"I've never…I've never been kissed."

"I'm glad I was yer first." He stroked her hair and held her.

Elsie had never felt more secure and loved than she did in the circle of Geordie's arms.

Too soon, their intimate moment was interrupted.

"There ye are, Geordie. Sorry to disturb ye." His friend Robin had a mischievous grin on his face, suggesting that he was much more amused than apologetic. "Good news, lad. The laird has asked us to stay until spring."

Geordie smiled at Elsie. "That is excellent news."

"Aye, it means we don't have to trudge into the teeth of winter to find another noble patron for a few weeks." His grin broadened. "I suppose having a warm lassie in yer lap is no harm, either. Good night, Geordie."

Chapter 3

With the feasts between Christmas and Epiphany over, there was no real reason for Elsie to go to the castle every night, but she and Geordie found time together every day. She loved every moment.

It felt as if she had been alone for so long. Elsie's da died when she was very young, and she couldn't remember him clearly. At the time, she hadn't understood what had happened. She remembered crying for him and being told to hush because it upset mama.

It had been much worse when her mama died of an illness that swept through the clan a few years later. Elsie had been a lass of ten by then and remembered crying buckets of tears. But so many people had lost loved ones to that illness, her tears were lost among the flood. She had no one to give her comfort. Elsie soon learned to hold back her grief. Tears had no purpose.

Dolina had taken her in. Elsie called her Aunt Dolina, but she was really a cousin of her father's who was just as alone in the world as Elsie. When Elsie was old enough, Dolina began teaching her healing and midwifery skills. Aunt Dolina provided for her well and cared for her, but perhaps having been alone so long herself, she was a detached, practical woman. She was not given to displays of affection and had little patience for the hopes, fears, and heartaches of her young cousin. Just as Elsie had learned not to cry, she eventually learned to keep her other feelings to herself.

The only time she really let herself go was when she danced. That it was a musician who finally reached her heart and began to set it free didn't come as a surprise. For the first time in years, her soul was fed with love, and she realized she had been starving.

January turned into February, and the affection between Elsie and Geordie grew. Aunt Dolina repeatedly warned her about the folly of loving a minstrel. "Wake up, lass. He will leave ye. *He will.*"

Elsie didn't tell her aunt that it would only take one word from Geordie for her to go with him. What's more, Elsie believed he would ask. The previous evening, she had slipped into the great hall to hear the minstrels perform for the laird. Afterward, when they had a few private moments, Geordie clearly had something on his mind.

"Geordie, what's bothering ye? Ye seem distracted."

"Aye, I suppose I am. There's something we need to talk about, love. Something I need to tell ye. I need to know yer thoughts."

"Ye can tell me anything."

He started several times, but seemed to have trouble finding the words. Before he could finish, one of the lassies from the village entered the hall looking for Elsie.

"There ye are, Elsie. My mam's time is here. Dolina said I was to run and fetch ye."

"All right, sweetling. Geordie, I'm sorry. I have to go."

"Ye like this, don't ye? Learning to be a midwife?"

"Aye, I do. I've only just started, mind ye. Bringing a bairn into the world is hard and frightening. So many things can happen. But holding that wee life, knowing ye've made a difference and perhaps brought some ease…well, there's nothing like it."

"Ye're glowing, more than ye do when ye dance."

"Am I?" She smiled.

"Aye, ye are."

"Perhaps I can see ye tomorrow and ye can tell me what's weighing on ye?"

He nodded. "Tomorrow will be soon enough." He gave her a quick kiss.

~ * ~

Just before daybreak, Elsie hurried toward the village priest's cottage, her heart aching. It had been a relatively easy birth, but as Kenna held her wee daughter in her arms, it became immediately apparent that something was dreadfully wrong. The bairn's fingers, toes, and lips had a bluish tinge that only got worse when she cried or tried to feed.

Aunt Dolina had pulled her to one side. Cradling Elsie's face in her hands, she said, "Go fetch Father Ian, Elsie. The wee lassie needs to be baptized."

"But—"

"Nay, lass. The bairn is going to die. Very soon. I'll stay with Kenna and her family. Go fetch Father, then go home. Ye're not ready for this yet."

She did as she'd been bid and watched Father hurry down the lane to the cottage where crushing sorrow was coming on the heels of great joy.

Her aunt had told her to go home, but she couldn't. She didn't want to be alone with her pain there. Instead she went into the little church, intending to pray there in the peaceful solitude.

But she wasn't alone.

Geordie knelt there.

"Geordie," her voice broke.

He turned toward her, clearly reading the grief on her face. He was on his feet and had his arms around her in a moment. "What's happened?"

"The bairn...something's wrong. The poor wee thing is struggling to breathe." She drew in a ragged breath. "She's dying, Geordie."

"Nay, isn't there anything to be done?"

Elsie shook her head. "Father Ian's on his way to baptize her." Elsie rested her head against his chest. She had no tears. It had been too many years. She couldn't stop trembling, and the pain building within her was nearly intolerable.

Geordie held her silently for what seemed like ages. The early morning light crept through the windows before she took one last deep breath and stepped back. "What…why were ye here?"

"Like I said last eve, I have something weighing on my mind. I couldn't sleep and thought perhaps I could find my answers here."

"You can tell me what it is."

He smiled. "It's not the time. We'll talk later. I'll walk ye home. You should try to get a little rest."

She nodded.

They walked in silence and when they reached Dolina's cottage, Elsie turned to face him. He took her hands in his. "Are ye all right?"

"Aye. Thank ye. I don't know what…well, thank ye."

He kissed her tenderly. "I've never met anyone like ye, Elsie. I love ye with my whole heart."

"Oh, Geordie, I love ye too."

He kissed her again before saying, "Go to sleep now, my precious lass. We'll talk later."

"Aye. Until later."

~ * ~

Elsie slept for a few hours, rising late in the morning. When she saw that Aunt Dolina still wasn't home, she made bannocks and prepared a pot of soup, hanging it over the fire to simmer. Finally, she tidied things up.

She had just finished sweeping when the door to the cottage swung open with force, banging against the wall. She spun around to see Drummond, one of the laird's guardsmen standing there. His sudden appearance startled her, and she took an involuntary step backward. She was a little afraid of the huge guardsman. In truth, she was more than a little afraid of him. He had a reputation for cruelty, and she was happy enough to stay out of his way.

It was impossible to avoid him with him filling her doorway. Not wishing to make eye contact, she glanced down. "Good afternoon, Sir Drummond."

"The laird has need of ye. Gather yer things."

"Why do I need to gather my things?"

"Because I told ye to, ye insolent chit. The laird is sending ye on an errand. If ye waste any more of my time with questions, ye'll go with nothing but the clothes on yer back."

An errand? Where? To do what? She didn't dare ask. This was not good, but she figured it was best to follow his bidding. She only had a few garments. Laying them on a linen sheet with her comb and a silver brooch that had belonged to her mother, she folded the sheet inward over the clothes and rolled them up, tying the bundle with a ribbon. She folded a blanket in half and rolled it around the bundle, securing it with a belt. She had barely wrapped her mantle around her shoulders when Drummond grabbed her arm, practically dragging her from the little cottage and up the lane through the village.

Elsie didn't complain. It would do no good and would likely result in worse treatment. All she could do was try her best to keep up. They were halfway to the keep when a horrific screeching sound assaulted her ears just before a searing pain tore through her skull. Gripping her head, she fell to her knees and dropped her bundle.

Chapter 4

"Elsie."

Elsie became vaguely aware of someone calling to her.

"Elsie, ye need to wake now."

Nay. Her head hurt, but she couldn't move it. Her body hurt. It hurt to breathe. She wanted to sleep.

"I know ye can hear me, child. Be a good lass, and open yer eyes."

Elsie blinked. The face of an elderly woman with white hair and kind eyes came into focus.

The woman smiled broadly. "There ye are."

Elsie looked around. She had no idea where she was. Just moments ago, Drummond was dragging her through the village. Now, she seemed to be in some sort of bed. Something was around her neck that prevented her from turning her head. Likewise, her left arm was bound to something rigid. The room was oddly bright, but she saw no torches or candles. Strange noises accosted her ears. Nothing was familiar. How had she gotten here? "What…where…," her voice sounded strange to her ears. She tried again, "What…"

The old woman leaned over Elsie and gently stroked her hair. "Sweetling, look at me. I know this place is strange to ye, and ye have a lot questions. I am going to try to help ye understand what has happened. But I need for ye to stay calm, and focus on what I'm telling ye."

Afraid to hear the bizarre sound of her own voice, Elsie nodded as much as the thing around her neck would allow.

"My name is Gertrude. I am...an immortal spirit. One of the ancients."

Elsie frowned. "An angel?"

"Aye, that's one way of understanding it."

"Have I died?"

Gertrude smiled warmly. "Nay, ye haven't. But yer soul has switched places with another."

Elsie became agitated. "What kind of sorcery is this?"

Gertrude stroked her hair again. "It isn't sorcery, lass. Far from it. Please try to stay calm while I explain. Will ye do that for me?"

"Yes," she whispered. Her voice sounded less strange as a whisper.

"I know this is hard to believe, but as I said, yer soul has switched places with another. Yer soul and memories have entered the body of a woman named Elizabeth, many years in the future. And her soul and memories have entered yer body in yer time."

"How?" she whispered again.

Gertrude reached in her pocket and pulled out a thick, gold disk attached to a chain. "This is called a pocket watch. It's a tool for marking hours that hasn't been invented yet in yer time. But this isn't an ordinary pocket watch. This unassuming device allows a soul who so chooses to temporarily change places with someone else."

"But I didn't choose this."

"I know, pet. Several unusual things happened this time. Normally, the person who accepts the pocket watch goes to sleep at night and then enters the body of someone who has made a choice that will result in their death. The time traveler whose soul enters their body does something immediately to change that. Then the time traveler has sixty days to experience and learn from a different life."

Gertrude pushed a button on the thing she called a pocket watch, and the disk opened. Inside was a white circle with markings around it. It also had one slender, black piece that pointed to a tick mark. "There are sixty marks around the face of this watch. Every day the hand moves forward one mark. The time traveler has a special word that he or she must say before the time is up in order to return to their home."

"And the other person goes back to their own body too?"

"Nay, pet. Normally, because that person was about to die, when the sixty days is up, their soul moves on. They are not even aware of what happened because while sixty days have gone by in the past, only sixty seconds—a single minute—pass where their soul is."

"You said, *normally*. Is that not what happened this time?"

"Nay, things were a bit different this time. Elizabeth was in an accident and lost consciousness instead of going to sleep. She also landed in yer body a bit earlier than intended."

Elsie could scarce take it in, but she understood the general idea. "So she stopped my death? What had I done?"

"That is another interesting wrinkle. Ye hadn't done anything…yet."

"I don't understand."

"I believe at the moment yer soul was brought forward, ye had been summoned by yer laird?"

"Yes, but I didn't know why."

Gertrude explained. "Shortly before Drummond came for ye, a group of men sent by Laird MacKenzie had spoken with yer laird. Ye see, Laird MacKenzie's wife has been pregnant four times, but each time the baby came much too early. She's pregnant again, and they want this baby so very much. Laird MacKenzie heard that Laird Macrae had an extremely talented midwife in his clan."

"My Aunt Dolina."

"Aye, yer Aunt Dolina. Laird MacKenzie hoped that Laird Macrae would let Dolina travel to Carraigile and see if there was anything she could do to help. Well, Laird Macrae believed there was absolutely nothing that could be done, but he thought he could fool Laird MacKenzie into thinking he was helping by sending someone else."

Elsie was shocked. Laird Macrae was not known for his kindness, but it was hard to believe that even he would be so callous.

"By yer expression, I can tell ye don't approve. But here is the worst part: he intended to pass ye off as yer Aunt Dolina."

Elsie frowned. "Me? I could never have done that. I couldn't pretend to be a midwife. I wouldn't give the poor woman false hope."

Gertrude smiled and nodded. "I know, pet. Ye would have taken the moral high ground, but he would have beaten ye severely for yer defiance. That punishment would ultimately have caused yer death. It may be the reason why the pocket watch didn't work quite like it usually does. It would have been tragic if yer noble choice had resulted in such a terrible outcome."

"But I still don't understand what happened."

"Like I said, normally, the watch goes with the person to whom it was given. Then for every day that person is in the past, only a second passes here."

"That didn't happen?"

"Nay, it didn't. The watch is here with ye, and time is equal. One day here is the same as one day in yer own time."

"Exactly where am I?"

"Ye're over seven hundred years in the future. It is about three o'clock, *none* that is, on the twelfth day of February in the year of our Lord, two thousand and six."

"Seven hundred years?"

"Aye, pet. Ye're in hospital, in a city called New York, across the sea from Scotland, in a place called America."

"In Elizabeth's body?"

"Aye. Elizabeth Quinn. She's a very skilled doctor. I will tell you everything I can, but there is one thing you must know first. Even as far in the future as we are, most people are unaware of the possibility of soul exchange. The people who are caring for ye don't know what has happened."

Panic rose in Elsie. "How do I explain not knowing anything about who I am? They'll think me possessed or a witch."

"Nay, lass, they won't. Most people here don't believe in such things. What's more, ye were in a bad accident and hit yer head. Head injuries can result in complete memory loss. It's called 'amnesia.' Other things can cause it as well. Time travelers have faced this for years, and when they encounter doctors, the doctors always manage to find a satisfactory explanation."

"Gertrude, I want to go home. Can't we just switch back?"

"Elsie, ye said ye would have accepted Laird Macrae's punishment rather than lie to the MacKenzies about who ye were."

"Aye, I would have."

"Well, the reason Elizabeth was sent into yer body was because she is a very special kind of doctor. She knows all about pregnancy and birth. She didn't refuse Laird Macrae's command because she has the knowledge and skill to possibly help Lady MacKenzie. But she hasn't had a chance to yet."

"So we must wait until she does?"

"The choice is yers, pet."

Elsie didn't know what to think, but her heart went out to the woman who had lost so many bairns. "If Elizabeth can help, I want her to."

"I was certain ye'd feel that way. So, ye must stay here, at least for a while, and pretend to have amnesia."

Elsie tried to nod again. She became aware again of

how much she hurt. She raised her right hand to touch the thing around her neck. There were clear flexible tubes attached to that arm. "You said I was in an accident. What happened? What is all this?"

"In this century, they have conveyances that people use to move from one place to another very quickly. But sometimes, those conveyances run into each other. It's called a motor vehicle accident or a wreck. People can be very seriously hurt when that happens. You were in a car that wrecked. Ye're left arm is broken. The doctors have splinted it to keep it still until they can put a cast on it and allow the bones to knit properly. This tubing," Gertrude motioned to the thing on her right arm, "is attached to a much smaller tube that goes directly into yer vein and the other end goes into a bag of fluid, see?" Gertrude pointed up and behind Elsie.

Elsie looked and saw the tubing went into a strange box. Hanging above the box was what looked like a clear wineskin full of liquid.

"This machine is called a pump. It pumps the fluid directly into yer body. Doctors in the twenty-first century have wonderful medicines that they can give ye this way."

"Why does my voice sound so odd?"

"Because it's Elizabeth's voice."

"And everyone here speaks Gaelic?"

"Nay. They speak English, but even it has changed a lot."

"How will I understand them?"

"Even though ye have yer soul and memories, some of Elizabeth's memories are still in her body. The language she speaks is one of them. Ye understand, and are able to speak English because of that. It will feel no different to ye than Gaelic. We're speaking English now."

"Really?"

"Aye. Ye may experience other strong memories from time to time as well."

"What is this thing around my neck?"

"It's called a cervical collar. It was put on after the accident, just in case ye had broken a bone in yer neck. Ye didn't. I expect they'll take it off soon."

"Where is the light coming from and what are those noises? Everything hurts so much. Can't I have some willow bark tea?"

"My sweet lass, I'm sorry ye're hurting. They don't use willow bark tea anymore, but they do have good ways of reducing pain. Unfortunately, the longer I stay here and answer questions, the longer it will be before someone can help with yer pain. I know it's all a bit overwhelming, but ye'll be fine. I'll come see you again when you need me, and we'll have another chat."

"You're leaving me? I don't want to be alone. Here." Elsie fought desperately not to cry. "I'm afraid," she added in a whisper.

"I know ye are, sweetling. But I promise, everything will be fine. I have to leave, but ye won't be alone for long. And I must warn ye, don't mention my visit to anyone. Ye see, no one actually needs to know that I've been here."

"Won't they see you leaving?"

"Nay, I have a way of coming and going unnoticed. It's a gift that serves me well. Also, I must tell ye the special word, the return word."

"But I agreed not to change places yet."

"Aye, but that is a choice you have made by your own will. You are always free to change your mind."

"I won't. Not until I know Elizabeth has done what she can."

"Still, you must know the word, even if only to ensure you don't say it accidentally. It is a most strange word and I think that unlikely, but we must take precautions. The word you mustn't say, until you are ready, is, *nintendocore*."

Elsie nodded. "I'm sure I won't say that by accident."

"I thought not. Now, you've made a courageous

choice. Hold on to that, and the universe will unfold as it should." With that, Gertrude left the room.

As she stepped through the door, it was almost as if she faded into a mist and disappeared. If it hadn't been for all of the other fantastical things Elsie had learned over the last few minutes, seeing such a thing would have been terrifying. But really, disappearing was mild in comparison to having one's soul yanked into someone else's body.

A woman with blue breeches and what appeared to be a short tunic out of the same blue fabric entered the room. "Oh, my goodness, Dr. Quinn, you're awake. You were in an accident and you're in the hospital in the ICU. My name is Jennifer. I'm your nurse. I'm going to get a set of vitals and then I'll let the doctor know. She'll want to examine you."

Although Gertrude had said Elsie would understand English, most of what Jennifer said made no sense. Elsie certainly didn't know how to respond, so she opted for silence. Jennifer pushed a button on one of the—Gertrude had called them machines—and a band that was wrapped around her upper arm began to tighten. It became uncomfortable and frightened Elsie. "Get it off. It hurts."

Jennifer touched her shoulder. "It's all right. It's just the blood pressure cuff. It's already going down." Her voice was calm and reassuring, but her brow was furrowed. "There, see? It deflated." Jennifer tilted her head to one side. "Do you remember what happened, Dr. Quinn?"

Elsie shook her head.

"That isn't terribly unusual. As I'm sure you know, people with head injuries often don't remember details of the incident. Do you know where you are?"

"You said I'm...I'm...in a h-hospital."

"That's right. But do you know what city you're in?" Although Jennifer's voice was light, she frowned. "Do you remember flying here?"

Flying here? Could people fly? Gertrude said nothing

about flying. She had mentioned a city, but Elsie couldn't remember it.

Jennifer must have read her stunned expression. "It's okay, Dr. Quinn. Don't worry about it for now. We are in the middle of a huge snowstorm and you were in an accident, but you aren't seriously injured. Can you tell me your full name and birthdate?"

Elsie looked at her blankly.

"Dr. Quinn? What is your full name?"

Elsie swallowed hard. "I don't know."

Chapter 5

After his chat with Chuck, Gabe crashed for a few hours in an on-call room and woke in the afternoon. He checked in with the emergency room before taking a quick shower. He had every intention of going to the cafeteria to get something to eat, but found himself heading up to the ICU instead.

When he walked into the unit, Jim, one of the nurses teased, "Hey, Dr. Soldani, are you lost? Peds is down a floor."

Gabe chuckled. "No, I'm not lost. Elizabeth Quinn is an old friend of mine. I thought I would check on her. Has anything changed?"

"She's conscious."

"Can I go see her?"

"Maybe you better talk to Dr. Harper first. There she is."

Christie Harper, the intensivist on duty, walked out of a patient's room. "Hey, Gabe, pediatrics must be quiet if you decided to come play with the big kids."

"It is, but I actually came to see Elizabeth Quinn. She's a friend. Jim said she's regained consciousness."

"She knows you?"

"It's been a few years, but yeah."

"Gabe, she's awake, but she seems to have profound retrograde amnesia. She doesn't remember anything."

"You mean about the accident?"

"I mean about anything—her entire life. She has no clue who she is or where she is. You'd never know she was a doctor. She has already freaked once when she realized she had a Foley in, and she almost pulled it out. I've called for a neuro consult."

"Dr. Levi is in with her now," offered Jim.

At that moment, a scream came from one of the patient rooms followed by a panicked, "Get away from me. Get away. Don't touch me."

Christie turned and ran toward the room.

Gabe did too. It was Elizabeth's voice.

Martin Levi was backing away from the bed, an ophthalmoscope in his hand. Elizabeth was sitting in the middle of the bed with her knees drawn up and her arms over her face. Her nurse was trying to calm her, but Elizabeth struggled against her.

Without thinking, Gabe strode across the room and took Elizabeth's hands in his. "Elizabeth, you're safe. Everything's okay."

She calmed a little, lowering her arms. Her brows drew together as she looked at Gabe.

"Do you remember Gabe?" asked Christie.

Elizabeth searched his face. "I-I think I do. I don't remember his name, but I think...I think I love him?"

All eyes turned to Gabe. "That's right, sweetheart. We loved each other." He put his arms around her and she rested her head against him, completely calm again. His heart melted. In response to the questioning looks from the others in the room he added, "We went to medical school together. We dated for a while."

"I'm afraid," she whispered.

"I know. Let me try to help you."

"I want this thing on my neck off. Please take it off."

Gabe looked over his shoulder. "Christie, can the c-collar come off?"

"Yes. The CT was negative. I just hadn't written the order to remove it yet."

Gabe released the straps and removed the collar. "Is that better?"

Elizabeth nodded, but glanced warily at Dr. Levi. "I don't want him to touch me with that thing."

Gabe glanced at Martin. Confused, Martin showed him the ophthalmoscope. "I need to check her fundi."

"Elizabeth, he's not going to hurt you. He's just going to look into your pupils."

"Why?"

"He's checking for signs of increased intracranial pressure."

"What's that?"

Holy crap, she really doesn't remember anything. He shifted into pediatrician mode to explain. "It's...well, it's a sign that you might have hurt your brain."

"He can see into my brain?"

"Not exactly. But with that light, he can see the backs of your eyes and if you have certain brain injuries, he can see signs of it there."

"The light isn't...it isn't hot? It won't burn me?"

"No, it won't. Martin, give me the scope so she can see it." Martin handed it to him. Gabe turned it on and showed it to her. "See, it's just a light, and a magnifying glass. Go ahead. Take it."

She reached for it cautiously, turning it over in her hand to look at it. She frowned, handing it back to Gabe.

"Will you let Dr. Levi look in your eyes now?"

She nodded. "Yes."

Gabe started to step away from the bed.

Elizabeth grabbed for his arm, panic rising again. "Don't leave me."

"I'm not going anywhere, sweetheart. I was just giving Martin room to examine you."

Martin shook his head. "Stay beside her. I'll work around you. I won't be able to assess anything if she doesn't stay calm."

Martin checked her eyes and went on to do as complete a neuro exam as possible. Gabe explained everything that was being done. When Martin finished, he said, "Everything seems to be normal. Dr. Quinn, I'm going to ask you some questions. What is this?" He pointed to the bed.

"A bed."

"Yes, and this?" he pointed to the curtain.

"A curtain?"

"That's correct. What about this?" he pointed to his lab coat.

"It's a garment."

Martin frowned. "But what kind?"

"I don't know."

"What are these clothes that all of us are wearing called?" He pointed to his scrubs.

"I don't know."

"Look out the window and tell me what's falling from the sky."

"Snow."

"Do you remember my name?"

"Martin Levi."

"Good. And this lovely blond lady?"

"Dr. Harper."

"Yes. Do you remember what we told you your name is?"

"Elizabeth Quinn."

"That's right. What about your nurse, do you remember her name?"

"Jennifer."

"And this bearded beast holding your hand?" Martin teased.

"His name is Gabe."

"And who is he?"

"I don't remember exactly. He said we went to medical school and we...we...dated? I don't remember that. I just know I love him."

Gabe's heart melted for the second time.

"What does it mean to date someone?" Martin asked.

"I don't know."

Martin's brow drew together. He picked up the patient welcome packet from the bedside table and pulled a page out of it. "Read this aloud for me."

Elizabeth took the page and frowned at it. "I can't read it," she said in a small voice.

"Is it blurry?"

"No. I can't read it."

"Then just tell me the letters in the first word on the page."

"I can't. I don't know what they are."

"Point to any number on that page."

Color rose in Elizabeth's cheeks and she shoved the page back to Martin. "I told you I can't."

Gabe's shock that Elizabeth, the girl genius, couldn't even recognize letters and numbers was mirrored on the face of everyone in the room. "Martin, what do you think is wrong?"

Martin frowned. "Elizabeth, there are rules that we have to follow. One rule is that your doctors and nurses don't talk about your condition to anyone but you unless we have your permission. Gabe is a doctor in this hospital, but he isn't your doctor." Martin smiled at her. "You're too old. He's a pediatrician. Do you know what that is?"

"No."

"He specializes in taking care of children. And he is a friend of yours. He was perhaps a very good friend a few years ago, but it has been a while. I cannot speak to him about what is happening with you or even speak to you in front of him unless you say I can."

Elizabeth frowned. "There is a lot I don't know, but I am absolutely certain I know and trust Gabe. You can talk to him."

"All right. Well your short-term memory seems to be okay. You were able to recall all of our names. But there are huge holes in your long-term memory."

"Can't that be explained by the blow to the head?"

Gabe asked.

"Yes. Amnesia can occur with concussion or as part of postconcussive syndrome. However, memory loss this severe is usually accompanied by significant brain trauma. Other than her extended loss of consciousness and amnesia, she has no signs of brain injury. Her CT and physical exam is normal. More disconcerting is that her memory loss is atypical. Profound retrograde amnesia most often affects both episodic memory and autobiographical memory, but not semantic memory—at least not to a great extent."

Elizabeth frowned and looked at Gabe. "What did he just say?"

Gabe explained. "Getting hit on the head can cause memory loss, which we call amnesia." Elizabeth nodded. "And there are three kinds of memory. Episodic memories are of things you have done or things that have happened to you. Autobiographical memories are details about who you are, like your name and birthdate. It is common to lose these kinds of memories with amnesia."

Elizabeth nodded, appearing to understand.

"The other kind of memory Martin mentioned is semantic memory. Language is part of semantic memory, as is the ability to recognize familiar objects and know what they're used for. Most people with amnesia don't lose much semantic memory. You were able to correctly identify the bed, the curtain and snow, and you associated light with heat. Those are semantic memories. But you panicked when Martin wanted to look in your eyes. Not recognizing the device he was using is an example of semantic memory loss. Not knowing that the clothes we are wearing are called 'scrubs' or that this is a lab coat," he motioned to the one he wore, "is another example of semantic memory loss. These are the standard clothes worn by doctors and nurses who work in hospitals. You would have known that from childhood because your father is a doctor."

Martin nodded. "Not being able to read or even recognize letters and numbers is another example of unusual semantic memory loss. These deficits are extremely rare and hard to explain without any evident brain damage."

~ * ~.

Elsie looked at the four people in her room. It was all overwhelming. She knew exactly why she couldn't remember certain objects or even letters and numbers. She had never seen those objects before, and she had never learned to read, but she couldn't tell them that.

What surprised her was that she remembered Gabe. Gertrude had said she might experience some of Elizabeth's strong memories from time to time. But strong didn't begin to describe it. The moment Gabe had touched her and she saw his face, images of him—younger and in a different place—flashed through her mind. Somehow, it was more than simply remembering his appearance. She felt a sense of connection that was instant and profound. She remembered his touch, his laugh, his embrace…his kiss. It was as if these things were all written on her heart and were as familiar to her as her feelings for Geordie. But even those paled now in comparison. She had only just begun to experience first love with Geordie—at least she thought it was love. She had wanted more and believed his feelings were as strong for her. Still, part of her feared loving him too much and perhaps losing her heart to someone who was destined to move on.

But if her love for Geordie had been like the warm glow of a gently crackling fire, what she felt for Gabe was as intense as the heat of a blacksmith's forge. She knew instinctively that he was infinitely important to her, and her heart was bound to his.

She looked into Gabe's eyes. She was afraid, but she found strength there. "I don't understand anything that's happening."

Gabe caressed her cheek. "I know you don't. If it makes you feel any better, we aren't sure what's happening either, but we are going to try to find out. Martin, could something have been missed on the CT?"

"Yes. Sometimes CT scans taken the day of injury are negative and an MRI performed later reveals the problem. For that reason, we will do an MRI, maybe tomorrow unless something changes. But even if there is a small amount of damage that the CT missed, I'm having trouble believing it's causing this massive deficit."

"So what are you thinking?" asked Gabe.

"A fugue precipitated by the physical trauma."

Again, Dr. Levi was supposedly speaking English, but every time he opened his mouth, Elsie didn't understand most of what he said. "What does that mean, Gabe?"

Gabe smiled at her. "It means you have amnesia that isn't caused by a brain injury, but it happened because of the accident."

"That's actually good news," said Dr. Levi. "Fugues don't usually last long and most of the time are completely reversible."

She frowned at him.

Dr. Levi chuckled. "I'm sorry. That means you'll probably get all of your memories back soon."

That was convenient. When she and Elizabeth switched souls again, her memory return would be expected.

Dr. Levi turned to Dr. Harper. "She is completely alert and stable. I don't think she needs to remain in the ICU. I will admit her to a neuro step-down unit and keep her under observation. I'll also request an ortho consult to take care of her arm."

Christie nodded. "Jennifer, go ahead and remove the Foley, and let's get her something for pain."

Jim poked his head in the room. "Dr. Harper, Dr.

Quinn's father, Dr. James Quinn, is on the phone for you."

"Elizabeth, may I speak to your father about your condition?"

Elizabeth frowned and looked at Gabe. "They have to ask if they can speak to my *father*? Is my father here?"

Christie shook her head. "He isn't here, he's on the phone. Maybe you would like to talk to him."

"But you said he isn't here." This was all so confusing. Tears welled in her eyes. "I don't know what I'm supposed to do. Gabe, what am I supposed to do?"

"Sweetheart, do you remember what a phone is?"

"No."

"It is a way of talking to someone who is far away. Your father is worried about you and wants to know you are okay. But just like you had to give your permission for Martin to talk to me, you have to give Christie permission to speak to your parents. Do you understand?"

Why would this be necessary? They were her parents, weren't they? In her time, if she had a father, she would have belonged to him. He would be the one to tell her what she could and couldn't do. She shook her head. "No, I don't understand. What should I do?"

"You have to make the decision, Elizabeth. You are an independent adult and free to make your own choices. But your parents will be very worried about you. If you don't want Dr. Harper to speak to them, you should."

Oh dear God, no. "I don't want to. I don't know what a phone is. I don't know what to say. I don't know them. Dr. Harper, you can speak to them."

"Alright, I will. Martin, you should be on the call too."

He nodded and left with her.

Jennifer smiled. "I'm going to bring you something for pain, then I'll take the Foley out."

When Jennifer left, Elsie lowered herself onto the pillows and closed her eyes for a moment. For some reason, she wanted to cry. That wasn't like her. She had cried out all of her tears long ago. She took a deep breath to try to regain some control. She needed to focus on the present and keep things together until she and Elizabeth could trade places again.

"Something for pain would be good. I have never felt like this. It hurts to simply breathe."

Gabe caressed her cheek. "You were in a bad accident. On top of having broken ribs and a broken arm, you have lots of scrapes and bruises. The pain medicine will help."

"What was the other thing she said?"

"She's going to take out your Foley."

"What is that?"

"It is the tube going into your bladder."

"Oh." That had terrified her when she first became aware of it. "I don't like it here."

He smiled. "But this is the best place to be until you are better."

She hadn't just meant this hospital. She wanted to go home to her own time as soon as possible. For an instant, she considered saying the word. *No, you can't do that. Elizabeth needs time.*

Jennifer returned. "Since you are awake and alert, Dr. Harper wrote for oral oxycodone. She's also ordered a regular diet, so I brought you some graham crackers and apple juice. Sometimes oxycodone can make you queasy, but eating a little with it helps. Normally, before someone gives you medication, they are supposed to ask you your full name and birthdate."

"But you know who I am. Apparently better than I do."

Gabe chuckled and Jennifer smiled. "Yes, I do know who you are, but I still have to ask. It's an extra step to make sure the right person is getting the right medicine. I know you don't know your birthdate, but can you tell me your full name?"

"Elizabeth Quinn." That answer felt so odd.

"Okay, Elizabeth. Your birthdate is January 31st, 1978.

See if you can remember that for the next time someone asks."

"I'll try."

Gabe helped her sit up and Jennifer handed her a small clear cup with a perfectly round white disk in it that was engraved with some symbols.

"What is this?"

"It's the oxycodone, the pain medicine."

Elsie frowned at it. "What do I do with it?"

"You swallow it."

"I don't think I can do that."

Gabe smiled. "It's easy. Take a drink of water first. Then put the tablet on the back of your tongue and take another drink. Just let it go down with the water as you swallow."

Elsie tried a couple times but the tablet, as Gabe had called it, stayed stubbornly in her mouth.

"Try one more time. Sometimes, it helps if you tip your head back as you swallow," said Jennifer. "If you can't swallow it this way, we can try putting it in applesauce."

Elsie tried again, and it finally worked.

Jennifer smiled at her. "Very good. It should start working soon. Dr. Soldani, if you'll excuse us for a moment, I'm going to cap her IV and take the Foley out."

Gabe started to leave. "Gabe, I...I don't want you to leave."

"I'm not leaving, sweetheart. I am just going to step out of the room to give you privacy. I'll come back as soon as Jennifer is done."

"It will only take a minute. I promise," said Jennifer. She proceeded to put on a pair of gloves that looked as if they were made of skin. The expression on Elsie's face must have prompted Jennifer to explain. "These are latex gloves. They protect my hands and keep germs off of them. Here, take a look at one."

Jennifer handed her the flimsy glove. Elsie turned it over in her hand, looking at it. She would have tried to put it on, but with the left arm splinted, she didn't think she could manage. "What are germs?"

"They are organisms that are so tiny we can't see them, but they make us sick."

Elsie wasn't sure she understood that, but she didn't ask more.

Jennifer explained everything she was doing as she did it, making Elsie much less nervous. When Jennifer was done, she made sure Elsie was comfortable, rolled a table into position over her bed and put a packet containing two brown squares and a small clear vessel filled with an amber liquid on the table. "If you need anything, push this button and someone will come to help you. I'll send Gabe back in."

"Thank you," said Elsie. She was examining the packet when Gabe returned. "Are these the *graham crackers* she mentioned?"

"Yes."

"How do I open the packet?"

Gabe took it from her. "You just tear the cellophane like this." He handed her the open package.

"But it's ruined then."

"It isn't intended to be used again. It's disposable." Perhaps realizing that she didn't know how to open the container of liquid either, he peeled back the lid and put it on the table.

She cautiously took a bite of one of the crackers. She smiled. "It's sweet. I like it."

Gabe chuckled. "I'll have to bring you some Italian tea cookies. You used to love them."

She took a sip of the liquid. "Mmm. I like that, too. It's like cider."

"Apple juice is cider that has been filtered and pasteurized."

Elsie smiled and nodded.

Gabe chuckled. "You don't know what that means."

"No, I don't."

"Elizabeth, don't be afraid to say so or ask." He went on to explain it to her. She liked listening to his voice. She found it soothing, like music.

"Can I ask you something else?"

"I said you can ask anything."

"Dr. Levi said something that confused me."

"What was it?"

"When he said I had to give my permission so he could talk in front of you, he said you had perhaps been a very good friend *a few years ago*. I'm certain I...I love you. Now. What did he mean?"

Gabe took her hand, smiling sadly. "The truth is, I love you too. I have for years. We went to medical school together, and were friends for most of that time. We started dating in our fourth year."

"What does that mean?"

"We spent a lot of time together. We did things together like going out to dinner or to a movie. Eventually, we slept together."

"Slept together?"

He chuckled. "Made love? Had sex?"

That's what she thought slept together meant. "And we weren't married?"

His brow drew together. "No, we weren't."

Perhaps Elsie should have been more shocked by that, but for some reason she wasn't. That must be Elizabeth's memories pushing through again.

"But I wanted to marry you. I was working up the courage to ask. We had matched at different hospitals, but I had been trying to change. There was an opening in pediatrics at the University of Cincinnati where you had matched, which hadn't been filled in the scramble. I was trying desperately to get it."

"I don't understand anything you just said."

He laughed. "I'm sure you don't. The short version is that you go to medical school for four years, and in your last year, you apply for a residency. A residency is more years of training in a specialty. You wanted to be an obstetrician—that is a doctor who delivers babies. I wanted to be a pediatrician. The whole selection process is complicated, but it's called *matching*. We could have tried to match as a couple, but we hadn't been dating long when the process started and we didn't discuss it."

"So we matched at different hospitals?"

"Yes. I was matched here at NYUHC and you were going to Cincinnati."

"And they are a great distance apart?"

"Yes, they are."

"And you weren't able to change?"

"I stopped trying."

Those words caused a lump to rise in her throat and her heart to ache. "Why?" she asked tentatively.

"Something happened. I said some things I shouldn't have, and we went our separate ways."

"No." That truly distressed her. She was certain Elizabeth loved him deeply. "What happened?"

"It's a long story."

"Please, tell me."

"Okay, but first, you need to understand who I am. My name is Gabriel Eduardo Soldani, and I grew up in a big, working-class, Italian family in New Jersey. You probably don't know exactly what that means." He chuckled. "Most people don't until they've experienced it, but family is very important. It is a defining feature of my life. I'm Natalie and Sal's son. I'm Joey, Nick, Tony, Luke and Angela's brother. I have aunts and uncles and cousins too numerous to list. At some point or another, they can all annoy the life out of a person, but I love them. They are my world."

Elsie understood that. Clan was extremely important.

"I didn't like your family?" Elsie couldn't believe it even as she said it.

"No, nothing like that. You liked them and they liked you. But for some reason, you kept your family...a secret."

"What do you mean? How could I do that? Why would I?"

Gabe sighed. "Elizabeth, you are the only child of an extremely wealthy and important family. Your mother is Charlotte Matheson Quinn. She is a partner with her father in a law firm that grossed over two billion dollars last year."

"What does that mean?"

"They make a huge amount of money. On top of that, your father is a very well recognized surgeon, as was his father. But every time I asked you about your family, you avoided the discussion. I had no idea who you were until the day we graduated—essentially our last day in medical school. And even then, it wasn't you who told me. I found out from the whispers when your family was recognized."

"So nobody knew?"

"Nobody. Not even the dean of the university. When I finally saw you later that day, I was angry and hurt that you had kept this huge secret from me. I thought you must have been ashamed of me, afraid I would embarrass you."

"Why would you think that? Did I say that?"

"No. You said you feared they would embarrass you."

"Did they?"

"Embarrass you? Not really. They were cold and formal—nothing like my family—but they were polite."

"If I liked your family, maybe I was embarrassed because mine wasn't like yours."

Gabe just stared at her. "I—I guess I never thought of it that way."

"Did I give you any other reason?"

Gabe nodded. "You said as long as people didn't know who you were, you could just be ordinary, but as soon as they found out, everything changed. At the time, I just couldn't understand why you would keep your family a secret. Like I said, my family is so much a part of who I am that I felt like you were hiding yourself from me. You said your family was not your identity, but I couldn't believe that. I said goodbye to you and left."

Elsie's heart broke. She was so certain they loved each other. Well, she was certain she felt Elizabeth's intense love for him. A tear slipped down her cheek—the first one she'd cried in years. "I'm sorry, Gabe. This sense that I know you and love you is the only thing that feels real to me in this place. I thought...I thought..."

"Oh, sweetheart, I do love you. I told you that. It's just that it took me a while to actually realize how much I loved you and how little that argument had meant. But it had happened at a crossroads in our lives, and we had already gone our separate ways. It was too late—or I thought it was. Maybe...maybe this is our second chance. Maybe we can figure this out."

Elsie sighed. She was absolutely certain Elizabeth still loved him. "I hope so. I'm willing to believe God's blessings come in unexpected ways."

That was true. Not only had Elizabeth saved Elsie's life by choosing to exchange souls, she was in a place where she could use her knowledge to help Lady MacKenzie. Elsie had no such skills and had been certain she had nothing to offer Elizabeth or anyone else in this century. Perhaps *this* is what she could do for Elizabeth. Elsie could bring her close to Gabe again so that when she returned, Elizabeth would have this lost love in her life once again. Then Elsie would go home to the man she was beginning to love and make sure they never parted.

Chapter 6

Gabe didn't believe he had ever thanked the Almighty for a snowstorm, at least not since he was a kid and had prayed for snow days, but this one could only have been a gift. Although there had been accidents, no one had been killed or even very critically injured. While he wished that Elizabeth hadn't been injured as badly as she was, he wouldn't have found her again otherwise, and he never would have known the deep feelings she still held for him—feelings that mirrored his own.

He had only fallen in love twice. Once when he had been young and stupid and had fallen for a girl he could never have. The second time was with Elizabeth. It turned out he was still pretty stupid then, too. When Elizabeth, suffering profound amnesia, had not only recognized him but said, *I think I love him*, he had prayed this was his second chance with her. He wasn't going to blow it. She was alone and frightened, and she needed him. He would be there for her. Dr. Sweeny had only called Gabe in as backup. Things were quiet now, so in the brief time Gabe had left Elizabeth to Jennifer's care, he'd received clearance to sign out. He would have the next six days off.

Christie Harper returned after she had spoken to Elizabeth's father. "Elizabeth, your parents are very concerned about you. Your father would have liked to speak with you, but I told him you weren't really up to talking. They will be coming up from Baltimore as soon as possible, but I doubt that will be before tomorrow morning."

"Is Baltimore far?"

Christie shook her head. "No. About two hundred miles."

"Two hundred miles? How long will the journey take?"

"Under normal conditions, without traffic, a little over three hours. But in bad weather, it could take much longer."

Elizabeth looked a little amazed and very happy, but said nothing.

"Dr. Levi has written orders and there is a bed available in the neuro step-down unit, so we will transfer you there shortly. I think Jennifer was trying to get a dinner tray sent up for you in the meantime."

The tray arrived a few minutes later. Elizabeth's brows drew together. She cautiously explored the contents. The first item to draw her attention was a white bowl of some sort with a lid. "What is this bowl made out of?"

"It's called Styrofoam. It keeps things warm or cool. Take the plastic lid off: there is soup in it. Sadly, it may be the best thing on the tray. Hospital food isn't usually very good."

She tasted a spoonful of the chicken noodle soup and smiled. "I like this, but what are these slippery worm-like things?"

"Those are noodles."

"I like them."

"Wait until you try my mom's homemade pasta. That's another word for noodles. You used to love it."

"If it's even better than these, I'm sure I still will."

When she finished the soup, she removed the cover from the plate. "What is this?"

"Chicken, rice pilaf, and green beans."

She scooped up a little rice with her spoon, tasting it. "Since those things are green, this must be rice pilaf? It isn't bad."

"You don't remember rice?"

"No, what is it?"

"Rice is a grain."

She nodded. "Like barley?"

"Yes, like barley."

She tried to scoop up a green bean with her spoon.

"It will be easier to pick them up with your fork."

She picked up a utensil. "Is this a fork?"

"Yes, it is."

She attacked the green beans with the fork. "These are a little odd."

"They are better when they are fresh."

The holes in her semantic memory were bizarre. She clearly knew what a spoon was, but not a fork. She knew what soup was, but not noodles. She didn't know what rice was, but she understood that it was a grain and compared it to barley.

She had eaten a few bites of everything when she looked up at him. "I feel…I feel…I don't feel right."

Gabe became immediately concerned. "What's the matter? Are you having any trouble breathing?"

"No, it isn't that. I feel…sleepy and a little light-headed."

He smiled. "The pain medicine you took is starting to work. It has that effect on most people. How is your pain?"

"It's better and I'm thankful for that, but I don't think I like feeling like this."

"We'll talk to your doctor about it."

His puzzlement only grew when they were finally ready to transfer her from the ICU. She had no memory of elevators and as they rode in one, she had a death grip on his hand that might have been appropriate on a roller coaster. In fairness, Elizabeth didn't like roller coasters, either.

When she was settled in the new room, the oxycodone made her even drowsier. "This bed is nice."

"Really? Most people don't find them overly comfortable."

"I'm having trouble staying awake."

"Then don't. You need plenty of rest anyway."

"You won't leave?"

"No, I won't." Gabe moved the recliner closer to the bed and took her hand.

She held on tightly. "I'm sorry I'm not braver. I will try harder, but everything here is so peculiar and I don't like to be alone. It scares me."

"I won't leave you alone, and you've nothing to be sorry for. I know how disorienting it is to be in a strange place, and I understand that you're afraid. Everything will be okay, sweetheart."

She sighed. "I think it will be. I want to remember it all when I go back."

Gabe had no idea what she meant by that, but assumed the narcotic had muddled her thoughts.

As she drifted off to sleep, although she continued to cling firmly to his hand, she looked relaxed and peaceful, a small smile resting on her lips.

He smiled, made himself as comfortable as possible in the recliner, and gave in to sleep.

~ * ~

Everything will be okay. Elsie wasn't sure why she so firmly believed that. The events of the day were almost too much to comprehend. At first, it seemed to be a dreadful nightmare, but now she was opening herself to the adventure. What had changed?

She smiled as she realized two things that helped her embrace this opportunity. First was Gabe. Not only did she feel safe when he was with her, she felt a sense of completeness she had only just begun to experience with Geordie. Elizabeth was a lucky woman, but Elsie believed the same depth of emotion would be hers as well when she returned to the man she was beginning to love in her own time.

The second thing was the chance to experience the love of a family again. Perhaps it was silly; after all, she'd lost her mother and father so long ago and she was a grown woman now, but the chance to feel the loving embrace of parents once more was beyond enticing.

Until recently, Elsie had existed in a world filled with duty and perhaps kindness, but not love. Today had been more frightening and overwhelming than anything she had ever experienced, but even in all its strangeness, a part of her was excited by the possibilities the next few days or weeks held. As she drifted off to sleep holding Gabe's hand, she knew she had been given an extraordinary gift. She would partake freely.

~ * ~

Several hours later, Gabe woke as people came into the room. He opened his eyes to see Elizabeth's parents.

"Who are you?" her father asked.

Gabe stood, but didn't let go of Elizabeth's hand. "Good evening, sir. I'm Dr. Gabriel Soldani."

"I remember you. You went to medical school with Elizabeth. You were the only friend she introduced us to the day she graduated," said Elizabeth's mother.

"Yes, we're friends. It's nice to see you again. We weren't sure you'd be able to get here before morning."

"As soon as the storm stopped, we flew by helicopter," explained Mrs. Quinn.

Dr. Quinn frowned. "Don't you think it is a bit unseemly for a doctor in this hospital to be sitting holding my daughter's hand while she sleeps?"

The conversation was evidently penetrating Elizabeth's slumber. She blinked and looked around as if trying to get her bearings.

"I'm a pediatrician, Dr. Quinn. I am only here as a friend."

"Well, we're here now. You can leave," said Dr. Quinn.

Wide awake now, Elizabeth's jaw dropped. "No!" she

said vehemently, reestablishing her death grip on his hand. "I don't want him to leave. Who are you anyway?"

"I'm your father, Elizabeth. We are going to have you transferred to Hopkins. We'll go by helicopter tonight."

Elizabeth couldn't have looked more shocked. "You're my father? I...I...I want to stay here." She looked scared.

"Don't be ridiculous. You'll come with us to Baltimore."

She turned terror-filled eyes to Gabe. "I don't want to do that." She glanced again at her father before asking Gabe, "Is what Dr. Levi said true? Do they need my permission to do this?"

"Yes, but Elizabeth, your parents are worried about you. Your father is on staff at Hopkins, so I'm sure he would be more comfortable with you there."

"But they need my permission?"

"Yes."

"Then I don't give it. I want to stay here." She looked at her father. "Please don't ask this of me. I don't know you yet."

"You don't know anyone," said her father.

"I know Gabe."

"Darling, we know your memory is foggy, but we only want what's best for you," said her mother.

"Is there something at this place...this *Hopkins*...that is certain to bring my memory back?"

Her father stood, clenching his jaw but her mother said, "Of course not, but it is a stellar hospital in Baltimore, close to home."

"I thought I lived in a place called *Cincinnati*."

"You do, but our home, your childhood home, is in Baltimore."

"Then, forgive me, but it seems it isn't necessarily what's best for me. I know it might be more convenient for you—"

"Elizabeth, you are being exceedingly thoughtless.

Ceci Giltenan

You know I have a busy surgical schedule. Your mother has important clients. Why would you choose to make things difficult?"

Elizabeth visibly recoiled as if she had been struck. "I'm sorry."

Gabe had remained silent during this exchange. It wasn't his place to interfere, but his heart fell when he heard her apologize and appear to capitulate. He reckoned this conversation was very like the heated discussion she had appeared to have with them after graduation.

Her father nodded. "I'm glad you see things our way. This is for the best. I'll make arrangements to have you transferred immediately."

Just like that, she was going to be gone from his life again.

She shook her head. "No. You misunderstand me. I'm sorry that my choice to stay here will make things difficult. But you have no idea what I'm going through. Everything is strange enough already. I don't know anyone there, and I don't remember you."

"As I said before, you don't know anyone here, either," countered her father.

"I know Gabe. I know we were friends—close friends. I have fleeting memories of him and a deep sense that he is important to me. I understand you have things you must do. Don't feel as if you need to stay here with me."

Gabe was speechless.

Her mother sat on the bed beside her. "My darling, it will really be better if you come to Baltimore. However, if it would make you more comfortable to delay moving a little, I'll arrange to stay for a day or two."

Her father frowned. "No, Charlotte. She has profound amnesia and is not mentally capable of making this choice. I will see that she has a psychiatric assessment and then we will move her to Hopkins. I'll call Howard Jacobs and have him put me in touch with the chief of psychiatry here."

"James, I'm sure when she's had some time, she'll come around."

"She'll have tonight. Considering how late it is on a Sunday evening, I expect it will take until tomorrow anyway. I'll get us a suite at the Fitzwilliam." He strode out of the room without another word.

Tears filled Elizabeth's eyes. "Can he do that, Gabe?"

"If he believes you aren't mentally capable of making a decision, he can attempt to have you declared incompetent. But he can only take the decision out of your hands if another doctor determines that you aren't able to make sound choices."

She blinked, clearly trying not to cry, but her lower lip trembled. "He must hate me."

"No, Elizabeth," said her mother. "Your dad doesn't hate you. He just thinks this is best and, really, it is."

The tears finally spilled down Elizabeth's cheeks. "He thinks it's best to make me so unhappy? He thinks it's best to move me from the only place where I know anyone?"

"He doesn't see it that way. He just wants you in his hospital, where he can—"

"—control me?"

"Elizabeth, that isn't fair. We're your parents. You make your own decisions. We are only advising you on what is prudent. Surely, you understand that."

"If I make my own decisions, then I should be able to make this one."

Elizabeth's mother patted Elizabeth's hand. "No one is going anywhere tonight anyway. Rest and perhaps you'll feel differently in the morning." Her mother kissed her forehead and left the room.

Elizabeth watched her leave and then started to sob.

"Oh, sweetheart, please don't cry." Gabe didn't know what to do, so he instinctively lifted her into his arms and sat on the recliner, cradling her on his lap and against his chest.

"I—never—cry," she said between sobs. But she wrapped her arms around him, continuing to weep.

He whispered soft soothing words, trying to quiet her sobs.

A nurse came into the room. "Goodness, what's the matter?"

Elizabeth continued to cry, so Gabe explained. "Her parents were here."

"Did she recognize them?"

"No."

"Is that why she's upset?"

"No. Her father is on staff at Johns Hopkins. He wants her transferred there, and she doesn't want to go."

"Well, she's an adult, she doesn't have to go, and you shouldn't push her into it."

"I'm not the one pushing her. When she told them she wanted to stay here, her father said he would have her evaluated by psych and declared incompetent."

"No." The nurse's tone was incredulous. She sat on the bed and rested a hand on Elizabeth's shoulder. "Dr. Quinn, don't let this upset you. A lot of things have to happen before anyone can make you do anything."

"Really?"

"Yes."

"And, Elizabeth, if your father gets his way, I'll go to Baltimore to be with you there."

He felt the tension leave her body. "You will?"

"Of course. I know you're afraid. I won't leave you."

She sighed and rested her head against his chest.

The nurse smiled. "Try to calm down a little now. I'll be back in a few minutes to take some vitals. Are you having any pain?"

Elizabeth nodded.

"Then I'll bring some pain medicine too."

She nodded again. "I don't like the way it makes me feel, but I am hurting a lot."

When the nurse left, Elizabeth snuggled against Gabe's chest again. He rested his cheek on the top of her head, content just to hold her.

"I wish I could sleep here."

Gabe chuckled. "So do I, but it's probably better if we tuck you into bed."

"Can you stay here all night?"

"Yes. I'll stay right here in this chair."

"Thank you, Gabe."

~ * ~

Elsie's disappointment in the callous way Elizabeth's parents—particularly her father—treated her was shattering. But as she regained control, it occurred to her that the ability to make her own choices was a heady power, so much so that the threat of losing that right steeled her determination to prevent anyone from taking it from her.

Chapter 7

The twenty-first century was loud and scary in many ways, but it didn't take long for Elsie to appreciate some modern marvels. The first being a little chamber called a *bathroom*. She had been introduced to it the previous evening when she needed to relieve herself. There were no pots to empty into cesspits. It wasn't even like a garderobe. The *toilet* was filled with water and everything was flushed away with the push of a lever. A wash basin was attached to the wall, and levers there caused warm water to pour out of a spout.

That was also when she saw her reflection for the first time. Elizabeth was shorter than Elsie had been. She had warm brown eyes and short, wavy, brown hair. It would have shocked her had she not already seen so many women in this time with short hair. Elizabeth had an ample bosom, a slightly rounded tummy, and curvy hips. Elsie smiled, thinking her body very attractive—at least men in her own time would find it so. Her face, on the other hand, was a bit of a mess. There was a scrape above her left eye and some ugly bruises, but they would go away with time.

Just after Elsie had awakened that morning, to her surprise, a *breakfast tray* was delivered. If she ate at all, her morning meal consisted of bread or a bannock and either broth or cheese. This tray had some foods she recognized. There were two pancakes, which were like bannocks but very soft and in the twenty-first century, eaten drenched in syrup. There was also bacon, cooked until it was crispy. She had never eaten bacon in the morning before. She seemed to amuse Gabe with her questions about everything else.

The large, curved, yellow thing was a fruit called a

banana. "Try it, but don't be surprised if you don't like that one," said Gabe. "It is a little green, and you like very ripe bananas."

She tasted it and made a face. "You're right. I don't like it. How did you know?"

He chuckled. "Because I like them green. You used to buy bananas, and I'd irritate you by eating them before they got ripe enough for your tastes."

She smiled, "You can have this one. And please eat one of these pancakes, I can't manage them both."

He gave her a warm smile. "We've done this before. You like pancakes, but you'd only ever eat one and they are usually served in a stack of two or three or more. I have never minded finishing your pancakes."

The tray also held a container of milk that was nothing like the milk in her time, and a container of *orange juice*. It was very tasty. But the thing that surprised her most was the cup of hot black liquid Gabe called *coffee*. The aroma was wonderful. She started to take a sip, but Gabe stopped her.

"You like milk or cream in your coffee." He poured some of the milk in.

She tasted it in awe. "This is…this is…delicious."

Gabe laughed. "You've loved coffee as long as I've known you. It sustained you through medical school."

"Is it very good for you? Does one drink it instead of eating?"

"You don't drink it instead of eating—or you shouldn't—that isn't what I meant by sustain. Coffee has something in it called caffeine. It is a stimulant." At her frown he said, "Having a cup of coffee when you're tired perks you up for a while. In medical school, we had a lot to do and didn't get as much sleep as we should have. We drank a lot of coffee."

"Do you want some of this?"

"No, thank you. You enjoy it and I'll get a cup later."

After breakfast, a nurse checked her *vitals*. Gabe had explained what they were yesterday. The nurse also removed the little tube in her arm that had been capped yesterday.

"I'm going to wrap that splint and have a nursing assistant help you shower."

"Shower?"

"Wash up," the nurse said by way of explanation. "Dr. Soldani, you can take a break for a while."

Elsie started to protest, but Gabe said, "You'll want privacy. I won't be gone long. I think I'll have a shower, too." She frowned, but he added, "There's a coffee shop in the lobby that makes a great mocha. It's a flavored coffee that you love. I'll bring you one."

"Okay." She was still worried that her parents might return before Gabe did, but she was determined to be brave.

The hot shower was one of the most wonderful things Elsie had ever experienced. She never could have imagined how heavenly it would feel to have delightfully warm water sluicing over her body. It soothed her aches. The *blow dryer* was marvelous, too. Her hair was completely dry and fluffy in a few minutes.

Finally, dressed in a fresh *gown*, she returned to bed. The head of the bed was raised so that she was in a semi-sitting position. She closed her eyes and dozed a little. The whole experience had been very relaxing.

She rested until someone entered the room. Opening her eyes, she expected to see Gabe, but it was a man she didn't know. He wasn't dressed in scrubs. She was immediately wary.

He smiled. "Hello, Elizabeth."

"Hello," she said tentatively. "Who are you?"

He smiled warmly. "My name is David Sinclair, and I'm a friend. A very good friend."

She shook her head slowly, wishing Gabe were here. "I don't remember you."

"That's okay. I didn't think you would."

"Where do I know you from? I don't live here. I live in a place called Cincinnati, and it's far away."

He nodded. "That's right. I live in Cincinnati too, and until a couple of days ago, I was your boyfriend."

At that moment, Gabe walked in carrying a cup in each hand. Elsie gave a sigh of relief.

"Excuse me, who are you?" asked Gabe.

"I'm David Sinclair." David offered Gabe his hand.

Gabe set down one of the cups and returned the handshake. "Dr. Gabe Soldani. Here, Elizabeth, I brought you the mocha I promised."

Elsie took the cup, but didn't taste it. On seeing David, Gabe became tense and that made Elsie tense too.

Gabe turned back to the new arrival. "If you *were* Elizabeth's boyfriend until a couple of days ago, what are you doing here?"

"Her parents called me. They told me what happened. They didn't know Elizabeth and I had broken up on Saturday morning."

"Then why didn't you fill them in?"

"Dr. Soldani, shall we sit down and I'll tell you what I know?"

Gabe nodded, motioning for David to sit in the recliner as he sat in the other small chair. "So, I'll ask again, if you and Elizabeth are no longer a couple, why did you fly here from Cincinnati this morning?"

Fly? There it was again. She had to remember to ask about that.

"I care about Elizabeth, but in the short time we dated I learned a few things that I didn't think would ever change. Elizabeth drives herself harder than anyone I know. After a while, I came to believe it was out of some need to please her parents. She aced the hardest courses in prep school, and was always first in her class. But these were simply her parents' expectations. I know you went to medical school with her, so you know she graduated as valedictorian. What you probably don't know is that it was her third time. She was valedictorian in both high school and college. Her parents didn't even attend those ceremonies."

Elizabeth didn't understand all of what that meant, but it didn't sound good.

Gabe put two fingers to his brow, as if he were in pain.

David continued. "Elizabeth, I believed your constant push to excel was to gain your parents' attention, which they didn't seem overly anxious to give. I told you that you would never be happy as long as you relied on their approval for fulfilment, and it broke my heart watching you continue to try. You were probably even dating me because it was expected. Your mother set us up."

"What does that mean?"

"It means I know your mother, and she suggested that I take you out on a date."

"But that still doesn't explain why they called you and why you dropped everything to get here," observed Gabe.

"They called me for several reasons. First, they said she remembered you and she believes she loves you. I guess they thought she might remember me. I was fairly certain she wouldn't because I don't believe she loved me. Still, they figured if she remembered me, I could talk her into going to Baltimore."

"I'm not going to Baltimore," Elsie said emphatically.

To her surprise, David grinned. "Good girl. Although your parents don't know this yet, the reason I came was to support *that* decision."

Gabe gaped at him. "Are you serious?"

"Absolutely. Elizabeth, I don't think we were meant to be together, but that doesn't change the fact that I care very deeply for you. It's rather ironic that it took losing your memory for you to stand up to them. I firmly believe that had you not, had you simply been injured, you would be in Baltimore this morning regardless of your feelings for

Gabe. And as to that, you've mentioned him to me in the past, but you've never told me what happened. I always suspected you had unresolved feelings, but had simply chalked it up as a love lost. It doesn't surprise me that he is the only person you remember. So that's why I came."

"Thank you, David."

"It's my pleasure. One of the last things I said to you on Saturday was that I hoped someday you could work your way free of *expectations* and allow joy to enter your life. Maybe this fugue state you're in will open the doors for that."

Gabe shook his head. "Holy freakin' cow, the fugue could have been brought on by this."

"I wondered as much. If that's the case, the last thing she needs is to be forced into something by her parents. If I need to tell all of this to the psychiatrist, I will." David turned to Elizabeth. "Now, drink your mocha: it's one of your favorite things."

She took a sip and was transported. "Oh my, that really is delicious. But can I tell you both? It's a little disconcerting that you know what I like better than I do."

Chapter 8

When Gabe walked into Elizabeth's room to find the boyfriend with whom she had apparently just broken up, his heart went to his throat. When he heard that her parents had called the man, he wasn't happy, but perhaps they were doing what they thought was best. After all, if she remembered an old boyfriend, she might remember a new one. The more her memory was jogged, the more likely it was to return.

But when David described Elizabeth's relationship with her parents, when he said they hadn't attended her high school or her college graduation, he became angry.

With himself.

Again, he remembered the conversation where he had confronted her about not telling him who she was until after he had learned the truth.

"I never dreamed they'd show up."

"What the hell, Elizabeth? You were graduating from med school. You were the freaking valedictorian for the love of God."

"You don't understand—"

"No, I don't."

"Gabe, please listen. My family isn't like yours."

He hadn't listened. He could never have imagined there was any doubt about her parents being there.

When they arrived shortly after David, things got tense quickly.

Her mother carried a bag from the hotel boutique. "David, it's lovely to see you."

Dr. Quinn shook his hand. "Yes, it has been a while, but it's very good of you to come. I'm sure Elizabeth appreciates it."

"I'm happy to help Elizabeth in any way I can."

Neither of her parents greeted Gabe.

Her mother sat on the edge of her bed. "Darling, I brought you some lounging pajamas, slippers, and a robe, so you don't have to wear a hospital gown. Gentlemen, if you'll give us a moment of privacy, I'll help her change."

"I'll change later, mother," said Elizabeth.

"Don't be silly, darling. You'll be much more comfortable in these. They're cashmere. And you've always called me mom, not mother."

Gabe had a hard time schooling his expression. *Cashmere pajamas?* For Pete's sake, who buys pajamas that need to be dry-cleaned?

Dr. Quinn leveled a glare at him.

Gabe simply motioned to the door. "After you, sir."

They were barely through the door and had it closed when Dr. Quinn rounded on Gabe. "What in the hell is your end-game, young man? Are you after her money? Are you hoping to convince her to marry you while she's in a fugue? Perhaps pay off your student loan debt before she remembers anything?"

Gabe became angry instantly. He summoned every ounce of self-control he contained and said, "No, sir. I have no *end game*. I care about Elizabeth and want what's best for her."

"Then why are you manipulating her to stay here?"

"Manipulating her? Me? Are you serious? *I* assumed she would want to go with you and was as shocked as you were when she said she wanted to stay here."

"Well, you made no attempt to convince her to do what's best and go to Baltimore with us."

"But that would be manipulating her. She's the one who wants to stay here. I haven't pushed her one way or the other. It was you who came in last night, threatening to have her declared incompetent if she didn't do what you wanted her to do. I was the one that comforted the sobbing, shattered girl *you* left without so much as a 'sleep well.'"

"Why don't you just leave her the hell alone?"

David stepped in. "Dr. Quinn, this is not necessary. We all want the same thing: what's best for Elizabeth. Do you agree?"

"Of course."

"Then let's let this play out. You requested a psych consult, did you not? Didn't you tell me the chief of the department will be seeing her this morning?"

The chief of the department? Christ almighty. Her father certainly played to win.

"Yes," snapped Dr. Quinn. Turning to Gabe again, he said, "And you can just clear off now, Soldani."

David shook his head. "As far as I can tell, Gabe has only been supportive. I know they were friends in the past because she has talked about him before. In fact, I have always been under the impression that they were very good friends. I absolutely believe she remembers him and what's more, she seems to take comfort from his presence. When she doesn't recognize anyone else, why would you deny her that?"

Because he has to be angry at someone, and I am the easiest target.

"Fine. But I swear to you, Soldani, if I find out you were the one pulling her strings, I will destroy you."

Elizabeth's mother opened the door. "James, you need to keep your voice down. You're upsetting Elizabeth."

Dr. Quinn cast one more quelling stare at Gabe before striding into the room past his wife.

David and Gabe followed.

Elizabeth sat in her bed, looking tense but very pretty in spite of her injuries. Pale pink cashmere pajamas might be impractical, but they looked cozy and soft, as did the delicate silk robe. The cream colored, cable-knit slippers by the bed looked suspiciously like cashmere too.

When her gaze caught his, the fear and vulnerability

Gabe saw there caused his heart to ache for her. She reached a hand out to him.

He took a step toward her, and Dr. Quinn grabbed his shoulder.

"Elizabeth, Dr. Gerald Rose, the chief of psychiatry will be up to see you shortly. I have some calls to make, and I think it would be a good idea if we all left and allowed you to rest until he arrives."

She nodded. "If you have something you need to do, I don't wish to keep you from it. But I would like Gabe to stay with me."

"I don't think that's a good idea."

"You've made that clear, but until after I have met with Dr. Rose, it is my understanding that I can make my own choices."

"I'm only thinking of what's best for you."

"I'm not certain you know what's best for me."

"This needs to stop," said Elizabeth's mother. "James, she's confused. Antagonizing her won't help. We both have calls to make. Perhaps by the time we're done, Dr. Rose will have an answer for us, and we can take Elizabeth home." She took her husband by the elbow, but before leaving with him, she said, "David, you have our numbers. Call if we're needed."

David nodded. "Certainly."

Gabe took the hand Elizabeth held out and then sat beside her.

She sighed. "It seems my parents already know the outcome."

"They're making an assumption, sweetheart. That's all."

David leaned against the window ledge. "Gabe, is Gerald Rose still the chief of psychiatry here?"

"Yes."

A slow smile spread across his face. "Then I think if Dr. Quinn wants Elizabeth declared incompetent, calling him in was a mistake. I know Dr. Rose. He's an old friend of *my* dad's. A resident might be intimidated, but there is no way Gerald Rose will do anything just because a high-handed surgeon from another hospital wants him to."

"What do you think, Gabe?" she asked hopefully.

"I've never met him, but Dr. Rose has an excellent reputation. I think he will make a fair evaluation."

"What if he says I'm not competent?"

Gabe leaned forward and kissed her forehead. "Let's not borrow trouble."

They didn't have long to wait. The chief of psychiatry arrived not long after Dr. and Mrs. Quinn left.

When Dr. Rose walked in the room, Gabe stifled a smile. If anyone could look more like a stereotypical psychiatrist, he wasn't sure how. Dr. Rose was a diminutive older man with graying hair, dark-rimmed glasses, and a neatly trimmed goatee that was also liberally sprinkled with gray.

The old doctor smiled broadly. "Good morning. I'm Dr. Rose. David, I certainly didn't expect to see you here." He had a rich Scottish burr.

David shook hands with Dr. Rose. "It's very nice to see you. I'm here because Elizabeth is a friend of mine."

"Is she? What a small world." He turned toward the bed. "So if I'm not much mistaken, you are Dr. Elizabeth Quinn.

Dr. Rose seemed to emanate warmth, and Elizabeth visibly relaxed. "Yes, I am."

"And you are?" he asked Gabe.

"I'm Gabriel Soldani. I'm a pediatric hospitalist here."

"And since Dr. Quinn isn't a wee lassie, I presume ye're a friend as well?"

"Yes. We went to medical school together."

Dr. Rose shook Gabe's hand. "It is a pleasure to meet ye, Dr. Soldani."

"Likewise, sir."

He turned his attention back to Elizabeth. "Do ye mind if I call ye by yer given name?"

Elizabeth smiled. "That's fine."

"Splendid. Now, Elizabeth, I understand ye're having a wee bit of trouble remembering things. Would ye mind telling me a bit about what happened?"

"I don't remember what happened. I've been told I was in an accident."

"And ye remember nothing?"

"I remember Gabe. We're old friends."

"And David Sinclair, do you remember him?"

She gave David a sad smile. "No. He seems very nice, but I don't remember him."

Dr. Rose smiled broadly. "He is a fine young man and the image of his father. David, were you in the city visiting yer dad?"

"No, I came specifically to see Elizabeth, but I intend to see Dad later today."

"Give him my best regards."

"Certainly, sir."

Dr. Rose turned to Elizabeth. "Now, ye said Gabe here is an old friend and based on the grip ye have on his hand, it appears ye're very confident of that. Can ye tell me why?"

"When I saw him, I had memories."

"Did ye? And did he look as braw as he does now?"

She chuckled. "Not quite. In my memories, he didn't have the beard. But I like it."

Gabe was shocked. She had never mentioned that.

"Ye look surprised, lad. Many a lass finds nicely trimmed facial hair attractive." He smiled, stroking his goatee.

Gabe laughed. "That's not what surprised me. This is the first Elizabeth has said that I don't have a beard in her memories. I'd forgotten it, but I didn't grow the beard until I came here for my residency."

"So ye knew each other in medical school. When did ye see her last?"

Guilt swirled in his gut. "Six years ago, on the day we graduated."

"I see. What else do ye remember about Gabe, lass?"

"The images are so fleeting, it's hard to focus on them. But the feeling I have is nearly overpowering. I'm certain he means the world to me and that I love him."

"I see." He glanced around the room. "I expected to find your parents here. They were so very concerned about ye."

Elizabeth's brows drew together for a moment. "They said they had calls to make."

"If you need them, I have their cell phone numbers," offered David.

"Nay, it isn't necessary. I just thought they'd be here. They told me you and Elizabeth are dating."

"We were, but we aren't any longer," David clarified. "Her parents don't know that yet."

"But ye came here—this morning, I presume— specifically to see her. Why?"

"Because I care about her. I believe her parents often railroad her, and she tries to make them happy by giving in. When they called me, I feared they were about to do it again, and I wanted to be here to support Elizabeth in any way I could."

"That's very thoughtful of ye." The old doctor canted his head. "And ye, Gabe, ye seem content to have her hand in yers. Why is that?"

Gabe sighed. "I love her. I think I have for years. It was my own stupidity that made me break up with her in the first place."

"I see." He surveyed both men for a moment. "Well now, Elizabeth, if it's okay with ye, I'm going to ask these two rogues to leave us for a bit."

"That's fine." She smiled at Gabe and squeezed his

hand before letting go.

~ * ~

Gabe and David left the room, and Elsie smiled hesitantly at Dr. Rose.

He smiled back. "Do ye mind if I take seat?"

"No, not at all."

He sat in the recliner, making himself comfortable. "Well lass, I suspect this has been a right harrowing few days for ye."

Elsie frowned. "I...It's..."

"I understand, lass. I know all about the pocket watch."

"Did Gertrude send ye?"

"Nay, I haven't seen her in years. When yer father described yer odd memory loss, I suspected ye were a time traveler. But when ye described the intense feelings ye have for young Dr. Soldani, I was certain. Where are ye from, lass? Or should I ask when?"

"I'm from the Highlands of Scotland. When I left it was the year of our Lord twelve-hundred and seventy-nine."

"Ye don't say? Bless yer wee soul, I've haven't encountered many travelers who came to the future. I have more experience with those who returned from the past. How old were ye when ye left?"

"I was twenty-one."

"And did ye know ye'd be coming forward so far?"

"I didn't know anything. I didn't accept the watch. Elizabeth did."

"And ye're alive? I've never heard of that happening."

"Gertrude said several things happened differently. I don't understand it all, but the watch stayed here instead of going with Elizabeth. And our souls changed places before I...well, before I..."

"Ah, ye hadn't done the thing that would have ended in yer death. Now that's very interesting. So, what's going to happen now?"

"In my time, Lady MacKenzie desperately needs Elizabeth's help. I want her to have it, and Elizabeth is willing. Gertrude says we can change back when the problem is resolved."

"And have ye a mission here?"

"I think I might. This feeling I have for Gabe—well, it's hard to describe. But I think Elizabeth cares very deeply for him. I reckon I can maybe help bring them together."

"Gertrude always has been a great one for making sure souls find each other if they're intended to be together."

"So, what now?"

"Well, Dr. Levi believes ye're in a fugue state and that is an excellent explanation for what everyone thinks has happened. So I will concur and suggest that ye meet with me once a week."

"But I'm not ill."

"I know ye're not ill, lass. I'm a Scot myself, and I want to find out more about where ye're from and what it was like then. And ye might have questions that ye'd rather ask someone who knows yer situation. Besides, we need to be seen to do something. It will smooth things nicely when Elizabeth returns."

"What about Elizabeth's parents? They want me declared incompetent."

"Those two are a puzzle. I do believe they care for their daughter, but she doesn't seem to be their priority, does she?"

"No." Elsie looked away for a moment.

"What is it, lass?"

"It's silly I guess. My parents died when I was very young. My aunt cared for me, but…"

"It wasn't like a parent."

"No, it wasn't. When I learned Elizabeth's parents were rushing to her side, I had rather hoped to feel a part of a family."

"And ye may still. Don't give up hope. Ye just never know."

Elsie smiled and nodded, unable to completely shake the sadness left by disappointment.

"Well, ye're perfectly competent, and ye need to stay here in New York. I suspect that isn't what yer da wants to hear, but so be it. We must make way for the course of true love." He winked and chuckled.

When Elsie and Dr. Rose had finished chatting, he went to fetch Gabe and David from a nearby lounge.

David called her parents. When they arrived, Elizabeth's father was as impatient as ever. "Now with the formalities done, can we take our daughter home?"

"Dr. Quinn, let's not be so hasty. Ye asked me to determine yer daughter's competence to make her own decisions."

"She has no memories. It seems open and shut to me."

"Well, it isn't quite as simple as ye think. *Open and shut* may be consistent with a surgeon's practice, but it is rarely the case in psychiatry. As ye're aware, the law requires us to respect a patient's wishes unless they are unable to adequately make choices for themselves. The evaluation of competence is intertwined with the decision the patient is being asked to make. The more serious the decision, the more carefully we have to make the assessment. Elizabeth has profound retrograde amnesia related to a fugue state, but that alone doesn't mean she isn't competent. She demonstrates the ability to reason, she holds appropriate values, and she understands her condition as well as the choices available to her. Furthermore, in this case, she is not refusing treatment. She is simply refusing to change hospitals. I find her perfectly competent to make that decision."

"She has no one to care for her here."

"She has agreed to meet with me regularly so I can

monitor her condition as long as she is in New York. If she returns to her home in Cincinnati, I will ensure that she is under the care of a trusted colleague there. It seems she has friends she trusts in both cities who are willing to help as needed."

"Who will manage her finances? She can't read. She has a massive trust-fund that could be wiped out in the blink of an eye."

"I can understand why that might concern ye. Elizabeth, would you be willing to have an attorney and an accountant act on your behalf regarding your financial matters? Someone both you and your parents would be comfortable with?"

Elsie frowned. "I'm not sure how to find people like that or know if they were skilled."

Before her father could jump in, David said, "Perhaps you would allow me to suggest some candidates. I'll take you to meet them. Then your parents can review and approve your selections."

Elsie looked to Gabe. "What do you think?"

"I think it is an excellent idea. David has the skills it takes to help guide you, and both you and your parents seem to trust him."

She looked back at her parents. "Does that make you more comfortable?"

Elizabeth's father glowered at her. "Your mother and grandfather own one of the largest legal firms in the country and you think it's a good idea to seek an attorney elsewhere?"

Elsie was stunned by his derision. "Why are you so angry with me?"

"Because you are being obstinate and unreasonable."

Elsie wasn't going to give in to tears again. In that instant, she steeled herself. She didn't want a single thing from this man. She turned to Gabe. "I hate to ask this, but would you help me for a little while, even if I have nothing? Just until I get my memory back?"

"Of course I will."

"Thank you." Turning her attention back to Elizabeth's father, she said, "There. You can appoint whomever you choose to manage my affairs. I want nothing to do with any of it. Keep it for when my memory comes back. If this is the way a father treats a daughter..." Her voice caught. She swallowed hard. She would not cry. "If this is the way a father treats a daughter, I don't need a father in my life."

"Elizabeth!" exclaimed her mother.

Her father turned his glare on Dr. Rose. "Do you still think my daughter is competent to make decisions for herself?"

"Absolutely. I'm inclined to agree with her. Ye've not shown Elizabeth a modicum of affection in my presence. When we spoke on the phone last night, 'twas clear ye were concerned about her, but the disruption to your schedule was as much a concern." He gave Elsie a warm smile. "Ye needn't worry about having nothing, lass. I'll help ye sort out things with yer employer. I'm absolutely certain ye have disability insurance that should provide a little income for ye until things resolve."

"Thank you, Dr. Rose."

"I've had enough of this foolishness," declared Dr. Quinn.

Elizabeth's mother put a hand on his shoulder. "James, you're not helping things. Elizabeth, there is no need to take such drastic measures. I need to rearrange a few things, but within a week, I could be set up to work for a limited time from the Manhattan office. I'll appoint someone to help you with your affairs. You don't need to rely on strangers."

"I know you mean well, but anyone you appoint will be a stranger to me. You both are strangers to me. And for some reason, I have the distinct impression it's been this way for a while. It seems you've raised me to be independent."

Charlotte Quinn inclined her head. "We have, but that is an admirable quality."

"I'm glad you think so, and I'm sorry you're both so upset with me. With that said, I'm not going to Baltimore. Since independence is such an admirable quality, I intend to remain independent. If you wish to stay here, I'd like that, but it's up to you. Please don't feel as if you must rearrange anything on my behalf. I'll be fine."

Her father stormed out of the room without a word.

Her mother sighed. "I'll return in a few days, and we'll sort things out." She kissed Elsie's cheek and left the room.

Dr. Rose released a frustrated sigh. "They are a disappointment." His face brightened. "But ye seem to have two very good friends, and, of course, me."

"Thank you, all of you."

"Now, I'm going to contact yer neurologist. He wants ye to have another scan of yer head called magnetic resonance imaging. Gabe will explain it to ye. I think that's a very good idea, just to make sure ye don't have a brain injury from the accident that was missed. I also understand an orthopedic doctor will put a cast on that arm today. When they ask ye what color ye want, be adventurous. After that's all done, I see no reason to keep ye here in the hospital. As we discussed, I'll see ye once a week. I generally take Wednesday afternoons off, but I am going to make an exception. I'll meet with ye at two each week. Call my office with yer schedule, young man," he said to Gabe. "If ye're working, we'll make other arrangements or I'll come to her."

Elsie smiled at him, tears welling in her eyes.

"Don't worry about a thing, lass, ye'll be grand."

Chapter 9

Gabe smiled when Elizabeth picked bright blue as her cast color. He wasn't surprised that she didn't like the MRI. The technicians let him talk to her through the intercom during the scan.

When all of this was completed and they were back in her hospital room, Martin Levi came to see her.

"Well, Elizabeth, your MRI is perfectly normal, so in the absence of a brain injury, I think the diagnosis of fugue is accurate. I have spoken to Dr. Rose and understand you'll be seeing him every Wednesday as long as you are in the city, so I am going to discharge you to his care."

"What does that mean?"

"It means you can leave the hospital. Do you have a place to stay?"

"She'll be staying with me," Gabe answered.

A happy smile spread across Elizabeth's face.

Martin nodded. "Then everything is set. I'll go write discharge orders, and you can get ready to go."

He left the room, and Elizabeth frowned. "What do I need to do to get ready?"

"You need to get dressed."

"But I am dressed, and these are the only clothes I have."

"The clothes you are wearing are pajamas and not normally worn outside, but I suppose they'll be good enough to get you home. You can wear my coat. I'll check the bags that were brought down from the ICU. There might be something usable from the clothes you were wearing when you were brought in. At least your shoes should be okay."

He found her purse, computer bag, and two white

patient belonging bags containing the remnants of her clothing. The only usable items were socks and ankle boots. "Yup, socks and shoes are about all that's salvageable. The rest of it can be thrown away."

"Actually, that is what I've been taking care of this afternoon," said David as he walked into the room with a shopping bag in one hand and a woman's coat in the other. "I assumed you had a suitcase in the cab, so I tracked that down. It was found when the cab was towed, and it was turned in to the lost and found at the 115th precinct in Queens. I have sent someone to get it and will see that it gets delivered to Gabe's apartment tomorrow. I also stopped in to see my father. He sent his executive assistant to Sak's to get you a few things to wear until you have your own things back." David put the bag on her bed.

"Sak's?" asked Gabe, incredulous.

"Should I have sent her to Barney's?" David sounded concerned.

Barney's? Was he out of his mind? "No. I would have thought something a little more affordable."

"Money isn't really an issue with me."

"Come on, money is an issue with everyone."

David gave him a puzzled smile. "Gabe, do you know who I am?"

"All I know is that your dad is acquainted with Elizabeth's mother. I figured he was a lawyer."

"Well, he isn't. My dad is Aldous Sinclair, owner and chief executive officer of Sinclair Amalgamated, and he's Matheson & Matheson's biggest client."

"Excuse me? Huge-multinational-conglomerate-with-ties-to everything Sinclair Amalgamated?"

"That would be the one.

"What does all of that mean?" asked Elizabeth.

It means you and your friends are way out of my league.

David waved a hand. "It's not important, Elizabeth. I'll

step out of the room so you can get changed."

Elizabeth had begun pulling items from the bag.

Gabe nodded. "I can leave too, unless you need some help."

She held up a very pretty pink bra and panty set. "I think I do. I don't know what these are."

"Those are, um, undergarments. I can ask a nursing assistant in to help you if you prefer."

Elizabeth blushed. "Didn't you say we have...um...made love?"

"Yes, we have."

"Then I don't guess there is any reason to be shy."

He chuckled. "No, I don't guess there is."

Aldous Sinclair's assistant had excellent taste. In addition to the undergarments, there was a pair of dark wash jeans, a loose-fitting, feminine blouse, and a slightly oversized, peach, cashmere cardigan that fit easily over the cast.

"What is it with you people and cashmere?" he teased.

"I have no idea unless it has something to do with how incredibly soft it is." she teased back, her eyes twinkling.

Helping her dress had been a bad idea. The attraction he felt was so strong that putting clothes *on* her was the absolute last thing he wanted to do. Through sheer force of will, he did.

Once she was dressed, David returned followed by a nurse with a wheelchair.

"I can walk," said Elizabeth, frowning at the chair.

"I know you can, Dr. Quinn, but even though you're going home, you are recovering from a serious accident and have broken ribs. You must take things easy, including allowing me to push you to the front door."

Elizabeth sighed, but sat in the chair with her purse, laptop bag, and the new coat David had brought her on her lap. They made one stop by the doctors' lounge so Gabe could get his coat. As they neared the front of the hospital, the nurse asked, "Dr. Soldani, do you have a car?"

"No. We'll need a cab."

"Actually, my driver should be waiting for us."

"Driver?"

"Sinclair Amalgamated, remember?"

This all made Gabe a little uncomfortable, but he wouldn't refuse David's assistance today. With her broken ribs, a drive in a high-end luxury car would be much more comfortable for Elizabeth than a cab.

However, when they rolled Elizabeth outside, her eyes went wide. "I—I don't think…Gabe, I can't…I don't want to get in that."

"Elizabeth, we talked about this. You saw the cars and buses from your window. It will be okay."

"But you said you usually walk to work. Can't we just walk?"

"No, sweetheart, we can't. It wouldn't be good for you."

David nodded. "Elizabeth, there is nothing to be afraid of. This is a very safe car with a skilled, professional driver. And Gabe is right: you cannot walk to his apartment."

The nurse narrowed her eyes. "Honestly, girl, you were brave enough to have that MRI today—I couldn't have done that, but I'd have no trouble at all riding in that fine vehicle."

Elizabeth still looked wary, but she nodded.

"That's my girl," said Gabe as he helped her into the back seat.

David climbed into the front seat as Gabe went around to get in from the other side.

"This is Jake," said David, motioning to the driver.

"Good afternoon, Dr. Quinn, Dr. Soldani. I'll have you home in just a few minutes."

Gabe glanced out the window. "The roads are remarkably clear considering how much snow we got."

"Crews worked all night, sir. They didn't even have to

close schools today."

They reached Gabe's building in a few minutes. He hopped out and ran around to help Elizabeth from the car.

David gathered her few belongings. "I'll help you get inside."

Gabe's building was one of the few in the area that had an elevator, for which he was very thankful today. When they reached his apartment, he invited David in.

"Thank you, I won't stay. I am flying back to Cincinnati tonight."

Gabe shook his hand. "I can't tell you how much I appreciate what you've done. Thank you for everything."

"You're welcome." He turned to Elizabeth and took her hands in his. "It is hard to believe that just two days ago you were mine."

She smiled sadly.

"But I suppose you never really were mine, and now I know why. I wanted joy to enter your life, and I think you have every chance of that happening now." He kissed her cheek. "Nevertheless, I will miss you."

"Thank you for coming to help me. I don't know what I would've done without both of you. We will see you again, won't we?"

"I expect so. I know you told your father you wanted nothing from him, and that's fine in the short-term. I'm sure you'll get your memory back soon, so it isn't likely to ever be an issue, but if it becomes one, I can help you. Also, depending on what happens, you may want help with your things in Cincinnati. You simply need to ask. Gabe has my card."

~ * ~

Elsie tried to be brave and take everything in stride, but this twenty-first century world just seemed to get bigger and louder and faster. Buildings grew too tall. She'd been aware of that based on what she could see from the hospital windows, but being on the ground and looking up was an entirely different perspective. And although the sun had set, there were so many lights that everything was visible— except the stars.

When the sleek, black, car pulled up to the doors, a memory flashed through her mind of a terrible screeching sound and instantaneous pain. She knew instinctively it was Elizabeth's memory of the accident. Elsie really wasn't ready to ride in a car yet, but both David and Gabe insisted, so she complied.

There were so many vehicles on the street that it was no wonder they crashed into each other sometimes. Apparently, they weren't going terribly fast, but she had never traveled at such a pace. In fact, she was accustomed to walking nearly everywhere she went.

Once they reached Gabe's building, she had to ride in another elevator. She didn't like elevators because they made her stomach feel odd, but she guessed she would have to get used to it. Climbing stairs to the heights of these buildings would take forever and be exhausting.

She stood just inside Gabe's apartment and for the first time since waking yesterday, she felt comfortable. They came in through a small entryway with a closet to one side, in which Gabe hung both their coats. The entryway opened into the main room, and there was a window in the opposite wall. A table and chairs were arranged just to the right of the entry and other furniture, the likes of which she had never seen, stood just beyond, closer to the window.

"It's very small—just one bedroom—but the location is ideal and it's all I can afford in this area."

The room was somewhat bigger than the main room of Aunt Dolina's cottage, and she nearly said so. Thankfully, she stopped herself in time. "It's lovely."

"Follow me. I'll show you the rest and help you put your things away."

"I thought you said it just had one room?"

"I said one bedroom, and it's this way." Carrying her bags, he stepped into a small corridor and motioned to an opening on the left. "The kitchen is in there." He indicated another door on his left and said, "I have a washer and dryer in there. I was crazy lucky to get an apartment with those."

She wondered what a *washer and dryer*, washed and dried. She reckoned she'd find out soon enough.

He motioned to a door at the end of the passage. "The bathroom is in there." Then he opened a door to the right. "And this is the bedroom. I'll make some room for your things in the closet before your bag is delivered tomorrow. You can have the bed in here. I'll sleep on the couch."

"The couch?"

"Yeah, the couch…uh…the long piece of furniture for sitting on in the living room."

Ah, she had assumed that was his bed when she thought there was only one room. "Gabe, I know you didn't plan on any of this. And I probably caught you off guard when I asked if you would help me. I don't want to take your bed."

"Stop it, Elizabeth. I love you, and I want to help you. I want you in my life. You will not sleep on the couch. You have a broken arm and broken ribs."

Elsie frowned. She really didn't like the idea of being alone, even if he was just in the next room, but she wouldn't argue now.

Gabe put the bag containing the *pajamas* on the bed. "You should probably change back into these. I'll heat us up something for dinner while you do. Do you need any help?"

"I think I can manage."

He opened two drawers in a chest and combined the contents into one. "You can put the clothes you're wearing in here. Then, come out to the kitchen."

She nodded, and he left the room, closing the door

behind him. She didn't like being alone. She tried to undress. The sweater was simple; it was loose-fitting. The blouse came off easily enough as well. But the thing Gabe had called a bra closed in the back. Between her broken arm and the pain in her ribs, she couldn't maneuver out of it. She managed to unfasten the *jeans,* but she couldn't get them off over the boots she was wearing. She tried to take the boots off, but unlacing them and working her feet out of them with one hand proved to be difficult. During the process, she lost her balance and fell. She found herself sitting on the floor in a bra and panties, jeans around her ankles, boots stubbornly tied, and ribs throbbing. She couldn't suppress her tears.

Gabe was through the door within moments. "Oh, God, Elizabeth, what happened? Are you all right?" He knelt beside her, putting an arm around her shoulder.

"I just...I just lost my balance." She swiped at her tears. "And I can't get the boots off. Or this bra thing."

He kissed her temple. "Please don't cry. Let me help you." He undid the bootlaces and pulled off her shoes before removing the jeans from her ankles.

"Let's get you up." He lifted her gently from the floor and sat her on the bed. Moments later, her bra was off and he helped her into the soft pajamas. "Come have some soup and then you need to rest."

He led her to the table and pulled out a chair. A strange beeping sound came from the kitchen. He smiled. "The soup's ready. Sit tight for a sec."

When he came back, he had two steaming bowls of soup. "This is my mom's minestrone. I always come back from their house with containers of leftovers. And while she will resort to dried pasta in a pinch, she says there is no excuse for canned soup."

Elsie didn't understand a word he had said.

"Let me get spoons. I'll be right back."

He made several trips to bring spoons, bread, butter,

and glasses filled with cold water. "I'd crack open a bottle of wine, but alcohol doesn't mix well with your pain medicine."

"This is fine."

"Dig in." He ate a big spoonful of soup.

Elsie looked at the soup for a moment. The broth was *red*. "What did you call this?"

"Minestrone."

"Why is it red?"

"It has tomatoes in it."

"What's a tomato?

"It's a red vegetable…or, I guess, technically a fruit. Do you recognize anything in the soup?"

"Beans and carrots. And this looks a little like the noodles I ate yesterday."

"That's right. Go ahead and try it."

She cautiously lifted her spoon to her mouth. The broth was tangy, flavorful, and unlike anything she had ever tasted. She smiled. "It is very good. I think I like tomatoes."

He laughed. "You certainly used to. Wait until the summer when we can get fresh New Jersey tomatoes. They're the best."

She wouldn't be here in the summer. She wouldn't be here for more than a few weeks. After all the pain, frustration, and overwhelming sensations she had experienced in the twenty-first century, that thought should've made her happy, but a pang of anticipated loss twisted in her gut instead.

When they finished eating, she helped him carry the dishes into the kitchen. There was a sink in the kitchen like the one in the hospital bathroom, only bigger. As he washed the dishes, she glanced around. There were *machines* that she didn't recognize. One very large one—the size of a small wardrobe—hummed quietly. As she looked around, she realized there was no fire and no source of heat of any kind that she recognized. And for that matter, there was no pot of hot soup.

"Where did the soup come from?"

"I told you, my mother made it. Every time I visit, she sends me back to New York with homemade food."

"But how…I don't understand. There isn't a pot anywhere." She wanted to say there was no fire either, but in her short time here, she had seen so many amazing things that she figured something must have replaced fire for cooking.

Gabe smiled. "You don't remember what a microwave is." He opened a door and a light came on inside. "This is a microwave. It heats food really fast." He closed the door and opened one of the doors in the big humming machine. Again, a light came on, revealing a variety of small containers. He handed her one.

"It's frozen." Elsie tried to cover her amazement, but it wasn't easy.

"Yup. This is a freezer. Mom puts soup and stuff in these plastic containers, and I freeze them so they will keep until I'm ready to use them. Then I just pull one out and heat it up."

She handed the container back to him. He looked at the writing on the lid. "Wedding soup. You'll love this. We'll have it for lunch tomorrow." He pulled out another container like the first one, shut the door, and opened the other door. Another light came on. This section was bigger than the first one, and it also held a number of containers.

He put the frozen soup on one of the shelves. "This side is a refrigerator. It keeps things cold, but not frozen. Milk, butter, cheese, meat, eggs, fresh fruits and vegetables, really anything that will spoil if it gets too warm. All of those kinds of things are kept in here." He opened a drawer in the bottom and pulled out two orange balls, slid the drawer back in, and closed the door of the *refrigerator*.

She watched him dig his thumb into one of the balls

and peel away the thick outer layer, releasing the most wonderful aroma. He handed her the whitish ball that remained while he peeled the other one. He put the peelings in a container under the sink. "I keep the garbage bin here." Then he dug his thumbs into the center of the peeled ball and pulled it apart. It seemed to be made up of multiple little segments. At her confused look, he popped a segment in his mouth and said, "It's an orange. Try it."

She did exactly what he had done, and the moment she bit into it, her mouth was filled with the most wonderful thing she had ever tasted. This must be the source of the juice she had drunk in the hospital, but the fruit itself was infinitely better.

Gabe grinned. "You like it?"

"I don't think I've ever tasted anything so delicious."

"Really?" A slow grin spread across his face, and he leaned forward and kissed her softly. He caught her lower lip between his teeth and sucked it gently into his mouth.

A pleasant fluttering started in her stomach, making her forget about the orange entirely.

When he pulled away, she was breathless. "Mmm. Yes, entirely delicious, but I'm not sure whether it is you or the orange."

~ * ~

Gabe adored this woman. How could he have walked out of her life five and a half years ago? He kissed her again. "As delicious as you are, I must stop kissing you and let you finish eating your orange."

She blushed, but didn't look away. "I like your kisses."

"Then I promise to give you many more. But not tonight. You need rest."

She didn't respond, but she frowned slightly.

When they were through with the oranges, he guided her into the bedroom and folded the covers back. "Let's get you tucked in."

Elizabeth's brow furrowed. "I don't want to sleep here."

"Sweetheart, you cannot sleep on the couch."

"I—I don't want to sleep on the couch. I don't want to sleep anywhere by myself. Everything is so strange, and I'm…" Her voice broke and she looked away.

"What is it?"

She turned her gaze back to him. "I'm afraid to be alone."

"I'll just be in the other room. You aren't alone."

"Last night, you held my hand while I slept and I felt safe."

"You are safe."

"Please, Gabe. I can't explain it. I'm sure things won't seem so strange after a few days. I just don't want to be alone yet."

"But, Elizabeth—"

"You said…you said we've slept together before. Would you sleep with me? I don't mean…well you know. I just don't want to be by myself. Please, Gabe."

He gathered her gently into his arms. "Of course I will."

Elsie sighed. She was the slightest bit embarrassed at having asked that, but nevertheless, she was extraordinarily relieved. She fell asleep curled up next to Gabe.

Chapter 10

As he lay in the dark with Elizabeth in his arms, Gabe tried to process all that had happened over the last two days. If last week someone had mentioned Elizabeth to him, he would have said she was an old girlfriend from medical school. He would have remembered her fondly—he might even have said that he had loved her once, but he also would have firmly believed that relationship was in the past. When he walked into her hospital room to find her cowering in fear, something long dormant awakened in him. He was filled with the profound need to keep her safe, to cherish her. The sensation was intense—more intense than anything he remembered feeling for Elizabeth.

When Martin had asked if she remembered him, she had said, *I-I think I do. I don't remember his name, but I think...I think I love him.*

Gabe had been instantly overcome with the sense that he absolutely loved her. Thinking about it rationally now, he couldn't understand why. Maybe time has a way of lending clarity to emotion, allowing someone to better understand the true depth of the love they once felt. Perhaps absence did make the heart grow fonder.

Since those first moments, his feelings for her had only grown stronger. And yet, with her profound amnesia, it was almost as if she were a completely different person. If she wasn't the same Elizabeth, how could his feelings for her be stronger?

He sighed. He didn't understand what was happening.

She snuggled closer to him in her sleep, and he thought his heart would burst.

No, there was no explanation for why he felt like this, but he didn't care. She was back in his life—in his arms—

and he would do whatever he could to keep her there.

That might be a challenge. For whatever reason, her father had taken an instant dislike to Gabe. That situation would require careful handling. Regardless of the fact that it was Elizabeth who had said, *if this is the way a father treats a daughter, I don't need a father in my life*, Gabe thought it important to try to mend this rift. Or, if that proved impossible, at least he didn't want to make things worse.

Furthermore, he couldn't deny that her father was right about some things: with no memories and being unable to read, Elizabeth was extremely vulnerable. For her own safety, she would need to learn certain basic skills until her memory returned. Gabe decided he would start teaching her in the morning.

He raised the subject right after breakfast. "Elizabeth, I've been thinking about something your father said yesterday."

She frowned. "I'm sorry. I don't understand why he was so angry and unkind."

"I think I might. I do believe he loves you and wants to keep you safe. I do too, but I think he doesn't trust anyone else to take care of something so important to him. I think one of his major concerns, one of the reasons he wanted you declared incompetent, is that you do not remember how to read, so you don't have the ability to manage your own affairs."

"I'm certain I'll remember everything soon."

"And you probably will. But until you do, I think it is a good idea for you to relearn some basic skills. I work a full week, and then I'm off for a week. On the weeks I work, I switch between working days and nights. So every other week, you will be alone from early morning to late evening, or from late evening to early morning for seven days in a row—from Saturday to Friday."

Her brow furrowed. "Completely alone? Here?"

"Yes, but I'm off today and I have the next three days off. I can start by teaching you the things you need to know to get by and be safe—like numbers and how to make a phone call and what to do in an emergency. You also might want to learn how the appliances work, so you can make meals for yourself or even just a cup of coffee."

She smiled. "I'm certain I want to learn how to make coffee."

"Then I'll teach you. But more important than making coffee is how to use a phone. You can get in touch with nearly anyone—me, Dr. Rose, your parents—simply by pushing a few buttons."

He spent the rest of the morning teaching her to recognize numbers from zero to nine so that she could dial a phone. It wasn't surprising that she learned them quickly—this was the girl who had graduated from medical school at the tender age of twenty-two. She not only learned the numbers well enough to read them and dial a phone, but she was also able to memorize Gabe's cellphone number and Dr. Rose's number. She also memorized Gabe's address and learned how to call 911 in an emergency.

He didn't want to overwhelm her with too much, but when she insisted, he also showed her how to make coffee and use the microwave. Elizabeth approached learning each new skill with an almost childlike awe, becoming elated when she mastered something.

Her suitcase was delivered that afternoon, just as David had promised, and Gabe helped her unpack it as they prepared for bed that night. It looked as if Elizabeth had been planning to stay for about four days. There was one beautifully tailored, light grey business suit with both a pencil skirt and trousers, a cream colored, long-sleeved silk blouse, a plum twinset, a pair of navy wool trousers, a white turtleneck sweater, several colorful scarves, four sets of undergarments and hosiery, a nightgown, and a pair of black pumps. In Elizabeth's standard, efficient style, everything went with everything else, nothing was particularly casual and, with the exception of the undergarments and nightgown, nothing was washable.

Elizabeth ran her hands over the clothes. "These are pretty."

"Yes they are. And it is exactly what I would've expected you to pack for a business meeting, but other than the jeans that David brought you and the cashmere pajamas from your mother, you have nothing particularly casual to wear."

"Casual?"

"You know, comfortable, everyday clothes. These are professional clothes. Clothes you would wear to work or a meeting."

"Why wouldn't you wear them every day?"

"Well I suppose you could, but they can't be washed easily, so it makes them a little impractical. We need to get you a few other things. You meet with Dr. Rose tomorrow. After that, we'll buy a few other things that are a little more serviceable."

Elizabeth frowned. "How will I buy things?"

"I'll take care of what you need tomorrow."

"Gabe, I don't want you to do that. Isn't there any way I can take care of things myself?"

"You do have some money in your purse and several credit cards. However, we should talk to Dr. Rose about the best course. At this point, I'd feel better just taking care of it. I don't want to give your father anything to complain about."

She gave him a sad smile. "I don't think that's a battle we can win. He doesn't seem to be a very nice person."

Gabe kissed her temple. "I know the last few days have been difficult and your father didn't make anything easier, but he is your father. I hope we can smooth things over."

She arched an eyebrow as if she sincerely doubted that

would be possible, but said nothing.

After they put her things away, they went to bed. Gabe once again had the overwhelming sensation that he adored her and wanted her in his arms forever.

He was drifting off to sleep, savoring this sweet perfection when she said, "Gabe, thank you."

"For what?"

"For everything. For taking me in, for teaching me all the things you did today," she paused for a moment. "For making me feel safe."

She was curled up against his chest, and he kissed the top of her head. "I promised I would help you."

"I know you did. But this is just … I can't really explain it. I think I would feel totally lost if I didn't have you."

He kissed her again, pulling her closer. "I know what it's like to feel out of place. But, sweetheart, please try not to worry. While I'm sure this fugue will resolve, I will take care of you as long as you need me to."

She nodded, turned her head up toward him, gave him a sweet kiss, and whispered, "Thank you."

~ * ~

With Gabe's arms around her, Elsie didn't care where she was or *when* she was; the sense of belonging was unlike anything she had ever known. *Elizabeth is very fortunate indeed.* In her heart, Elsie knew she would feel the same—just as safe and comfortable—when she returned to Geordie. This was a lovely thought to drift to sleep on.

She woke several times during the night to the city sounds. Gabe had explained what *sirens* were, so they didn't scare her anymore. She slept more soundly than she had in the hospital, and she was able to go back to sleep easily enough. At one point, she woke with the need to relieve herself. She rose quietly and slipped into the bathroom. Of all the modern things she had experienced so far, she still liked the bathroom the best—although coffee was a close second.

Before returning to bed, she went to the window and peeked out the curtains to see what time it was. Dawn was just beginning to pink the sky. In her own time, she would rise to start the day, but Gabe was still asleep and the cozy bed called to her. She climbed under the covers and nestled close to him. She wasn't able to fall back asleep, so her thoughts turned to all that she had learned the previous day. She could count before and do simple sums, but now she knew the symbols that represented those numbers. She was inordinately proud of this.

It hadn't been so difficult. Gabe had taught these to her so that she could use a phone and the *microwave oven,* which she could do now. However, she wondered if he would teach her more. Of all the things she might learn about in this time, the only thing that she could take with her that might be really valuable was the ability to read. Of course, she supposed she would only learn to read modern English, but it still might be nice to know.

When she asked him the next morning, his face split with a warm smile. "I would love to teach you to read. I think it would be a very good thing to learn, even if you do get your memories back soon. I was going to take you shopping for some casual clothes, after you see Dr. Rose, but we can go to a book store too. They make all kinds of workbooks to help children learn letters and how to read. We'll pick up some to use as a starting point."

Elsie was glad that Dr. Rose had suggested seeing him regularly. He was right: simply the thought of spending time with someone who knew her circumstances was comforting.

When they arrived at his office a few minutes before two, no one was at the reception desk, but the door to his private office was open and he called to them. "Come right in. As I told ye, I usually take Wednesday afternoons off, so my staff is off, too."

Dr. Rose's office was large and well-appointed with comfortable furniture. He came around his desk and shook Gabe's hand first. "Good afternoon, Dr. Soldani."

"Good afternoon, sir. Please, call me Gabe."

"Then please don't call me sir. I'm Gerald."

Gabe laughed. "I fear that might be a hard habit to break, but I'll do my best."

Dr. Rose turned to Elsie and took both of her hands in his. "Elizabeth, my dear, how are ye feeling?"

Elsie smiled. "I'm feeling better. My ribs still ache a bit, and I'm still getting used to this cast, but all in all, I'm well."

"That's good to hear."

"She doesn't seem to have recovered any more memories, but clearly can form new ones. Yesterday, she learned to read numerals so she could use the phone."

"And the microwave," she added with a smile.

"Well done, lass."

"And I learned how to make coffee. I quite like coffee."

"I've always preferred tea, myself."

"Tea?"

"Gabe, lad, ye must give her a balanced education. I'll make a proper pot of tea for us and we'll have a cup as we chat."

"Shall I leave you then?" asked Gabe.

"Not immediately. There are some general things to discuss first, then Elizabeth and I will chat alone."

Elsie found the tea delicious, but she still thought she preferred coffee. Dr. Rose also put out a plate of things he called biscuits, but Gabe called them cookies.

She didn't care what they were called, but she liked them. "Did you make these?"

Dr. Rose chuckled. "Nay, lass, I bought them. They are

called Nutter Butters and are a particular weakness of mine."

"I've never tasted anything like them. They're delicious."

Gabe laughed. "You always were a big fan of peanut butter. I'll have to make a peanut butter and jelly sandwich for you."

"Aye, like I said, a balanced education."

As it turned out, the general things Dr. Rose wanted to discuss concerned Elizabeth's employer, and Elsie didn't completely understand it all.

"Elizabeth, as we discussed, I contacted the University Hospital on your behalf to tell them about the accident and explain your condition. The head of human resources will be calling in a few minutes. You will need to give her permission to speak in front of me and Gabriel. She is going to explain your disability insurance."

"What does that mean?"

"You are a doctor, employed by the hospital in which you work. In addition to being paid a salary for the work you do, there are other benefits. You have health insurance that pays for medical care, such as that which you received in the hospital here. You also have something called disability insurance. It pays you part of your salary if something happens that prevents you from working."

Elsie had only been in this century for a few days, but it hadn't taken long to realize that modern life revolved around money. Everything had a price, and people worked in exchange for money. Without money, they didn't have a roof over their head or food in their bellies.

She also knew that Elizabeth had quite a lot of money. It was what her father had gotten so angry about. She looked from Dr. Rose to Gabe. "I said I don't want to use any of her—I mean, my money while I have no memory. I don't want my father to accuse anyone of trying to take my money."

Dr. Rose shook his head. "I know ye were upset by your father's attitude and ye can leave the bulk of your wealth untouched, but ye really do need to have access to some money. We're going to arrange for you to receive your unemployment insurance."

"But—"

"Nay, lass, you need this."

Elsie frowned, but said no more.

The call with the *human resources* person didn't take long. Elsie didn't understand much of what was said, but she gathered that she would receive a certain amount of money twice a month as long as she had no memories. She just wasn't sure she understood how that would happen.

When the call was over, she asked, "How will I get the money?"

"It will go directly into your bank account, just like your salary does."

Dr. Rose smiled indulgently at Gabe. "Lad, I think it's safe to say Elizabeth only seems to understand very concrete things." He proceeded to explain what a *bank account* was and how it worked.

"But if the benefit money is just going in with all of the rest, won't my father get mad if I use it?"

"You have several different kinds of bank accounts, and one of them is called a checking account," explained Gabe. "I suspect you don't keep large amounts of money there anyway, but if it makes you feel better, I can help you make sure you only use the funds from the disability insurance. I'll even teach you how to do it yourself."

Elsie would rather just stay completely away from Elizabeth's money, but if she did that, it would mean Gabe would have to completely support her. That didn't seem fair, either. She nodded. "Okay."

Dr. Rose nodded, obviously satisfied with the plan. "Now that all that is sorted, Gabe, I'll ask ye to step into the waiting room and give me a few minutes alone with

Elizabeth."

"Certainly." Gabe stood and brushed her temple with a kiss before leaving. That little gesture created a warm glow within her.

As the door shut behind Gabe, Dr. Rose cocked his head to one side. "Ye quite like that young man."

"Elizabeth does, and it feels pretty wonderful."

"Perhaps."

"I'm certain of it. When she comes back... if she is able to help Lady MacKenzie, she will deserve the happiness."

"And ye, Elsie?"

She blushed and smiled. "I think happiness awaits me."

He smiled warmly. "Good because ye deserve it, too. This has not been easy. I can promise ye, most travelers find going backward tolerable, but coming forward is frightening and disorienting."

"It has been that. I don't want to be alone. I... I asked Gabe to sleep with me. Even so, when I wake up in the night, it takes me a few moments to get my bearings."

"I imagine." Dr. Rose considered her for a moment. "You are aware that Gabe can't stay with you all of the time. He has to work."

"I know. I keep hoping Gertrude will find me and tell me to say the word before too long. Gabe works seven days in a row starting on Saturday."

"And what if Gertrude hasn't returned by then?"

"I'll..." What would she do? "I guess I'll figure out how to be alone. At least it will be during the day. Surely by the time he works at night, everything will have been put to rights."

"Perhaps it will be. And perhaps by then you will be more comfortable here."

Elsie nodded, but she wasn't sure she would ever be very comfortable.

"Elsie, there is something else I want to discuss with ye. Elizabeth's mother has already contacted me. She knows I cannot break patient confidentiality, but she wanted me to give you a message. She is making arrangements to work from her company's Manhattan office. She will be here by Monday at the latest. She would like to see you."

"I don't...I'm sorry Dr. Rose, but I don't want to see them. Elizabeth will be back soon and then everything will be resolved."

Dr. Rose steepled his fingers under his chin. "This whole pocket watch thing is not always easy to understand. You believe that Gertrude does what she does for very specific reasons, don't you?"

"Yes, I think so. Elizabeth is where she needs to be to help Lady MacKenzie."

"She is. Still, that could have happened without you coming here. The exchange could have taken place as it usually does—with you losing your life."

"But the accident changed things."

"So Gertrude said. But maybe the accident wasn't really so much of an accident. Maybe everything happened exactly the way it was supposed to. Maybe Gertrude had a plan for ye that is bigger than just bringing Elizabeth and Gabe together."

"What do you mean?"

"I think it is fairly obvious that Elizabeth and her parents don't have a very close relationship. And didn't ye say ye'd rather hoped to feel a part of a family?"

"I did, but..."

"Elsie, perhaps that's part of your role here. Maybe ye're intended to bring Elsie and her parents together again."

"How can I do that? I don't know them, and they don't seem happy with me right now."

"I think ye may be able to do it precisely *because* you

don't know them."

"I don't understand."

"Well, based on the way her parents, or her father at least, acted, they expected Elizabeth to simply fall in line. I suspect she avoids them because of this. She would never have challenged them, but you did."

"That doesn't seem to be the best way to improve their relationship. It seems to have sent them away angry."

"I think they were more stunned than angry."

"I'm pretty sure her father was angry."

Dr. Rose chuckled. "He was frustrated." At Elsie's look of doubt he added, "And perhaps a little angry too, but I suspect it was more at the whole situation than anything else. His irritation will cool, and when it does, he may begin to see Elizabeth as an adult with a will of her own. That might be a very good thing. If ye approach it with a loving heart, ye may be able to help them grow to respect her independence. This little episode may also wake them up to the fact that they had lost their daughter."

"She isn't lost to them. She is coming back."

"Elsie, I've spoken to Elizabeth's parents on several occasions now. From everything I've learned, they lost Elizabeth a long time ago. Ye've allowed them to find her in a way that she never could have. For all intents and purposes, ye're an innocent. Elizabeth's past, both good and bad, has ceased to exist. I don't think they realized how distant their daughter had become. Now they have to deal with the reality that in order to have her in their lives, they have to rebuild a relationship from the ground up."

"But maybe they'll just wait until she's back and she remembers them."

"That clearly isn't the case because her mother wants to see ye. And *they* have no assurances that the old Elizabeth will come back."

Elsie looked away for a moment. "I've already told you how afraid I am, but there is more to it than encountering things that are foreign to me."

"What's bothering ye?"

"The fact is that I am living one big lie. I have not lost *my* memories. They are all absolutely intact. I'm pretending to be Elizabeth with amnesia while trying to make sure that my own memories don't inadvertently reveal that I am not Elizabeth. For whatever reason, I feel safe with Gabe. Maybe it's because his memories of Elizabeth aren't terribly recent and maybe it's just because I trust him. Regardless of the reason, I am at ease with him. But Elizabeth's parents make me uncomfortable. If I slip in front of them, they might use it against me. They might be convinced that I've lost my mind."

"I suppose I understand that. But I think it would be a mistake to shut her parents out. What if I'm with you, at least the first time?"

"I guess that would work."

"Then perhaps on Monday, when Gabe is working, I'll clear my schedule and we can meet her for lunch. I'll come to Gabe's apartment to fetch you."

"Gabe is worried about Elizabeth's parents too. I suppose it is for the best."

"I think so. I'll make the arrangements and call Gabe with the details."

In the rest of their time together, Dr. Rose asked her questions about her home. Elsie found it very calming. He also explained how canonical hours translated into the numbered hours Gabe had explained to her.

Afterward, Gabe took her to a clothing store. She had only ever worn clothes that someone had made for her or she had made herself, and except for the fabric color, all of her garments were alike. The sheer variety of clothing available was mind boggling, but Elsie couldn't deny that she enjoyed *shopping*. Trying things on was fun, and she had never seen looking glasses—*mirrors*—as large as those in the changing rooms.

Gabe helped her pick two more pairs of jeans and tops to go with them, and one of the girls working in the shop helped her pick some more undergarments. As they were going to *check out*, a rack of beautiful skirts caught her eye. They were a lot longer than the one in Elizabeth's bag, while still being shorter than what she was accustomed to wearing. She fingered the soft, lightweight fabric reverently.

"Would you like to try one on?" asked Gabe.

"They are very pretty."

"Then try one on."

"But we already have enough."

"Elizabeth, try it on."

She grinned. She really did want to see what one would look like. She picked one with a dark purple floral print, and along with a white, lace-trimmed blouse the shop girl said was "perfect for the boho chic look," she went back to the dressing room. When she had the garments on, she stood and stared at herself in the mirror for a moment before stepping out of the dressing room to show Gabe. She felt beautiful.

"You look lovely, Elizabeth, and by the expression on your face, I'd say you like the outfit."

"Oh, I do. I don't think I have ever worn anything this pretty."

He cocked his head to one side, appearing slightly amused. "Then you must have it," he said simply.

"We can put something else back."

"No, we can't. I want you to have these things."

"Ballet flats would be just the thing to finish off the outfit," said the girl who had been helping her.

"What are ballet flats?"

"You know, flat black shoes like dancers wear."

"Oh, I don't need shoes."

The girl laughed. "I've literally never heard a woman say that."

Gabe laughed. "At the risk of starting a bad habit, I think she is right. There is a discount shoe store near the book store. I suspect we can get a pair there."

By the time they were finished shopping, Elizabeth did indeed have a pair of comfortable, flat, black shoes and *workbooks* from which she could learn to read and do sums.

Before going back to Gabe's home, they stopped at a *restaurant* and Gabe ordered a *pizza* for them. It was perhaps the most delicious thing she had ever tasted. But then again, everything she tasted seemed like the most delicious thing she had ever tasted.

~ * ~

Elizabeth fell asleep almost instantly that evening. Gabe lay beside her, watching her as she slept. Today had been an extraordinary day. She seemed to have so much fun shopping even though she never really had in the past. The truth was that she'd always been too busy to simply spend the day shopping. But today, she had appeared lighthearted and happy.

My sweet girl, it seems losing your memory is what it took to slow you down. To make you stop and smell the flowers. You need more of that in your life.

That gave him an idea. He couldn't do it this week, but next Saturday morning, he would take her to the flower district.

Chapter 11

Over the next two days, Elsie poured herself into learning everything she could to better function in the modern world. The machines were amazing. She conquered the *washer* and *dryer* first.

On Thursday morning, Gabe said, "I'm going to do laundry. Would you mind getting the dirty towels for me?"

Dirty towels? "None of them are *dirty* Gabe."

He smiled at her. "I know they aren't actually soiled, but I mean the towels and wash cloths we've used."

"Oh. Okay, I'll get them."

When she came out of the bathroom with them, he stood in front of the *washer and dryer* he'd said he was lucky to have. *So a washer must be for washing clothes and linens.*

"How does it work?"

"It's pretty easy. You put the stuff you want to wash in this bottom part. You don't want to pack it in or nothing will get clean." He showed her how much to put in. "Then you measure out the detergent." The *detergent* was a thick, bright green liquid he poured into the machine before shutting the door. "Then you select your water temperature. Hot water is for whites, warm water is for colors, but if the colors are very bright or the fabric might shrink you use cold. Then you turn this knob to here and push it in."

When he did that, the machine started to fill with water. For a few minutes she watched through the glass door in amazement. "What happens?"

Gabe chuckled. "The laundry tumbles in the soapy water first. Then the machine pumps the dirty water out before filling with rinse water and tumbling some more. Then that water is pumped out and the drum spins very fast to get out as much water as possible. You'll hear when it starts."

When the washer finished, Gabe moved the damp clothes to the *dryer* and showed her how to turn it on. Then he started another *load* in the washer.

The dryer turned out to be even more remarkable. When the timer buzzed, Gabe opened the door to remove the towels. She picked up one of the towels and couldn't help but bury her face in it. It was delightfully warm and fragrant.

"This is wonderful." She looked up to see Gabe watching her with a grin.

"Yeah, laundry fresh from the dryer is one of life's simple pleasures."

"I think I like doing laundry."

Gabe laughed. "I'm sure that is the first time those words have ever crossed your lips."

"I didn't like it before?"

"No. You hated doing laundry. A lot of your clothes had to be dry-cleaned, so you went to a cleaner who also offered a fluff and fold service."

"Fluff and fold?"

"Yeah. Essentially, you paid to have everything laundered except your undies."

"Undies?"

"You know, underwear—bras and panties."

"I can't imagine why I did that." She blushed. "I mean I can see why I might not want someone else washing my *undies*, but it's so easy to do laundry. I can't imagine paying someone to do it for me."

Gabe smiled. "You were always busy, always in a hurry. You didn't like spending time doing mundane things."

Elsie shrugged. "Until I remember that I don't like it, I think I'll enjoy it."

Gabe laughed. "Be my guest."

In addition to the washer and dryer, Gabe also showed her how to use the stove although she didn't really know how to cook the modern food he had. She wanted to learn, but he said it would be easier to do that after she could read, so she focused on reading.

Then, there was the television. As soon as she recovered from the shock of pictures that moved and talked, she became enthralled. And then bored. Gabe enjoyed sporting events and watched the *winter Olympics* a lot. She didn't find it quite as thrilling. There were no tests of strength or sword fights. Although sliding down the side of a mountain at breath-taking speeds did have its appeal.

On Friday evening, after dinner was over and the dishes washed, Gabe said, "I'm going to watch some TV and then go to bed early. Seven days of days start tomorrow. Do you want to watch with me?"

She didn't actually want to watch TV but she did want to curl up next to him on the couch.

They were watching *snowboarding*, and something occurred to Elsie. "Gabe, what do you watch on TV when there is no snow?"

He gave her a puzzled look. "I'm sorry, what did you ask?"

"Well you called these the winter Olympics, what do you watch on TV when winter is over?"

"Elizabeth, there are lots of other things to watch, on other channels. Do you want to see something else?"

"I'd love to."

He pushed buttons on the *remote* and the image on the screen changed rapidly. He would stop for a bit every once in a while and watch for a few minutes before moving on. "There isn't much on."

"You're joking right? You keep going past lots of things."

He laughed. "You used to hate it when I channel surfed. But what I meant is, the shows that are on will be hard for you to understand without a lot of explaining. Maybe there is an on-demand movie we could watch."

He went to another channel that just had lots of words. He shook his head a lot before, his eyes went wide and he looked truly excited. "Star Wars. I love Star Wars. Do you want to watch that?"

"It's something about war? I don't know." She couldn't imagine anything more gruesome.

"No, it isn't real. It's science fiction. Basically it is a story that is completely made up about far away worlds."

Elsie was dubious, but it had to be better than the Olympics or *channel surfing*.

Gabe explained a few things as they started to watch, but oddly, it didn't take much. After she watched for a bit, she began to follow the story. By the time it was over, she was completely enthralled.

"Well I'd start the next one but it's really too late."

"There's another one?"

"There are five more."

"And you'll watch them with me?"

"Of course I will."

She sighed, contentedly. "I think sitting on the couch with you, watching a movie, is my new favorite thing."

He smiled at her. "I had fun too."

"Did I like it before?"

"I don't think we ever did it before. We were in medical school and there was always work and studying to do. You rarely just kicked back and watched TV."

"Well I like it now."

Gabe showed her how to use the remote and find shows. It turned out the range of entertainment available was both shocking and mind boggling. There were channels devoted to everything from history to cooking. There were even shows to help children learn things. Gabe wrote down the numbers for the channels she liked so she could find them if she wished to watch something while he was at work. Thus, by the time Saturday morning rolled around, she felt relatively comfortable staying alone while Gabe worked.

~ * ~

Elsie awoke when Gabe had the next morning. After he left for work, she'd indulged in watching a little TV, but she also worked diligently to complete some pages in her workbook. Just after midday she stopped to make a peanut-butter sandwich for her lunch. She had taken the first bite when the front door buzzer sounded. She wiped her hands and went to push the intercom button as Gabe had taught her.

"Hello?"

"Good afternoon."

"I'm sorry, Gabe isn't home at the moment."

"I'm not here to see Gabe. I'm here to see you, Dr. Quinn. My name is Aldous Sinclair. I am David's father."

"I'd rather not let someone in who I don't know."

"I understand. That is a good rule to follow, but this is rather important. Perhaps I could get David on the phone and you'll feel better after speaking with him."

She thought about it for a brief moment. He was David's father, so what harm could there be? "No, I don't suppose that's necessary."

She buzzed him in.

A few minutes later, the doorbell to the apartment rang. She looked through the peephole and smiled to herself, remembering what Dr. Rose had said. The well-dressed man waiting for her to receive him was indeed a slightly shorter and older version of David. The man standing directly behind him, though, was huge and a little scary.

Elsie opened the door. "Good afternoon, Mr. Sinclair. It's nice to meet you. Please, come in."

"Thank you, Dr. Quinn. It's lovely to meet you too.

This is Dixon, the head of my security team."

"Good afternoon, Dixon."

"Good afternoon, Dr. Quinn."

"What exactly is a security team? Something like guards?"

Mr. Sinclair smiled. "Yes. That is precisely correct. The members of my security team are my guardsmen. Dixon doesn't like to let me out of his sight, but he will wait just outside the door."

"He's welcome to come in."

"That is kind of you, but there are some things I want to discuss with you privately. Thank you, Dixon."

Dixon inclined his head and shut the door.

Elizabeth couldn't imagine what Mr. Sinclair had to discuss with her, and it made her a little nervous. "Can I offer you a cup of coffee, or tea? Or maybe a peanut butter sandwich? I was just making one for myself."

"A peanut butter sandwich and a cup of coffee sound wonderful." He followed her to the little kitchen.

"I like my bread toasted."

"So do I."

She popped four slices of bread into the toaster oven. "We have strawberry or peach jam. We also have fluff. Gabe loves it. I think it is atrocious, but he assures me that other people really do eat fluffernutters, as he calls them."

Mr. Sinclair chuckled. "Well, he's right, people really do eat them. I think David was fond of them as a youngster, but I'm with you. I don't care for fluffernutters, either. Peach jam would be perfect."

"That's my favorite."

They exchanged small talk while she finished making lunch and laid it out on the little dining table. "Please, sit down."

"After you, Dr. Quinn."

"Just call me Elizabeth. I don't exactly remember how to be a doctor anyway."

"No, I don't expect you do." He took a bite of his sandwich. "It has been ages since I've eaten a peanut butter sandwich. Sometimes, they really hit the spot."

Elizabeth took a nibble from her sandwich, then a sip of coffee. She couldn't help but wonder why he was here. "You said you had some things to discuss with me?"

"Yes, I do. First, I want you to know that I have known Dr. Rose for years, since we were very young men. He would never break a patient's confidentiality; I only know you are seeing him because David told me. Over the years, Dr. Rose has occasionally suggested that someone contact me."

"Why is that?"

"I have a little experience with...memory loss. That's why I'm here. David told me about your accident and amnesia. However, he doesn't know I've come to see you, and I would rather keep it that way."

"But when you were downstairs, you said you'd call David if it would make me feel better."

"It was a bluff. I was hoping you wouldn't ask me to."

Elizabeth frowned. "Why?"

"Because there are some things that are better kept secret. The pocket watch is one of them."

"The pocket watch? You know about it?"

"Yes, I do because I chose to use it, too. I'm a time traveler."

"I didn't actually choose to use it."

"What do you mean?"

"Elizabeth accepted the watch, but something unusual happened. Evidently, she had the watch in her hand at the time of the accident. Our souls changed places when she hit her head and lost consciousness instead of when she went to sleep, and she dropped the watch. With the watch here, and her in the past, time became equal."

Mr. Sinclair looked amazed. "I have met a few time travelers over the years, but I have never heard of that happening."

"It seems that I hadn't done the thing that would have resulted in my death yet. Gertrude thinks that might be part of the reason things didn't happen as they normally do."

"Why would that be part of it?"

"As I understand it, my laird intended to ask me to do something terribly dishonest and cruel. I wouldn't have done it, and he'd have whipped me, causing my death. Gertrude also thinks things might have happened differently because my choice was morally right."

"Your laird? You came from Scotland?"

"Yes."

"But if you hadn't refused to do the dishonest thing, does that mean Elizabeth did?"

Elsie smiled. "Yes, but it was neither cruel nor dishonest for her—quite the opposite. My laird intended to pass me off as an expert midwife to someone who desperately needed one. I was only an apprentice, but Elizabeth—"

"—is an obstetrician. Brilliant!" Mr. Sinclair laughed.

Elsie smiled. "There is a certain elegance to it."

"That there is."

"You said you used the watch? Did you go backward in time?"

"No, I came forward."

"Like me? But you stayed?"

"Yes, I did."

"How long have you been here?"

"Nearly my whole life. In my time, I was a young man, just twenty-one, but I landed in the body of seven-year-old Aldous Sinclair in the year 1948."

"A little boy?"

"Yes. It seems he was a bit of a handful—a brat. The Sinclairs were wealthy and lived on a beautiful, waterfront estate in Newport, Rhode Island. Wealthy people are often targets for criminals, so spiked, wrought iron fencing enclosed the entire property. Aldous wasn't supposed to leave the grounds alone, ever. Being the defiant little monster he was, he disobeyed that rule and snuck away often."

"If the grounds were fenced, how did he accomplish that?"

"There were plenty of trees on the property, some with branches that reached over the fence. He was in the habit of climbing one, crawling out on a limb, and dropping down outside the fence. The soul exchange occurred when he was climbing the tree on one of these excursions. I lost my grip and fell. It wasn't terribly far, but I bumped my head and funnily enough, broke my left arm."

She smiled at his reference to her broken left arm. "What would have happened had you not exchanged souls?"

"Gertrude was never specific about that. She said he might have slipped and impaled himself on the fence. She was there when I hit the ground."

Elsie was appalled. "Impaled? How horrible."

"Yes, and as it turns out, he had been injured many times doing the same thing. But had he made it to the other side that day, Gertrude implied something even worse might have happened. It didn't really matter which terrible fate would have been Aldous's. I was scared enough to never try that again. She told me what I needed to do and walked with me until we were in sight of the mansion. My memory loss was attributed to the head injury." He smiled. "It never returned."

"But Aldous was only seven."

"That's right. I have no memories of early childhood— at least of Aldous's early childhood. Most people's earliest episodic memories are from about the age of three, so while I am missing these actual memories, over the years I have been told enough that there is really no gap for me. Of course, I have my own memories, but they have faded some over the years."

"Why did you decide to stay? You were a grown man, thrust into the body of a child. That couldn't have been easy."

"I was a grown man, but I was a peasant, a commoner. I had no power, no voice, no opportunity to advance. Regardless of how bright I was, unless I had chosen the religious life, there was no future for me other than a life of physical labor that could be cut short in any number of ways. I was in the body of a child who had absolutely every advantage life could offer and had essentially thrown it away. He had never been mistreated in any way. He had any toy or book he could possibly want. He was adored by his parents and had servants who took care of his every need. He had very few limits on his behavior, but he wanted none. His only reason for leaving the estate was for sport—because it was a challenge. One simple rule and he couldn't follow it. His life was over and limitless opportunity stretched before me. I couldn't go back."

"Did you have a family?"

"I did. I had a wife and a child."

"Do you know what became of them?"

He nodded slowly. "Leaving them was my only regret. As soon as I learned to read, I searched every history book I could find to try to learn their fate. Unfortunately, it was so long ago that finding any surviving record of the lives of two inconsequential peasants was futile. Gertrude occasionally popped into my life. She always she assured me that they were well, but she would never give me details. Each time I begged her to bring them forward. Her standard answer was, 'That isn't the way the pocket watch works.'"

"And that is all you learned?"

"No, Elizabeth. If I gave up that easily, I wouldn't be where I am today."

"So what did you do?"

"I started researching memory loss. I learned everything I could about it. I looked for news reports of people with amnesia and kept records. In almost every case I read about, the person's memory eventually returned. I hoped to find someone, who, like me, appeared to have lost all memories permanently because that person might be a time traveler. But up until college, I had never found a report of that happening. Then I met Gerald Rose."

"Dr. Rose?"

"The same."

"He said you were old friends."

"We were assigned as roommates during our first year, and we instantly became close friends. He was amused by my fascination with amnesia and repeatedly tried to find out why. One Saturday night early in our second year, I told him."

"About the pocket watch?"

"Yes. Funnily enough, it turned out that he had been offered the watch once."

"Really? He didn't tell me. Where did he come from?"

"He went back in time and returned. It happened just before he came to college."

"It's amazing that of all people, the two of you ended up as roommates."

"Not really. I suspect Gertrude had something to do with it. She nearly always has a hand in coincidences like that. The January after I told Gerald about my experience with the watch, something truly amazing happened. He and I were at a party. Judith Olivia Carson, a young woman we both knew casually, was there. She'd had a very loud fight with her boyfriend and stormed out of the party, intending to drive home. Although the public shouting match should have been a dead giveaway, no one knew she had been drinking heavily and was in no condition to drive. Evidently, she wasn't really in any shape to walk. High-heeled shoes and ice only made it worse. She fell, knocking herself out before she reached the car. When she came to, she made her way back to the party, but she wasn't Judith anymore. Gerald and I were the first people she ran into. Her head was bleeding and she had no memory. We took her to the hospital, but recognizing the signs—specifically, semantic memory loss—we asked her about the pocket watch before we got there."

"She was a time traveler?"

"Yes, she was. As it turns out, after regaining consciousness, Judith would have gone on to the car. Had she driven off in the state she was in, drunk and with a head injury, she would have wrecked and been killed in the accident. She might have killed someone else, too."

"My goodness."

"As I suspect you are becoming aware, Gertrude doesn't just give the pocket watch to someone for a lark. There are always reasons."

"So where was the woman from?"

"My village. She was my wife."

Elsie was amazed. "Gertrude gave her the watch after all? That's wonderful, but what about your child?"

"That was the heartache of it all. There had been a terrible sickness passing through the village that winter. Jo was dreadfully ill and dying when Gertrude gave her the watch. Accepting the watch meant she could have sixty days with me and, under normal circumstances, could return sixty seconds later to be with our child. But in this case, even if she had done that, the outcome would have been the same. She would have died within hours of her return."

"So she stayed here?"

"Yes. But our child has weighed heavily in our hearts all of our lives."

"You've never learned what happened?"

"No. As I mentioned, when Gerald encounters someone who has used the watch to travel through time, he puts them in touch with me. I keep hoping to meet someone who travelled to or from my era who might know something."

"How do they find him?"

Mr. Sinclair smiled. "Gertrude, of course. As you can imagine, traveling with the watch can result in having to make some heart-rending decisions. It helps to have someone who understands and can assist a returning traveler in coming to terms with their decisions. So, when needed, Gertrude sends them to Dr. Rose."

"Have you ever met anyone who knew what happened to your child?"

"No, but that's why I'm here. Would you tell me your story? Maybe you are the link I have searched for. Where did you come from?"

"The Scottish Highlands, in the year 1279."

"Jo and I came from the Highlands, too. You are the first person who I've ever encountered from that far back. I left in 1260 and my wife in 1268. What clan do you belong to?"

"I'm a Macrae."

Aldous Sinclair went white. "We were Macraes. Maybe you knew our daughter, surely you did. How old are you? In your own time, I mean."

"Twenty-one."

Aldous frowned as if concentrating for a moment. "That means you would be about her age."

"What was her name?"

"Elsie."

Chapter 12

Could this be possible? Could this man really be her father? Elsie didn't want to get her hopes up. "Did you have a cousin named Dolina?"

"Yes, I did. Do you know her? Do you know Elsie?"

"Sir, I am Elsie, the daughter of Dolina's cousin Alder, but my mother's name was Jocelyn, not Jo. Not only that, my father died only nineteen years ago and my mother eleven years ago. You can't be my parents."

"Oh, my sweet girl, time travel doesn't work that way. Things aren't equal. Your mother joined me eight years after I left, but I had been here for thirteen years. Time isn't linear, and it only seems to connect at certain points. Nineteen years have passed for you since I left, but I have been here for fifty-eight years. I was Alder, and Jo was my nickname for your mother, Jocelyn."

Tears filled her eyes. "You're really my father?"

His eyes were bright as well. "I really am." He stood and opened his arms.

Completely bewildered, Elsie stepped into the embrace, returning it. She could no longer suppress her tears.

"Oh, my darling girl, please don't cry. I am so very sorry I abandoned you. I was young and the opportunities this world offered...but I never should have stayed."

"You're wrong. Mama was able to come here because you stayed. Illness would have taken her from both of us had she not accepted the watch. Not to mention all the other lives who would have been affected."

"But you were left alone."

"I wasn't alone. I had Dolina. I can understand your choice. Things here are truly wonderful. You said it a moment ago. In our time, commoners have no power, no voice, and no opportunity to advance. You have used your gift to do great things. If Elizabeth hadn't changed souls with me, I would have been beaten to death by my Laird simply because I wouldn't perpetuate a cruel lie. Da, I understand your choice."

His arms tightened around her and she felt him tremble, tears spilling down his cheeks. "Your mother and I have always loved you, Elsie."

After a moment, he released her. They sat back down, but he took one of her hands in his. "To honor you, we started a charity here to provide college tuition to young women in need. For years, your mother attended the college graduation of every girl who received the scholarship. There are simply too many now."

"Mama is still here? I thought maybe since you came alone…"

"No, your mother is very much alive. However, I've never told her of my attempts to find out what happened to you. She doesn't know I have met so many time travelers. I never wanted to raise her hopes only to dash them—it has been hard enough for me."

"Can I see her? Will you take me to her?"

"Of course you can see her, my darling. I would take you to her now, but I wouldn't want to take you away without Dr. Soldani knowing where you were. I imagine he calls to check on you when he can, and he would worry if you weren't here. Does he know? Can you call and tell him?"

"No, I haven't told him about the pocket watch, and you're right, he does call often."

"So it would be nearly impossible to explain to him why you were going anywhere with me."

"I suppose it would be, but I may not have much time here. I want to spend as much as I can with you both."

Her father's face fell. "I had just assumed you would

want to stay."

She smiled sadly. "It's not my sole decision to make."

"Ah, that's right. I'd forgotten about Elizabeth."

Elsie's heart ached. "I doubt she will want to stay in the past. You know what it's like there. She is a modern woman and a doctor. She belongs here. Besides, I think my mission is to repair the relationship between Gabe and Elizabeth. The feelings I have...well, I'm certain we, or rather they, belong together. There is also someone in my time who is important to me."

Her father nodded. "I understand. The blessing your mother and I have been given by your presence here is priceless. We will accept what we have and rejoice in it rather than mourn what we cannot have."

She squeezed his hand. Elizabeth's parents had been such a disappointment; Elsie had felt sorry for her. She had lived most of her life without parents, but somehow having parents who were so detached seemed worse. Being given valuable time with her parents now, no matter how brief, was a gift beyond anything she could have ever hoped for. But it also hardened her resolve to help repair the relationship with Elizabeth's parents. She had the opportunity to give the same gift she had been given.

"I agree with all my heart." She smiled broadly. "So when can I see my mama?"

"I understand Gabe is working twelve-hour days this week. Is that correct?"

"How do you know that?"

He cocked his head and smiled. "I am a very wealthy man. I have contacts."

"Well then, you know it's correct."

"Cheeky lass."

She laughed. "It is one of the wonderful things about the twenty-first century. I don't always need to hold my tongue."

"Then enjoy it while you're here. God knows you'll

have to mind it well when you return. I know Gabe will be at the hospital every day until late in the evening, so I will tell Jo about you this evening. I expect she'll be here at the crack of dawn to see you, and I won't be able to get a word in edgewise. So, unless you have other plans, I'd like to spend the rest of the afternoon getting to know you."

"I'd like nothing more."

Aldous did indeed spend hours with her. She learned that since he had been here for so many years, he had long since stopped thinking of himself as Alder. On the other hand, Jocelyn found it harder to think of herself as *Judith*. Since *Jo* was a pet name anyway, and Judith's first and middle initials were J.O., she started going by that name and it stuck.

She also learned that they had four children. Caroline was their oldest daughter. She was thirty-eight, married, and had three children. Three years younger than Caroline was Jennifer, who also was married and had two children. Xavier, their oldest son, was thirty-two, and David was their youngest at thirty.

As Aldous told her about his other children, he became thoughtful. "I want you to meet them, but we need to think about how best to handle this. Biologically, they are the children of Aldous and Judith Sinclair, and thus certainly not Elizabeth Quinn's siblings. But from a spiritual, philosophical standpoint, all five of you are the children of Alder and Jocelyn."

"I assume none of them know?"

Aldous shook his head. "No one knows that I traveled here from the past except Dr. Rose and the other travelers I've met. Dr. Rose alone knows about Jocelyn. As advanced as things are in this century, there is no room for mysticism. Modern people believe in science. Every phenomenon must have a sound, logical explanation. Very few people are willing to accept anything on faith. Thus, if the story of our experiences with the pocket watch were to get out, your mother and I might be written off as lunatics."

"David is a friend of Elizabeth's, maybe you can use the accident as an excuse. After all, both you and Mama have experienced amnesia."

"Actually, no one knows that about me. My parents kept it very quiet to avoid any sensationalism. I was young, and it was easy enough. It would have been impossible to keep Jo's accident a secret. Although it was so many years ago, much of the buzz died down before our children were born. It isn't a secret, but we never really discussed it with them. You're right though, that may be just the thing. But first, let's deal with Gabe. You can tell him that David informed me about your amnesia and I thought it might be helpful for you to speak with Jo but being cautious about my family, I wanted to meet you first. That will give you and excuse to spend time with your mother."

"That a good plan and it makes me feel better. I wasn't sure what I was going to tell him, but I didn't want to hide it from him, either."

"Then you can come to our home to visit. That way I wouldn't have to leave members of my security team standing in the hall for ages."

"Oh, good heavens, I forgot. Dixon has been out there for hours."

"No, he hasn't. I'm certain when it became clear that I was going to be a while, he sent for backup and they have been switching out. But it is getting late, and I should be going. Has Gabe taught you how to read numbers and use a telephone?"

"Yes, and I'm learning letters, too." She couldn't keep the note of pride out of her voice. Only a commoner from her own time could appreciate the wonder of that.

He smiled warmly. "Excellent." He took out a small card and wrote a number on the back. "This is my business card. If you call any of the numbers on the front, someone will answer, but it will not be me. In most cases, they can find me or take a message. However, if it is urgent, call this number on the back. It is my private cell phone number. Only a handful of people have this, and I always answer it personally."

"Why would I need to call you urgently?"

He smiled sadly. "We don't know when Gertrude will come and tell you it's time to exchange souls again. I don't want you to leave without telling me. I want to be able to hug you one last time and say goodbye, and I know your mother will as well. Promise me."

Again, the idea of her time here ending caused her heart to ache, but she nodded. "I promise."

He hugged her. "And if you just want to talk to your da, call. That's urgent enough for me." He kissed the top of her head.

She sighed. "I'll see you tomorrow, Da."

He smiled and kissed her cheek. "Yes, my sweet girl, I'll see you tomorrow."

When she shut the door behind him, she leaned against it for a moment, swallowing at the lump in her throat. She had been given a tremendous blessing: time with a parent who she had thought was dead. She didn't want to seem ungrateful, but now the thought of saying goodbye forever in a few weeks was almost too much to bear. Thoughts of Geordie and the family they would have together were the only things that kept her from breaking down.

Chapter 13

Although a twelve-hour shift was supposed to be seven to seven, Gabe rarely finished before eight or later. He arrived home at a quarter to nine that evening to find Elizabeth sitting at the table, doing pages in her workbook. He kissed her. "I missed you today."

"I missed you too."

"How did you spend your day?"

"I worked in this book a lot this morning, but I had a visitor this afternoon."

Gabe was instantly wary. "A visitor? You let someone in?"

"Yes. It was David's father, Aldous Sinclair."

"Why on earth would David's father visit you?"

"It seems that many years ago, David's mother had a serious head injury and suffered permanent amnesia."

"Why didn't David mention that?"

"I think it was so long ago—when his parents were still in college—it wasn't really something they talked about much. And even then, their children didn't fully understand the extent of it. He said memories sort of get filled in. People tell you so many of the important things that it feels like a memory eventually."

"I guess I understand that. But why did he come instead of David's mother?"

"He's...cautious. He wanted to talk to me first. If it is alright with you, he is going to bring her to visit tomorrow."

"That's fine. It's a good idea actually, talking to someone who has experienced what you're going through."

"I'm glad you agree. How was your day?"

"Busy. I'm tired. I'm going to take a forty-five minute

power nap and then a quick shower."

"If you're tired, why not just shower and go to bed for the night?"

"I would, but tomorrow's Sunday. I missed Mass last week because of the snowstorm and I can't go to a regular Mass working seven am to seven pm tomorrow. But there is one church in the city, St. Malachy's, which has a very late Mass on Saturday nights. I usually go there on the weeks I work days."

"I can't imagine many people go that late to Mass."

"Actually, there are quite a few. The church is in the theatre district. It's also called the Actors' Chapel. Mass is late so that performers and theatre patrons can go after shows are over."

"Can I go with you?"

"To Mass? This late?"

"You're going."

"Yes, but you aren't even Catholic."

"What do you mean? If I'm not Catholic, what am I?" She looked horrified.

"You're Episcopal, but you didn't practice much of anything when we were in med school."

"What's *Episcopal*?"

"It's a Protestant religion."

"No," she said vehemently. "I'm Christian. I know I am."

"Sweetheart, Protestants are Christians, too." This was another odd hole in her semantic memory. "It's just…well, it's really kind of a long story—too long for me to explain now. I would love for you to come to Mass with me if that's what you want."

She nodded, but her brows were drawn together.

"Don't worry about it. You'll like St. Malachy's." He kissed her before heading to bed.

Gabe was too tired to think much more about it, but the power nap and shower revived him sufficiently. Normally, he would have taken the subway, but he wasn't sure Elizabeth was up to that this late on a Saturday night, so he hailed a cab.

Elizabeth was enchanted by the gothic revival church, dwarfed by the high-rise buildings surrounding it. Upon entering the church, she seemed to be a little surprised.

"Is something wrong?" Gabe whispered.

She shook her head. "No, it just isn't quite what I expected."

He guided her into a pew. She didn't genuflect on entering the pew and glanced curiously at him when he did. Her insistence that she was Catholic confused him. Maybe she had become Catholic in the last few years. He guessed that she might remember her new faith and still have forgotten some of the rubrics.

He lowered the kneeler, and Elizabeth knelt to pray beside him. But what she did next absolutely floored him.

She made the sign of the cross and whispered, "*In nomine Patris, et Filii, et Spiritus Sancti. Amen.*" Then she continued her whispered Latin prayers with the Our Father.

> *Pater noster qui es en caelis sanctificetur nomen tuum adveniat regnum tuum fiat voluntas tua sicut in caelo et in terra panem nostrun quotidianem da nobis hodie et dimmitte nobis debita nostra sicut et nos dimmitimus debitoribus nostris et ne nos inducas in tentationem sed libera nos a malo. Amen.*

And she ended with the Hail Mary.

> *Ave Maria, gratia plena, Dominus tecum. Benedicta tu in mulieribus, et benedictus fructus ventris tui. Sancta Maria, Mater Domini nostri, ora pro nobis peccatoribus, nunc, et in hora mortis nostrae. Amen.*

Gabe was nearly too stunned to say his own prayers. She can't read, she didn't remember being Protestant, and yet she prayed in Latin. Maybe she became Catholic and worshipped at a church that offered a Latin Mass. Honestly, it was the kind of thing the girl genius would do. He could almost hear her saying that if one was going to switch religions, one may as well learn another language at the same time. He thought he would ask her about it after Mass, but changed his mind. There was no getting around it: the things she remembered and didn't remember were bizarre, and pointing them out often distressed her. This was confirmed by the fact that she became confused at several points during the Mass, and it flustered her. It was better to just let it drop.

In the cab on the way home, Gabe put his arm around Elizabeth and she snuggled against him, resting her head on his shoulder. This felt so right. It was even better than it had been in medical school. The idea that this could be his future, his forever, filled him with warmth. He kissed the top of her head and she sighed.

"How are your ribs feeling?"

"They hurt a little tonight."

He frowned. He had ensured that she iced them several times a day and took a nonsteroidal anti-inflammatory whether she had pain or not. "Did you use ice and take the medicine I gave you?"

"I did in the morning, but I forgot to while Mr. Sinclair was visiting."

"And you didn't take the medicine and use ice after he left?"

"No. I didn't think about it because I wasn't very uncomfortable."

"Elizabeth, you weren't uncomfortable because you had been icing and taking the medicine regularly to keep the pain away. It takes four to six weeks for broken ribs to heal, and they can be quite painful for a while."

"It isn't bad. I can stand it."

"That isn't the point. When your ribs hurt, you move less, and you breathe less deeply. Those two things can result in other illnesses developing. Also, if you are already in pain, it may take stronger medicine to relieve the pain. And you don't like the way that medicine makes you feel."

"I'm sorry. I didn't know that."

"I know, and I should have explained it better. We'll take care of it when we get home. You should feel better by morning, and tomorrow you can get back on a schedule again. But if you are still hurting by noon, I want you to call me."

"I will."

"I mean it, Elizabeth. Even if the Sinclairs are visiting, you need to do it. They'll understand."

"I will. I promise."

"Speaking of the Sinclairs, your social schedule is filling up. They'll be here tomorrow, you and Dr. Rose are meeting your mother for lunch Monday, and you have your regular appointment with Dr. Rose on Wednesday."

She laughed, looking up at him. "Three appointments in otherwise empty days is hardly a full schedule."

"Well, just in case you get any more invitations, I want you to keep Saturday free for me."

"I won't schedule anything on a day you are off without checking with you. What are we doing on Saturday?"

"It's a surprise. I think you'll like it."

"I'm certain I will."

Chapter 14

Again, Elsie woke early the next morning when Gabe rose for work. Although he told her to go back to sleep, and she tried, she simply couldn't. She was too excited at the prospect of being with her mother again—something she never dreamed would be possible this side of heaven. Still, it wasn't daylight yet, and it would likely be hours before the Sinclairs arrived.

She got up and decided to take a shower. Gabe had said she could get the cast a little wet, but it might be more comfortable if she didn't. He had wrapped it in *plastic wrap* when she had showered earlier in the week. She found the box containing the thin, clear film and tried to do the same thing. It wasn't nearly as easy by herself with one hand, but she managed.

By the time she had washed and dressed, the sun was up—barely. She remembered what Gabe had said about applying ice to her ribs and taking the pain medicine, so she did that and ate a little breakfast.

Elsie had to find something to occupy her time, or she would go mad with waiting.

She tried doing pages in her workbooks, but couldn't focus. Watching television didn't hold her attention either. Elsie had such wonderful memories of her mother. For years after her mother died, when Elsie longed for her so badly it hurt, she would close her eyes and relive a memory. Nothing extraordinary, for those only made her more keenly aware of her loss. She would relive something simple, like tidying the cottage or preparing a meal.

That was it: Elsie would try to cook something. It would keep her busy, and she'd have something to serve her parents for the midday meal. She searched Gabe's kitchen for something she recognized. She found several cans that, based on the pictures, contained small, white beans. He had showed her how a *can opener* worked when he opened a tin of ground coffee. She found carrots, celery, and onion in the refrigerator.

It wasn't easy with one arm in a cast, but she chopped the vegetables, put them in a big pot with some butter, and put it on one of the stove's *eyes*. She turned it on and stirred the contents until the onion was soft. She added water until the pot was about half full. She opened the cans of beans, but when she saw them, she wrinkled her nose. They were covered with a slimy liquid. She gave them a sniff. They didn't smell bad, so she tasted one. It tasted fine. *They must eat them this way.* She shrugged and dumped them in the pot. She found the salt and pepper—it still amazed her that salt was no longer valuable—and added some of each to the pot. She found some other small jars, some of which looked as if they contained dried herbs. She opened them, sniffing each jar to identify its contents. She added thyme and rosemary. She also added a white powder that she couldn't identify, but it smelled savory.

She would have liked a nice, meaty joint to flavor the soup with, but found nothing like that. She did, however, find a couple of cans of something that had a picture of a bowl filled with clear broth on the label. She opened one, sniffed it, and smiled. It was chicken broth. She added both cans to her pot.

She wasn't sure what to do when the pot began to boil. At home, she would swing the pot to the side of the fire where there was less heat, and allow it to cook slowly for several hours. The dial controlling the eye had numbers on it. She turned it to "1" and watched to see what happened. Initially, it seemed as if it didn't make a difference, but the boiling slowed to a low simmer after a minute or so. She smiled. *That will work.*

Feeling pretty chuffed about her pot of soup, she

decided to try one more thing. One of her mother's favorite things had been a pudding made of apples and raisins. There were apples in a bowl on the counter, and she had seen a box with a picture of raisins on the label in one of the cabinets. She needed milk, honey, and flour, all of which she had seen.

She peeled and sliced four apples, put them in another pot with a few handfuls of raisins, and added water. She cooked them just until the apples were tender and then drained the water off and mashed the fruit. She added milk and honey. She had found ginger and cinnamon in her search for seasoning for her soup, so she sprinkled in some of each. The last ingredient was the flour. She made a paste with a little bit of milk before mixing it in. Then she cooked it, stirring constantly until it became thick. She sat it on a cold eye to cool. Her mother would have put it on the window sill. *But she didn't have a refrigerator.* Elsie smiled. When the pudding had cooled a little, Elsie put it there to chill.

By nine o'clock, everything was done and the apartment smelled delicious. The buzzer for the front door sounded at half past nine, and Elsie ran to answer it. "Hello?"

"Good morning, Elsie, it's Aldous Sinclair."

"Good morning." She hit the button that unlocked the door. "Come in."

She could barely stand the brief wait while they rode the elevator. She wanted to meet them there, but she knew the door would lock behind her if she left the apartment. By the time she found the key to take with her, they would be here and she wouldn't need it.

Within a minute or so, a knock sounded at the door. She opened it. Maybe it was because she knew it really was her mother, but she had nearly the same intense feeling she'd experienced when she first saw Gabe. It was as if her soul recognized her mother's in spite of her outward appearance.

Elsie threw her arms around Jo Sinclair, so full of joy she could scarcely contain it. "Mama, it's you."

Her mother, eyes bright with tears, returned her embrace. "Oh, my sweet girl. You are so deeply embedded in my heart, I would have known you anywhere."

"Let's take this inside, ladies," said Aldous.

Too late, Elsie realized this had played out in the open doorway. She glanced around quickly, but saw no signs of a guard.

Her father chuckled. "I thought there would be no containing either of you, so I suggested that Dixon could keep an eye on things from outside the building. But still, it is better to keep from prying eyes."

Elsie ushered them in, shutting and locking the door behind them.

Aldous took a deep breath in through his nose. "Something smells wonderful."

"I made a pot of soup for our midday meal." Elsie felt suddenly shy. She remembered that it had been many years since either of them had been in the thirteenth century, and they were wealthy. They were probably accustomed to finer fare. "You don't have to eat it if you'd rather not."

"Nonsense," said her mother. "It is a perfect day for soup. In fact, if you have the ingredients, I can show you how we make bannock now. Is the kitchen this way? We can talk while we work."

At this, Elsie burst into tears.

Jo Sinclair gathered Elsie into her arms. "Sweetling, don't cry. What's wrong?"

Elsie clung to her mother. Between sobs she said, "Nothing…I've just…I've just missed you…so very much. And this…just being with you and doing ordinary things…is what I've missed the most."

"Well then," said her mother as she stroked Elsie's hair, "we shall have to do a lot of ordinary things together."

When Elsie had regained her composure, she showed her mother into Gabe's kitchen. "I don't know if he'll have what you need."

"It doesn't take much. Turn the oven on first so it heats up. I'll show you how to make a kind of bannock they call soda bread. I'd normally use a whole grain wheat flour, but this white flour will do." She looked through the cabinets and found a bottle with a brown liquid in it and a yellow box. "Vinegar and baking soda, perfect. Is there plenty of milk?"

Elsie pulled the plastic jug from the refrigerator. "It's half full."

"That will be enough, but if Gabe is anything like my sons, he uses a lot of milk." She called into the front room where Aldous had turned on the Olympics. "Aldous, dear, have Dixon send someone to the store for milk. I don't want to leave an empty jug."

He chuckled in response. "Certainly, Jo. But perhaps I should wait until you are done to make sure there is nothing else."

"Suit yourself."

Her mother showed Elsie how baking soda reacted to vinegar. "See how it foams up? That makes the bannock lighter." She added some vinegar to the milk, causing it to curdle. She stirred baking soda and salt into the flour. "Add the sour milk to the flour all at once. Then, work fast. You don't want to overwork your dough."

As they finished making the bread, her mother asked questions about clan members, told Elsie about her other children, and just chatted as mothers and daughters do.

That is how Elsie spent the rest of the day: talking with her parents, learning about their life, and telling them about hers. Along the way, she learned so much more about modern life and the world. They answered every question and explained things she didn't comprehend. Her father had a *laptop* with him. He could pull up images of anything imaginable to help her understand everything from airplanes to the bottom of the ocean. She saw images of Scotland taken from a *satellite*.

He pointed to the area where their clan had lived, but it was empty. Nearly all of the Highlands were deserted. "What happened?"

"That, my darling, is a very long, sad story. It won't happen in your lifetime and since you intend to go back, it might not be something you want to know about."

She nodded. "I suppose not."

At their midday meal, her mother had been delighted with the apple and raisin pudding. "I haven't had one in years."

The afternoon slipped into evening. Her parents insisted on taking her out to dinner.

"Gabe left you with a cell phone number, did he not? And he knew we were coming?" asked her father.

"Yes."

"Then you can call him to let him know where we'll be. You'll likely be home before he is anyway."

Truthfully, she didn't want the evening to end, and she could only serve them soup again. Besides, she would be eating in a restaurant tomorrow with Elizabeth's mother and Dr. Rose, so she wanted to know what to expect. "Okay. I'd like to go with you."

When she dialed Gabe's number, she heard his voice say, "This is Gabe, leave a message."

He had taught her how to do that, so after the beep she said, "Um...the Sinclairs are...um...taking me out to dinner. And...well...they don't expect we'll be out long. So...uh...I'll see you later...uh...when you get home."

When she hung up, she realized her parents were grinning at her.

She blushed. "How long before things like this stop feeling so bizarre?"

Her mother laughed. "Months, even years. But I fell in

love with some things right away. Like—"

"—the bathroom," they both said in unison before bursting into laughter.

Amused, Aldous shook his head. "Come, ladies. Dixon and Jake have brought the car around."

~ * ~

Gabe had been surprised to get the message that Elizabeth was going out to dinner with the Sinclairs, but when he returned home that evening and they were still there, he wasn't sure quite what to make of it.

Elizabeth introduced them, and they exchanged small talk for a few minutes. She seemed perfectly at ease with them, which was nice to see.

Soon, Aldous said, "Well, I know you're probably tired and have to work again tomorrow, so we'll be going. Elizabeth, I know you said you were meeting your mother with Dr. Rose tomorrow. Would you like to spend the day with Jo on Tuesday? I can send a car for you."

"I'd like that a lot. You don't mind do you, Gabe?"

"No, of course not." But he didn't quite understand why.

As if reading his confused expression, Jo Sinclair said, "When you lose your memory, it is easy to feel, unmoored, out of step. Sometimes, just having someone around who understands and can help a little is comforting."

"I'm sure it is, and thank you so much for helping Elizabeth with this."

"It is my pleasure, but very small in comparison to what you are doing for her."

He put his arm around Elizabeth's waist. "I would do anything for her. I love her."

Elizabeth blushed, but rested her head against him.

Jo smiled broadly. "Clearly."

Aldous took his wife's elbow. "We'll say goodnight, but we'd like to have you both to dinner. Are you free this weekend?"

"We have plans on Saturday," said Gabe.

"Then how about Sunday?"

Gabe glanced at Elizabeth, who smiled up at him and gave a little nod. He smiled back. "Sunday is perfect."

Mr. Sinclair nodded. "Excellent. I'll send a car for you around five."

Send a car? "We could just grab a cab."

"Nonsense. I'll send a car." His tone brooked no refusal.

The Sinclairs each shook Gabe's hand and embraced Elizabeth as they left.

When they were gone, Elizabeth turned to face him, positively beaming. If this was what spending time with them did for her, he didn't begrudge her a minute.

"I made soup and m—uh—Mrs. Sinclair showed me how to make soda bread. Would you like some?"

He grinned. "I'd love some. I'm just going to take a fast shower first. I'll be out in five minutes." He gave her a quick kiss before heading to the bathroom. He didn't quite understand what had happened today. As he understood it, the Sinclairs had spent the entire day with Elsie. That seemed odd, but Aldous Sinclair was a client of her mother's. Perhaps he felt he owed it to Mrs. Quinn. Ah well, he wouldn't worry about it. Elizabeth seemed relaxed and happy.

The soup she made was delicious. His mother would have put pasta in it, but otherwise, she would have approved. The soda bread was also very good slathered with butter. That was one thing he was certain his mother had never made.

"I've never come home to hot soup and fresh bread after a long day. I could get used to this."

Elizabeth looked genuinely pleased. "I'm glad you like it. I like to cook, although it is a little hard with this." She motioned to her cast.

"Speaking of that, did you use ice and take your medicine today?"

"Yes, I did."

"And how do you feel?"

"I'm a little sore and tired, but not as bad as last night."

"Good. You should ice it one more time before we go to bed."

"I will. I'll just put things away first."

"Leave it. I'll take care of the dishes and leftovers. Ice your ribs."

"You're bossy." She leaned in and, to his surprise, kissed him, igniting his desire.

When she broke the kiss, he grinned at her. "You're stalling."

"But I like kissing you." She kissed him again, fanning the flames.

He gave into the kiss for a moment. She was warm and sweet and wonderful. His right hand slid around her waist to pull her closer, brushing against her cast. *And she has broken ribs.* With great effort, he pulled away. "You're still stalling. Ice. Now," he said with mock sternness.

She pouted. "Okay."

After he put the kitchen to rights, he joined her in the bedroom. She was wearing the beautiful but insanely impractical cashmere pajamas and lying with ice packs on her right side.

She frowned at him. "You know, this kind of hurts."

"I know. But it keeps the swelling down and makes it hurt less in the long run."

"I believe you. Thousands wouldn't."

"They always say doctors make the worst patients."

Sadness flitted across her features for a moment. "But I'm not really a doctor. At least not now."

"Your memories will return, sweetheart. I'm sure they will. But even if they don't, you know that doesn't matter to me."

"I know. And you're right. My memories will come back soon."

"That's the way to stay positive. Now, I think that ice has been on for at least fifteen minutes. I'll put it away and then I'm ready to sleep."

When he returned to the bed, she curled up next to him. If he counted the night in the hospital room—and he did—this was the eighth night he had slept by her side. His desire for her grew with each passing minute. He wouldn't act on it, not until her ribs had been allowed to heal a little longer, but he hoped going to bed with her soon would mean more than just sleeping.

Chapter 15

While she had been excited the previous day to see her parents, she dreaded lunch with Elizabeth's mother. Still, if Dr. Rose was right, she needed to do this. She dressed in the skirt and blouse that Gabe had bought for her. She smiled at her reflection. She really did love the outfit.

She was to meet Dr. Rose in front of the building at fifteen minutes before twelve. She was standing just inside the lobby door when he drove up. He leaned across the front seat and opened the door for her. "Are you ready?"

"I suppose. As ready as I'll ever be."

"Well, lass, ye look lovely. Hop in."

When she was settled and buckled in, he said, "Ye have nothing to worry about, Elsie. Just be yourself, and everything will be fine."

Elsie nodded, but had trouble tamping down the butterflies in her stomach.

"I understand ye met Aldous and Jo Sinclair over the weekend, and everyone had a bit of a surprise."

At the thought of her parents, Elsie smiled. "Yes. I never, ever imagined that they were time travelers."

"I have to admit. I thought it amazing when Jo found Aldous, but that you have turned out to be their lost daughter is mind boggling. Just when I think I have Gertrude's plan sorted out, something else pops up."

"That's the truth."

"You know, Elsie, in many ways, Elizabeth's parents are a bit like Aldous and Jo. They made choices in their lives that led them away from their daughter. Now, they realize just what they have lost and are trying—at least Elizabeth's mother is trying—to find her and connect with her again."

Elsie nodded. "I guess I can understand that."

"So, you'll give it a chance? You'll try?"

"Yes, Dr. Rose. I'll try."

Charlotte Quinn was already seated when they arrived at the posh French restaurant in SoHo. She stood and opened her arms, a nervous, hopeful look on her face. "Elizabeth, darling, how are you feeling?"

Elsie hugged her. "Better, thank you. My ribs still hurt some, but not nearly as much as they did."

Charlotte turned a warm smile on Dr. Rose. "Dr. Rose, it's lovely to see you again. Thank you for arranging this."

"It was my pleasure, Mrs. Quinn."

"Please, call me Charlotte."

"Charlotte, then. Shall we sit down?" He held Charlotte's chair and then Elsie's before seating himself.

"Elizabeth...I...well, darling, I'm sorry for the misunderstanding last week."

Of all the things Elsie thought the woman might say, an apology was the last.

"We were so worried about you. Truly, we were. And your father—you know how he can be. But, no...I guess you don't. When something is very important and things aren't going well, when he is worried or scared, he shifts into command mode. He trusts *his* ability to handle anything more than he trusts anyone else. Darling, I have never seen him as upset as he was when the officers came to the house to tell us you had been in an accident. He wanted to leave immediately, but we were in the middle of a terrible snowstorm. He had our driver and helicopter pilot on standby. He wanted everyone ready to leave the minute the heliport was open. I am so sorry it took something as dreadful as this to...well...bring us together. I don't want a misunderstanding to tear us apart. We love you, Elizabeth."

As Elizabeth's mother rambled on nervously, Elsie realized everything Dr. Rose had said was true. Charlotte was fully aware of the distance that had developed between them, and she wanted to repair the relationship.

Elsie smiled. "I know you do."

Dr. Rose cleared his throat. "Perhaps we should order before we dive too deeply into this."

Elsie looked blankly at the menu and frowned. She had learned all of the letters and was beginning to be able to read small words, but this menu had no pictures.

Charlotte said softly, "You've always liked the eggs benedict. You are also fond of lamb, and there is a lamb sandwich on the menu. Also, today's special is *lapin à la moutarde*." At Elsie's frown, she added, "Rabbit in a Dijon mustard sauce."

She wasn't sure what *eggs benedict* was and she did like lamb, but she *loved* rabbit. "I think I'd like the rabbit."

While they ate over the next hour, Charlotte kept the conversation going with inconsequential things. But eventually, she brought the topic back around to Elizabeth.

"Darling, it seems even though you haven't recovered your memories yet, you are becoming a bit more comfortable than you were in the hospital. Wouldn't you rather stay with me at our suite at the Fitzwilliam than be a burden to Dr. Soldani?"

Elsie stiffened. Was she a burden to Gabe? She remembered his words from the previous evening: *I would do anything for her. I love her*. She shook her head. "I am not a burden to Gabe. While I appreciate the offer, I would prefer to stay with him."

"I know you better. I can help you remember things."

"My memory will come back when it does. I like being with Gabe. I *love* him."

"But—"

"No. Gabe helps me, too. He is teaching me to read and do math."

"He isn't family."

"I don't want to argue about this. I would love to see you again and spend time with you, but I am going to continue living with Gabe for now." Elsie's tone was gentle but firm.

Dr. Rose stepped in. "Charlotte, ye have clearly raised your daughter to be a strong, capable woman."

"But she isn't able to be independent now."

"Not completely, no. But forcing yer will on her is only going to make her more dependent, not less."

Charlotte took one of Elsie's hands in hers. "I don't want to lose you."

Elsie squeezed her hand. "You won't."

Charlotte smiled and nodded. "Okay. Are you free on Wednesday?"

"I meet with Dr. Rose on Wednesday afternoons."

"I could pick you up and take you to lunch before your appointment."

Elsie smiled. "I'd like that."

"Afterward, we can go shopping. I'm not sure where you got that outfit, but Boho-chic is passé and not your style."

Elsie shook her head and laughed. "If this outfit is Boho-chic, then it is my style. I don't care if it's passé—whatever that is—because I love it."

Charlotte pursed her lips as if poised to criticize, but stopped herself. She gave Elsie an indulgent smile. "You're right. If you like it, it's your style."

When Elsie was in the car again with Dr. Rose, he asked, "How do ye feel that went?"

"Okay, I guess. I see what you meant now about Elizabeth's parents being afraid."

"I thought ye handled things beautifully. Ye were kind and accessible, but you stood firm where ye needed to. I suspect Elizabeth would have had a bit more trouble with that."

"It's a little surprising. I come from a time and place where I have few, if any, choices."

"Indeed. In fact, most of the people I know who travel

back in time—especially the women—struggled quite a bit with that. When they return, they usually have a newfound appreciation for their personal freedoms."

"I'm not surprised. Once I learned I could make my own choices, I really didn't want to give that authority to anyone else." Elsie sighed. "It will be hard to lose that when I return."

As soon as she said it, she knew it wouldn't be the hardest thing to lose. She would lose her parents again. And Gabe. Her mind was filled with images of the man Elizabeth loved. *I could love him too. Nay, Elsie, don't go there. Ye'll have Geordie when ye return. Don't make leaving even harder by giving yer heart to Gabe.*

"Are you all right, Elsie? You became very quiet all of a sudden."

"I'm fine. I was just thinking about my parents…and Gabe."

"Ah, yes. We should talk about that more on Wednesday. This won't be easy."

"No, it won't be."

"Maybe I can help you prepare."

"That's a good idea."

Dr. Rose pulled up in front of Gabe's building.

"Thank you for going with me, Dr. Rose. It helped a lot, having you there."

"Ye're comfortable enough to spend time with her on yer own now. That was the goal."

"And thanks for pushing me in the first place. I think I understand a little more now."

"Good. I'll see ye on Wednesday then."

She nodded and got out of the car. "I'll see you on Wednesday."

~ * ~

When Gabe came home that evening, Elsie told him every detail of lunch with Elizabeth's mother that she could remember. He seemed genuinely pleased to hear things had gone well and that they had plans for Wednesday.

"I was wondering the best way to get you to Dr. Rose's office. It's good that you and your mother are spending some time together."

"That's important to you?"

"Of course it is. I know you don't remember this, but I have always thought family was important. In medical school, it was hard for me to understand why you were so distant from yours. It is a little clearer now, but I still think it is a great opportunity for you to bond."

"Bond?"

He chuckled. "Spend some time getting closer."

"I see. And do you *bond* with your family a lot?"

He laughed outright. "Sweetheart, if my family were any closer, we'd be attached at the hips."

"But you haven't spent any time with them since I...uh...since my accident."

"No, my parents' home is in New Jersey, about an hour away by train. I usually go down there at some point during my days off."

Guilt rose in Elsie, and she looked away. "And I kept you from that?"

Gabe put a finger under her chin, drawing her gaze back to him. "I don't always go. Taking care of you was important. And I usually talk to at least one member of my family every day. On my walk to work in the morning, I usually talk to Joey, Dad, or Mom. They are all very early risers. When I walk home in the evening, it's usually one of my other brothers. Angie is all tied up in high school stuff during the week, but I nearly always talk to her on Saturdays. Nick is an architect with a big firm not far from NYUHC. Once in a while, he meets me at the hospital for lunch. I saw him yesterday."

"You did? You didn't mention it."

"I guess I didn't. The Sinclairs were here when I got

home, and it slipped my mind. But we're going to go out to dinner with him on Saturday evening."

"That's why we couldn't have dinner with the Sinclairs?"

"Exactly. I was also planning to go down next week for a couple days if that's okay."

"I…I suppose so. I…uh…I am a little afraid to stay by myself, but I'm sure I can manage."

Gabe took her hand. "I didn't intend to leave you here, sweetheart. I was hoping you'd go with me."

Elsie brightened. "And meet your family? I'd love to."

"Good. We'll go down Thursday morning and come back on Friday."

"That's over a week away."

He grinned and canted his head sideways. "Is that a problem?"

Just that Gertrude might come and send me home before then. "No. I just…well, we could go on Monday."

"We could, except Thursday is my birthday and my mom would be very upset if I didn't come home for it."

Go with him to his home? She wanted to meet his family. At that moment, she vowed that even if Gertrude came before next Thursday, Elsie would not say the word until after she had met Gabe's family.

~ * ~

The next day when Elsie visited the Sinclairs' home, she was stunned. She had been aware that they were very well off, and she remembered that Gabe had described himself as coming from a "working class" family, which she'd assumed meant they had more modest means. She'd thought Gabe's apartment was quite nice, but she assumed the Sinclairs' might be larger. She was not prepared for the reality.

Dixon called for her as her parents said he would. The driver stopped in front of a large building like Gabe's, but fancier. Dixon escorted her `past the doorman and through the main lobby to a set of glass doors. A guard in this private lobby let them in.

"Good morning, Dr. Quinn. I've notified the Sinclairs that you've arrived. You can go right up."

"By myself? Where do I go?"

The other guard frowned, obviously confused. Dixon's stern demeanor slipped for a moment, and she caught a brief glimpse of a smile. "You'll be fine. The elevator only goes to one floor and opens directly into the Sinclairs' home."

Sure enough, when the elevator doors opened, her mother and father were waiting to greet her. The Sinclairs' apartment, which she learned was called a *penthouse*, was huge. Gabe's entire apartment would have fit in the living room with plenty of room to spare. For that matter, she thought perhaps the entirety of Castle Macrae could fit inside their home. There were more rooms than Elsie could count, including one room that contained a beautiful pool of water that was for swimming.

"The water is warm. We'll swim later if you'd like to," said her mother. "We can wrap your cast. Jennifer and Caroline leave clothes here. I'm sure there is a bathing suit that will fit you."

"I think I'd like that." The water did look inviting.

"I'd like to show you something, Elsie." Her mother took her hand and led her back to the entryway where the elevator was.

Aldous followed, closing two large, carved, wooden doors. They had been open when she arrived, and Elsie hadn't paid them much heed.

Aldous ran his hand lovingly over the carved surface. "I had these doors commissioned years ago. In fact, every home we own has front doors like these. No two are exactly the same, but they all have several things in common."

Now that they were closed, Elsie realized that the two

halves came together to make a beautiful tree with roots that spread out as broadly at the bottom of the tree as the branches did above.

"This is called a tree of life," said her mother. "Your father had certain important symbols carved into the tree."

"Some are obvious." He pointed to the base of the tree where the roots began to branch out. "Here is the trinity knot, a Celtic symbol of the Holy Trinity. Our family is rooted there. And here, in the middle of the trunk is a knot. If you look carefully, you can see sixty tick marks around the edge."

"The pocket watch?"

He smiled and nodded. "Exactly. The pocket watch. Half of it is on the left door and the other half on the right." He pointed to one of the upper branches on the right door, "Carved into the grain of the wood here is the motto of Clan Sinclair: *Commit thy work to God.* But if you look carefully in the roots of the tree on the left door, you can see a Latin word, *fortitudine*, which means: *With fortitude*, the motto of Clan Macrae."

Her mother squeezed her hand. "You see, sweetling, the left door represents our roots, our beginnings. The right door represents our present and future." She pointed to four birds in flight at the top of the right door. These birds symbolize our children: Caroline, Jennifer, Xavier, and David. But there is one more little bird that often goes unnoticed. See there, perched on the nest in the branches on the left? That bird was our way of remembering you, the little one we left behind."

"We have remembered you and prayed for you every day of our lives," said her father.

Elsie was speechless. She reached out and touched the carving of the bird on the nest. The wood was smooth, as if it had been touched often.

"The rest of the family understood the Celtic knot, the motto of Clan Sinclair, and the four birds in flight were fairly obvious," said Jo.

"Only a few people ever questioned *fortitudine*. It isn't very obvious, and it seems like a good place to be rooted, so it was easily explained," said her father. "And no one knows about the pocket watch except for Gerald Rose, but he didn't even notice it at first."

Her mother smiled. "However, the little bird on the nest has been the source of speculation for years. Some people think it represents me with an empty nest."

Her father laughed. "That rather leaves me out of the picture, but it's understandable."

"When the children were still young, they thought we hoped for another child. Other friends and family members have believed this over the years too, or they believed that I had miscarried a child at some point."

Aldous nodded. "We simply allowed people to speculate. Only Gerald, your mother, and I knew how very real the little bird in the nest was and how very much we missed her."

Tears filled Elsie's eyes as her fingers caressed the symbol of her parents' love for her. Dear God, she didn't want to leave. There was nothing for her in the past. Her parents were here. The man she loved was here. *Nay, Elsie, the man Elizabeth loves is here. Someone does wait for ye.*

Chapter 16

Gabe always loved his first day off after working seven in a row. He usually slept in and did nothing except catch up on laundry. But today he awoke with the woman he loved in his arms and the sure knowledge that the day would not be spent doing nothing.

Although he had joked with her about her social calendar at the beginning of the week, it turned out that her days had been filled while he worked. Her mother had taken the whole day off to spend with her on Wednesday. He didn't think anything about it until that evening when he'd asked her about the day.

"It was very good. We had a lovely lunch and then went shopping."

"Sounds like a typical mother-daughter day."

"Does it? My mother said we'd never done that."

"Really? That's hard to believe."

"It's what she said. I'm not sure why it surprises you. You said you didn't think we were close."

"I know I did, but lunch and shopping—or pedicures—with mom is my sister's favorite thing to do. Hands down."

"Pedicures? What's a pedicure?"

He smiled. Frankly, he wondered if Elizabeth had ever taken time for a pedicure. "A pedicure is a foot treatment. You soak your feet in warm water for a while and then someone rubs the dry skin off, trims the nails, massages your feet and lower legs and finishes by putting polish on your toenails."

Elizabeth had looked incredulous. "Really? And women like this?"

"In my experience, they do."

"Maybe I should get my mother to go with me for a

pedicure."

"It would probably do you both good."

Elizabeth had spent Thursday and Friday with Mrs. Sinclair, who had taken her to see a variety of attractions in the city. Elizabeth's favorite had been the Central Park Zoo.

"There were so many animals I'd never seen before."

"You probably have seen them, you just don't remember."

"Right...that's what I meant. But I loved it. Mrs. Sinclair says that the Bronx Zoo is even bigger. She's going to take me there the next week you work nights."

"If you thought the Central Park Zoo had a lot of animals, wait until you see the Bronx Zoo. It's the largest zoo in the United States."

Her eyes lit with a youthful exuberance that was both charming and insanely attractive. It made him want to be the one to take her there. Still, there were plenty of new experiences to share with her. *Not if she gets her memory back.* He tamped that little voice down. *If all of her memories returned today, it would be a blessing.* But even as he had that thought, a small part of him was falling in love with this version of Elizabeth. He had to admit, if only to himself, that he wasn't anxious for things to change.

Today, however, he had her to himself for most of the day, and he'd planned a few things that he was sure would please her.

He rose up on one elbow, brushed the hair from her face, and gave her a gentle kiss.

She blinked her eyes, looking confused for a moment before her face split into a wide grin. "Good morning."

"Good morning, sweetheart. It's time to get up."

She glanced toward the window. "The sun's barely up, and you don't have to work today. Let's go back to sleep." She closed her eyes and snuggled into her pillow.

He kissed her again. "Ah, but we have things to do."

"If those things include more kisses, we can do that right here."

The comment followed by a suggestive smile ignited his desire. How he would love to spend the day in bed kissing her…making love to her. "As hard as it is to turn down that delightful offer—and I assure you, it's hard," he grinned at his rude pun, "your ribs are still healing. We should give it a little more time."

She smiled up at him. "Do you have any idea how attractive it is when you become the protective doctor?

His brows drew together. "What?"

"When you do little things to take care of me, when you think about my wellbeing before my wants or even your own, I feel cherished. I like it. I don't think I've ever felt that."

"Really?"

She blushed and nodded. Then her face split into a salacious grin. "Of course, when I feel cherished, I want to stay in bed with you even more."

"Well, you can't." He gave her a quick kiss. "But someday, we will." He kissed her again a bit more languidly.

When he pulled away from her lips, the sweet smile on her face delighted him. "Now you do have to get up. I promise you'll enjoy what I have planned."

When they were dressed, she started into the kitchen. "I'll make coffee."

He stopped her. "Not this morning. Grab your coat."

"Gabe, surely you don't mean to leave the house before I've had a cup of coffee. I love coffee."

"I know you do, but we're going to have breakfast at a great diner where there will be lots of coffee. Then I have something to show you."

"A diner?"

"It is a kind of restaurant that serves all kinds of food, and they usually have particularly good breakfasts."

"Okay."

It wasn't far, so they walked to the diner. It was still early enough that the restaurant wasn't too busy.

Elizabeth smiled when she saw the menu.

"Do you see something you like?"

"Yes. Pictures."

He laughed. "Pictures are good, but you're reading improves every day."

She beamed at his praise.

"So do you see something you'd like?"

"I like eggs." She pointed to another picture. "But these look like strawberries."

"They *are* strawberries. That's a waffle."

"How can there be strawberries on it? It's the middle of winter."

He wasn't sure he would ever get used to the odd holes in her memory. "They are grown in warmer places and brought here."

When the time came to order, she was still having trouble deciding, so he said, "Bring us the big breakfast platter." It came with three eggs, bacon, sausage, home fries, and biscuits. "And we'll also have a Belgian waffle with strawberries and a side of scrapple." He smiled at Elizabeth. "We'll split it, and you can try a bit of everything."

"What is scrapple?"

"It's a little hard to explain. It doesn't sound very appetizing, but it is really good and I know you used to like it."

"But what is it?"

"It's a mixture of cooked pork scraps and organ meat that have been ground up and mixed with cornmeal and spices."

She smiled. "That sounds like...well, I don't know what it is called, but I think I do like it."

She did like it. She liked it all. The strawberries, in

particular, delighted her.

Note to self, buy some.

Once fortified with breakfast and several cups of coffee, they headed toward the destination he had planned over a week ago: the wholesale flower markets.

There were literally thousands of flowers from all over the world. It was an impressive sight, and Elizabeth stared in awe. "They're beautiful—but it's winter. Is this like the strawberries?"

"Yes, exactly like the strawberries. Flowers are brought here from all around the world."

As they wandered through the markets, she appeared enraptured. At one point, she stopped in front of buckets of blue irises. "I've never seen anything so beautiful before." She reached a hand toward them, touching one tentatively.

"What do they mean?"

Gabe's brows drew together. "I'm not sure what you're asking. They don't mean anything."

"You're wrong there, young man," said an older woman who appeared to be working there.

"Pardon me?"

"The young lady is right. Flowers speak a language of their own. They all mean something."

Elizabeth turned toward her. "What are these? What do they mean?"

"They're blue irises, and they represent faith and hope."

"They're beautiful," she said, her eyes shining.

"I think that's your cue, young man."

Gabe laughed. "Yes. We'll take some."

"Be sure to pick stems that have some unopened buds. They will bloom over the next few days."

This seemed to thrill Elizabeth. He selected a dozen stems, all with buds in varying stages of flowering, and had them wrapped.

They continued to walk through the flower district,

Elizabeth simply captivated by the beauty around them. "Well, it's settled. I'll take you to the Macy's flower show. These flowers are just in bins, but they're transformed into artwork at the flower show."

"You've seen it?"

He smiled sheepishly. "I've seen pictures. I would love to see it with you, though." The truth was, he'd probably spend more time watching her passionate responses to the show than the flowers.

"I'd love to go. Is it soon?"

"It's in April."

Her face fell. "April? That long?"

"It's only a little more than a month away."

"I expect I'll have my memory back by then, but I'm sure I'll enjoy it."

He had trouble imagining the Elizabeth he knew from medical school spending hours wandering through flower markets or a formal flower show.

Eventually, she began to show signs of tiring, so he lured her away with the promise of a stop at the bookstore to buy some more workbooks and a fancy coffee shop for a mocha. They also stopped at a shop where he could buy an inexpensive vase for the irises.

Once home, he tried to talk her into resting. "We're going out again later to meet Nick."

"I'm not as fragile as you think I am, Gabe."

"I don't think you're fragile, but I know you have broken ribs that still cause you pain."

"Just a tiny bit. Curling up next to you and working in one of my new books while you watch the last day of the Olympics is not going to hurt anything."

He opened his mouth to argue, but stopped. "Now that you mention it, I can think of no better way to spend the rest of the afternoon."

In spite of her assurances that she didn't need a nap, she dozed off after a few minutes, her head slipping into his lap. *I could get used to this.*

Eventually, he had to wake her. "Elizabeth, wake up, sweetheart. We need to leave soon."

She stirred and yawned, resembling a drowsy kitten. "Leave?"

"Yes, leave. We're meeting Nick for dinner, remember?"

She became fully awake. "Oh, right. I need to get dressed."

"What you're wearing is fine."

She frowned. "I don't want to be wearing trousers to meet your brother."

She disappeared into the bedroom, appearing again in a few minutes wearing the skirt and blouse he had bought for her.

"You look beautiful."

She beamed. "Thank you. This is my favorite outfit."

~ * ~

They took a cab *uptown* to meet Gabe's brother at a small Italian restaurant. Nick was waiting for them outside.

Gabe paid the cab driver, then gave Nick a hug.

"Since when do you take cabs? There's a subway station on the corner."

"Elizabeth has broken ribs. She doesn't need to be jostled in a subway car." He turned to Elizabeth. "Elizabeth, this is my brother, Dominic. Everyone calls him Nick."

She took his hand, as Jo Sinclair had told her to, and said, "It's lovely to meet you."

Nick leaned in and kissed her cheek. "It's nice to meet you too, Elizabeth. Although technically, I have met you before."

Although his words were polite, she sensed a coolness in his greeting that made her uncomfortable. "I-I suppose we have. I'm sorry. I don't remember."

"That's what I hear."

Looking at Gabe, he said, "Shall we go in? Our table should be ready."

Once they were seated, they were given menus. Elizabeth looked at hers, but there were there no pictures, and she couldn't recognize any letters.

"See anything you like, Elizabeth?" asked Nick. "No, I don't suppose you do. After all, you've forgotten how to read."

Elizabeth felt herself blush profusely.

"Why are you being an ass, Nick?"

"I'm sorry, Gabe, I just *forgot*."

Gabe hit his brother's shoulder with the back of his hand. "*Stunata*, what the hell's the matter with you?"

Tears prickled behind her eyes, and she blinked rapidly to keep them from spilling. She wasn't sure what was happening or how to handle it. She would have left, but there was no place to go.

"Lighten up, brother, I was just joking."

"It's not funny."

"You don't think so? The little girl genius that walked out of your life, stomping on your heart as she left, is in a little accident and can't even remember how to read? I think it's very funny and highly unlikely, but somehow she's managed to suck you back in."

Was that what his family thought of her?

"God damn it, Nick. Stop. You don't know what you're talking about."

"Look me in the eye and tell me that isn't true."

There was an older couple sitting at a table across from them. The woman waved her hand at Elsie. "*Signorina. Scusa, signorina*. Would you mind helping me?" She had a faint accent of some sort. "I need to use the ladies room, but I'm a little unsteady on my feet." Then she nodded toward the man at the table and winked at Elsie. "My husband, he's not so steady, either."

She wasn't sure what the *ladies room* was, but she'd take any escape. "I'd be happy to help you." Standing, she glanced at Nick, his angry gaze piercing hers for a moment. Crushed, she looked away. "Excuse me."

She left the table to help the woman. She could tell Gabe and his brother were still arguing, but she didn't look back.

The *ladies room* turned out to be a bathroom. When they reached it, the old woman just stood there.

"Do you need help...uh..."

"No, *bella ragazza*. I don't need to use the toilet. You looked like you needed a moment, and the brothers can fight without you there to take the blows. They'll work it out in a minute."

"How do you know?"

"I'm a mother of boys. They love each other. Sometimes they want to kill each other, but they love each other."

~ * ~

"Nick, why are you doing this?"

Nick's gaze followed Elizabeth as she helped the old woman to the restroom.

"Nick!"

"I'm sorry, Gabe. I just..."

"What?"

"You were so torn up after she left you."

"She didn't leave me. *I* left *her*."

"I've never believed that, and I've always been pissed off with her for hurting you so badly."

"That's what this is about?"

"You have to admit that total memory loss right when you walk back into her life is hard to believe."

"But I do believe it. And I'm the doctor. Remember? We've been through this."

"I know, but I had to see it."

"See what?"

"The look in her eyes."

"You're some great expert who can tell someone is lying by looking at them?"

"No. But I'm fairly sure when they're completely innocent."

"So what's it going to take to convince you?"

"Nothing. I just saw it. She's shattered, and I did that. I'm sorry, Gabe."

"God damn it. I should go get her."

Nick grinned, shaking his head. "No, let the *nonnina* handle it."

When Elizabeth returned the old woman to her seat and came back to the table, Nick stood up. "I'm sorry, Elizabeth. I love my brother. I had to know for sure that you weren't playing him."

She cast Gabe a puzzled look. "*Playing* you?"

"He was worried that you were pretending to have amnesia to gain my attention."

She looked back at Nick, shaking her head. "I'd never do that. But I understand. I wish I had brothers or sisters who would show such concern."

With the initial upset over, things settled down and they had a wonderful meal.

"Not as good as Mom's," Gabe qualified.

"But better than almost anywhere else," added Nick.

"Hey, are you coming home for my birthday?"

"Christ, Gabe, Mom would kill me if I didn't." Nick raised the pitch of his voice, imitating their mother. "*It's just a little train ride, Dominic. You can take an evening away from the city to celebrate your brother's birthday.*" He shook his head. "She's going to have kittens when she finds out Tony has to be in San Diego all week."

"He hasn't told her?"

"Nah. He'll find his balls just before he gets on the plane."

Gabe laughed. "Well, there's no way he's getting out of Joe's birthday."

"Yeah, it's on a Sunday. Wait, if you're off today," he counted quickly on his fingers, "that means you have to work on Joe's birthday."

"Actually, I will be there. I switched some shifts to get off. It means working two weekends in a row, but then I'll be off two in a row."

"When is Joe's birthday?" asked Elizabeth.

"March nineteenth," said Gabe.

"The feast of Saint Joseph," added Nick.

"Birthdays are very important?"

Gabe shrugged. "Not in all families, but we kind of have a family tradition that started when we were little."

Nick grinned. "Mom always makes the person's favorite meal, whatever it is."

"Yeah, once, when Nick was about six, he liked hot dogs, tater tots, and macaroni and cheese." At her puzzled expression, Gabe added, "It isn't what you'd call fine dining. You can buy hot dogs from street vendors, tater tots come frozen, and the kind of mac and cheese he liked came from a box. I think it nearly killed Mom to serve that."

Nick laughed. "But she did because it was what I wanted."

"Do you still like those things?"

"I'm not so into tater tots or boxed mac and cheese anymore, and while I love a good hot dog, I wouldn't waste my birthday dinner on it."

"What will your mother be making for you this year, Gabe?"

"Chicken Francese with pasta. It's a sort of fried chicken cutlet with lemon sauce. I also asked her to make broccoli."

Nick looked askance. "Why did you ask for that? No one likes broccoli."

"I like broccoli."

"You do not."

"Well, I don't hate it, and mom loves it."

"Suck-up." Nick shook his head. "I wish I'd thought of that."

"I'll remind you of it in August."

Elizabeth appeared amused as she watched the back and forth banter. "So you celebrate a birthday with a feast. It sounds like fun."

"Serving our favorite dinner is only part of the tradition. Mom decorates the table with confetti, and there are always noisemakers and birthday hats."

Elizabeth cast Gabe a confused look. "Birthday hats?"

Gabe laughed. "Yup, birthday hats. They are essentially cardboard cones with a rubber band strap to hold them on."

Nick nodded. "The rule is that you have to wear it. You cannot sit down at the table without one."

"You don't have to wear it on your head, mind you," said Gabe, "but you do have to wear it."

"Oh, and the dinner has to be on your actual birthday if possible," added Nick, "except for Angela's."

"Why?"

"Her birthday is on Christmas Eve," he answered. "We always have fish on Christmas Eve, so she gets to pick another day that week for her special meal. I remember ages ago—she must have been four or five—she begged Mom to get princess crowns instead of regular hats for her birthday."

"It was the Christmas she turned six. I'll never forget it," said Gabe.

"Yeah, that's right. She wanted to wait until you were there, so she had it the night after you came home from college."

Gabe nodded. "There was nearly a mutiny that year. I knew better, but you four idiots marched into the kitchen and announced that you would not wear princess crowns."

"To which Mom said, '*Then you won't eat dinner.*'" Nick shrugged. "If it had been hot dogs or something, we might have held firm, but Angie asked for lasagna. There was no way we were going to miss lasagna."

"That's when the *you-don't-have-to-wear-it-on-your-head rule* was born," said Gabe.

"I think Gabe was the only one of the boys who actually did wear it on his head."

Elizabeth smiled at him. "That was sweet of you."

He shrugged. "It's what Angie wanted, and it was a small enough thing."

"No, Elizabeth is right. It was sweet of you, just like asking for broccoli," said Nick. He turned to Elizabeth. "Gabe's probably the nicest guy I know."

She put her hand over Gabe's. "I have to agree."

Gabe looked into her eyes, and for a moment, nothing existed but the two of them. The bond of love he felt fed his soul. He smiled. "Well, I think all of the Soldanis are nice," he cast a pointed look at Nick. "Most of the time."

~ * ~

When they were back at Gabe's apartment that night getting ready for bed, Nick's initial reaction to her weighed heavily on Elsie. Finally, she asked, "Is your whole family going to hate me because of the way we broke up?"

"No, of course not.

"Just your brothers?"

"No, Elizabeth. And I'm really sorry about the things Nick said."

"It's okay. He loves you, and I've hurt you in the past. Having someone stand up to protect you…it's a wonderful thing. I haven't had that in a while." Elsie thought of her life in the thirteenth century. Who did she have there? Aunt Dolina. Perhaps Geordie. No parents or army of brothers and sisters.

He pulled her into his arms. "You have it now,

sweetheart."

Actually, Elizabeth has it now. "I know. I just wanted to be sure about your family. Forewarned is forearmed."

"It won't happen again. It's just that Nick, Joey, and I are really close. I think they were the only ones who fully understood how upset I was. I guess Nick never believed me when I said I ended the relationship. He always thought it was you who left me. We straightened a lot of things out tonight. I'm sorry you were hurt in the process."

"I wasn't hurt."

Gabe arched an eyebrow at her.

"Okay, I was a little hurt, but once I understood that he was just looking out for you…that made it better."

Gabe kissed her. "Still, I'm sorry it happened."

"And you don't think Joe will be as irritated?"

Gabe snorted. "Joe? You don't have to worry about Joe. He's the forgiving type."

Chapter 17

When he was alone with Elizabeth, Gabe thought of her as an ordinary person, just as he had in college before graduation. But when she had returned from shopping with her mother, who had spent more on one or two articles of clothing for Elizabeth than his mother and sister would spend in a whole year, he was reminded that she wasn't ordinary.

This hit home again on Sunday night when they went to dinner at the Sinclairs' penthouse.

Up until it was time to leave, it had been a quiet, ordinary day. They had gone to an early Mass. She still insisted she was Catholic, but asked why the statue of Mary was holding a string of beads. How could she not know what a rosary was?

After Mass, they stopped for bagels before going to a flea market in Brooklyn. It was her first ride on a subway, and just as it had been with elevators and cars, she was a little in awe once she got over her initial trepidation.

She had loved the flea market. And to his surprise, when a vintage marcasite and garnet cross caught her eye, she haggled with the vendor.

That evening, when they were getting ready to leave, she once again donned the gypsy skirt and peasant blouse—her *favorite outfit*—but added the new piece of jewelry to the mix.

Curious, he asked, "You don't want to wear the new clothes your mother bought for you?"

Elizabeth smiled. "I'll wear them the next time I see her because she loves them. But I feel prettier in this."

Again, ordinary Elizabeth. A bit more girly than she had once been, but completely ordinary.

Then, a bodyguard wearing a dark suit who Elizabeth greeted as Dixon arrived and escorted them to a waiting, chauffeur-driven Lincoln.

Not ordinary.

The car took them to a very posh address in SoHo.

Not ordinary.

Dixon escorted them to a private elevator that took them into the Sinclairs' penthouse.

Definitely not ordinary.

The Sinclairs, who were among the richest people in the world, greeted her as a dear friend. But what's more, unlike Elizabeth's parents, they greeted him—ordinary, middleclass, grandson of an immigrant Gabe Soldani—just as warmly. Mr. Sinclair led them through carved wooden doors. Elizabeth glanced at the doors, touching the left one almost absently as they passed. They walked through a colossal living room and down a hall to a cozier room with a fireplace, dark paneled walls, and butter-soft leather furniture.

"Please, sit down. Make yourselves comfortable. Dinner will be ready soon," said Mrs. Sinclair.

Mr. Sinclair stood and stepped behind a wooden bar in one corner. "What can I get you to drink? I can offer nearly any kind of spirit, several nice beers and ales, a variety of wines, or something non-alcoholic if you prefer. Elizabeth, what will you have?"

Gabe glanced at Elizabeth. To his surprise, she said, "I like ale."

"Excellent. I believe I'll have one, too. I have a Belgian Trappist ale I'm sure you'll enjoy. Now, Jo, my love?"

"I think I'll have a gin and tonic."

"Hayman's or Caorunn?"

She smiled at her husband. "Need you ask? Caorunn."

Mr. Sinclair chuckled. "It pays to ask. You might decide to run rogue someday. Now, Gabe?"

"A gin and tonic sounds good. But I'm sorry, I don't know the difference between Hayman's and Caorunn. I don't think I've ever heard of them."

"Frankly, I don't taste much of a difference. Jo swears Caorunn is the finest gin made, but between you and me, I think that's because it's made in Scotland."

Jo gave a huff of mock disdain.

Gabe's brows drew together. "Scottish gin? I didn't know there was such a thing."

Mr. Sinclair laughed. "Trust me, son, if it can be brewed or distilled, someone in Scotland can make it."

Gabe nodded. "All right. I'll try the Caorunn."

Aldous winked. "Good choice." While he prepared and served the drinks, a middle-aged woman entered the room with a tray of hors d'oeuvres.

Mrs. Sinclair asked about their weekend, and Elizabeth launched into an animated description of the trip to the flower market. With that, the surreal nature of the evening evaporated. They were just having drinks and dinner with old friends.

Ordinary.

After a great meal and a lovely evening, Gabe could almost convince himself that the ride home in the Lincoln was really just like a cab—until Dixon insisted on escorting them to the door. "It isn't necessary," he assured the bodyguard. "We can usually manage to make it safely to our apartment."

"I understand, sir. However, you are not usually seen leaving the Sinclairs' building with Mr. Sinclair's driver and bodyguard. That alone could make you and Dr. Quinn a target."

"I hadn't thought of that."

"It's perfectly understandable, sir, and it's why Mr. Sinclair employs me—to minimize the danger in even the most innocuous situation."

Not quite as ordinary.

Once they were safely in his apartment again, Elizabeth put her arms around him. "I had a delightful evening."

"So did I. The Sinclairs are very nice. But after meeting David, I really shouldn't have been surprised. Frankly, he was unbelievably kind and helpful when you had your accident. And you had just broken up with him."

"Actually, the story I heard was that he broke up with me, but it really doesn't matter. I couldn't have loved him. I love you." She snaked her right hand behind his neck, pulling his head down for a kiss.

~ * ~

Elsie wasn't sure when it happened, but at some point in the last two weeks of wonderful hours spent doing wonderful things together, and even more wonderful hours doing absolutely nothing together, she wanted more. She didn't want to just lay with her head in his lap on the couch or snuggle next to him in bed. She loved the closeness that had developed between them; it meant everything to her, and yet, it was not enough. She wanted him to make love to her.

She had been in this time long enough to know that things were different. It might have been another matter if Elizabeth had never been with a man before, but she had. She had been with Gabe, and Elsie wanted that.

She had argued with herself for days, maintaining that she shouldn't, that Gabe would be making love to Elizabeth and not to her. Finally, she stopped the internal argument. If it was wrong, it was wrong.

As she walked past the carved doors into her parents' home and saw the knot in the tree that represented the pocket watch, it sent a jolt of realization through her. Days were ticking by. Gertrude could come at any time, and Elsie would have to leave. She would be leaving behind so much more than Elizabeth's body. She cherished every moment she'd had with her parents, and she would hold the memories of them in her heart. Being loved by Gabe was one more memory that she wanted—and she wanted it with every fiber of her being.

She pulled his lips down to meet hers. She would've liked for it to be smooth and romantic like she had seen on television, but that was hard with a cast on one arm. Still, she poured every ounce of desire in her into that kiss.

When their lips parted, he whispered, "Elizabeth."

"I want you, Gabe."

"But, sweetheart, your ribs…"

"Are so much better. And you are so loving and caring, I know you won't hurt me. Please, Gabe."

He groaned, kissed her again, and then lifted her into his arms to carry her to the bedroom. He lowered her onto the bed and captured her mouth in a kiss. She kissed him back, pulling at his shirt with her good hand and making absolutely no progress.

He chuckled. "Maybe I'd better take care of this." He pulled off his shirt, dropping it to the floor and kicking his shoes in the general direction of the closet.

He turned his attention to her. He untied the drawstring at the waist, then caught the waistbands of both her skirt and panties, easing both garments down. She raised her hips a little to help. He pulled off her shoes, grinning as he threw them over his shoulders. He slid his hands from her calves all the way up her legs to her hips, causing her to shiver with pleasure.

His hands continued their upward journey underneath her blouse. He gently raised her up. "Raise your arms for me."

She did as he asked, and he pulled the blouse off, tugging it gently over her cast. Once free of the garment, he captured her head in his hands and kissed her more deeply and passionately than he ever had.

She was lost.

He trailed kisses along her cheek to her ear, then down her neck. He reached around her to unhook her bra, baring her breasts to his gaze. He rubbed his thumbs over the peaks, which pebbled under his touch. Taking first one and then the other into his mouth, he sucked gently, igniting a fire in her core that took her breath away.

His hands drifted lightly over her ribs. He raised his head, his gaze following his hands.

"Stop being a doctor. I'm fine."

"I can't stop being a doctor." He kissed her again. "But you like that. Besides, I can't bear the thought of hurting you."

"You won't."

"You'll stop me if I do?"

"You won't hurt me, Gabe."

"Elizabeth, I need your promise."

She smiled and rolled her eyes. "Fine. I promise that if you hurt me, I'll tell you."

Gabe kissed her again and laid her back down on the bed.

She was completely exposed to him.

"You are beautiful."

She blushed. She'd never thought of herself as beautiful, although she thought Elizabeth was very attractive. Still, the adoration in his eyes made her feel like a goddess.

Gabe stripped off his jeans and briefs and pulled something small and flat from his nightstand before climbing onto the bed beside her. Capturing her lips again, he kissed her passionately before planting kisses down her neck and breasts to her tummy. She delighted in every gentle caress of his lips. He continued past her navel toward her most private parts.

Her hands came up to stop him. "You don't mean to...to...kiss me there, do you?"

He chuckled. "Of course I do. Elizabeth, you like this."

Well, that's absolutely true. She did like it. And when he flicked his tongue against her sensitive nub, she lost all rational thought. The sensation was divine. The moan of pure pleasure she heard could not have escaped from her lips...but it had.

He licked and sucked, driving her ever higher—toward what, she knew not. But she had to get there or surely perish. Just when she was certain it was within reach, he stopped.

"No, Gabe, please..."

He gave her a wicked smile. "Not yet."

He started again, and she gave herself over to the bliss of pure sensation.

His hands slid under her bottom, lifting her toward his mouth. Her desire built to a fever pitch. Just a little bit more was all she needed.

He stopped again. "Please, Gabe, I can't stand it. I need...I need..."

"My beautiful girl, I need, too." He took the flat packet, tore it open, and covered his hard length with it.

She was too caught up in the moment to care what it was.

He touched her again on the spot that drove her insane until she was writhing with the pleasure of it. Then he knelt between her legs, lifted her hips slightly, and joined with her in one firm stroke. She rose to meet him, lost in the primal act. He drove into her again and again until she was overcome with shuddering waves of ecstasy. The muscles at her core contracted repeatedly around him, and he too found his release.

He held his weight off her as he caught his breath, clearly concerned with hurting her. Gabe gently withdrew from her and lay beside her on the bed, still panting. "Elizabeth...I...God, I've never felt like that."

"I never have either."

He smiled at her. "You wouldn't remember if you

had."

"No, I'm fairly certain I'd have remembered that."

"It was as if our souls were entwined."

Our souls. Dear God, what have I done? But how could it be wrong? She had never experienced anything so perfect.

~ * ~

Gabe held Elizabeth in his arms as she drifted to sleep. Making love to her had been pure bliss.

Absolutely extraordinary.

Chapter 18

Ever since Elsie had made the decision to make love to Gabe, she became intensely aware of time and just how little she had. One minute he was making love to her in the early morning light on Monday, the next they were leaving Ash Wednesday Mass to go to her appointment with Dr. Rose. And the next, it was Thursday morning on the train to New Jersey.

She was nervous. Although he had assured her that another incident like the one with Nick wouldn't occur, she couldn't help but worry.

"Tell me about your home, your family."

"I've already told you about my family."

"Tell me again. Tell me more."

"Home. Well, my parents moved into their house in Hamilton, New Jersey the year after they were married. They wanted a large family, and they started right away. I was born during their first year there."

"Is it a big house? A little house?"

"Little. It is a classic Cape Cod."

"What's that?"

"Well, it's a kind of house that was commonly built in a place called Cape Cod. It is sort of a cute, little, box house. Typically, Cape Cods have a kitchen, dining room, living room, one bedroom and a bathroom on the main level, and two bedrooms and a bathroom upstairs. It's kind of perfect for a little family."

"And they filled it up?"

"Not right away. I think my mother must have had some trouble, maybe a miscarriage or even two. I'm not certain, and it isn't the kind of thing she would ever talk about, but my brother Joseph didn't come along until I was four. After that, there was a new Soldani every two years. First Nick, then Anthony—we call him Tony—and finally, Luke."

"When was Angie born?"

Gabe smiled. "When mom was expecting Luke, it was pretty obvious she wanted a girl. She started redecorating one of the bedrooms as a nursery, which was kind of funny because Tony was only a year and a half, still very much a baby. And the bedroom he and Nick shared was essentially a nursery. She redecorated anyway and while it wasn't pink, the nursery had a definite feminine flair. But another Soldani brother was born."

"Was she very disappointed?"

"No, but she still wanted a little girl. Don't get me wrong—she loves her sons with everything in her, and she never would have said anything, but I was getting old enough to notice things."

"Like what?"

"Like when she'd be shopping in a department store and stop to admire little dresses or gaze wistfully down the doll aisle of the toy store while her five boys only had eyes for cars and action figures. But after Luke, she didn't get pregnant again for years. Then it happened, and on Christmas Eve five years after Luke was born, Angela Rose graced the world. I was fifteen at the time, and just like everyone else in the family, she wrapped me around her little finger from the first moment I saw her."

"Wrapped you around her finger?"

He laughed. "It means we adored her and would move heaven and earth to make her happy."

"Except wear princess crowns."

"Well, yeah. On our heads at least." He grinned. "Actually, she is a surprisingly sweet girl considering how we spoiled her, but Mom always said you can't actually spoil a child with love."

"I wouldn't think so. How old is Angela now?"

"She is eighteen and a senior in high school."

Elsie sort of knew what that meant because she had a basic understanding of modern schooling.

"So the house did fill up."

"Yup. After Nick, my dad finished the basement, making a rec room where their rowdy sons could play."

Elsie wasn't sure what a *basement* or a *rec room* was, but she was getting better at reading context clues. It was obviously a place to play.

"After Tony was born, they built an addition on the back of the house, making a master bedroom with a bathroom upstairs and enlarging the kitchen and dining room into a great room downstairs. The downstairs bedroom became the guest room."

"Did you have a lot of guests?"

He laughed. "Hardly any. Overnight guests, anyway. We have a lot of extended family, but most of them live within an hour's drive. Before we had a guest room, on the rare occasion that we did have overnight visitors, my brothers and I got to sleep in sleeping bags on the floor of the rec room. We liked doing that."

It sounded much like the way people working in the castle slept every night, on a pallet on the floor of the great hall.

"When Mom became pregnant with Luke, she wanted a nursery, so she moved Joey and I into the downstairs bedroom and put Tony and Nick in our bedroom."

"No more guest bedroom?"

"Nope, but like I said, it didn't matter."

"Tell me about your parents."

"My dad is an electrician, and my mom took care of our home and family."

"Isn't that normally what a wife and mother does?"

He frowned at her. "Some mothers do, but most have other jobs too, like your mother."

He told her more about his family and what growing

up with them was like. He talked about going to Catholic schools and big Italian family parties and being a kid in the suburbs.

Before long, the train rolled into Hamilton Station.

She looked around. This was definitely not the city. "How do we get to your house?"

"Someone's going to pick us up." He glanced at his watch. "It won't be Luke or Angela. School isn't over."

"Is Luke still in school?"

"Sadly, yes." Gabe's eyes twinkled with mirth. "But now he's a teacher...in our old high school. Angela hates it. She gets away with nothing."

"*Gabe*," someone called as they walked out of the station.

Gabe grinned. "It's Joe. Hey, Joey," he yelled to a man leaning against a rather beat-up car.

It only took a moment for Elsie to register Joey's clothes. "He's a priest?"

"Didn't I mention that?"

"No," she hissed.

"Well, he's a priest. Come on, I'll introduce you."

When they got to the car, Gabe hugged his brother. "It's good to see you, Joe. I've missed you the last few times I've been home."

"It's good to see you too."

"Elizabeth, this is my brother Joe."

"It's nice to meet you, Father."

"It's okay to just call me Joe. By your stunned expression, I figure Gabe thought this would be a fun surprise."

"Springing my priest-brother on people is always fun."

Joe just looked at her and rolled his eyes with a *what-can-you-do* expression.

Gabe ruffled Joe's hair, which was thick and bushy. "I bet Mom *loves* this."

"How do you get away with long curls and a beard and

172

I get: *Joseph when are you gonna get a haircut?* Just wait. I came straight here before stopping at the house. She'll say it as soon as she sees me."

"First, my long hair is cute, and yours is…well…not. It's so bushy you could make a topiary out of it."

"Thanks."

"You asked."

"And what's the other reason?"

"I would have thought you'd have learned this by now. I'm just a doctor who saves children's lives. You, little brother, are a *priest*. Appearances must be maintained."

Joe laughed. "Get in the car."

The drive to the Soldani house only took a few minutes. Since arriving in the twenty-first century, Elsie had only experienced New York City—loud, crowded, bustling New York City. She had seen suburban areas on the television, but they paled in comparison to this pleasant reality. The street where they lived looked much more like a village than a city, and she instantly fell in love. The *little* house Gabe had described was huge by medieval standards—and even compared to his apartment—but tiny compared to the Sinclairs' penthouse.

Gabe's mom was in the kitchen. She was a shorter woman than Elizabeth, with dark hair and dark eyes, which Elsie was sure never missed anything. She hugged both of her sons, but just as Joe predicted, she said, "Joseph, when are you gonna get a haircut?" She flicked her hand lightly against the side of his head. "*Brutto.*"

"Mom, I'm a grown man and a priest, for the love of God. I can let my hair grow if I want to."

"But you don't want to. Trust me on this. It's not a good look for you."

Gabe looked like he was trying desperately not to laugh, but he failed. His mother flicked his head in the same way. "Don't be rude to your brother."

She turned her attention to Elsie. "Elizabeth, I know

you don't remember me, but I'm Gabriel's mother."

"It's nice to meet you, Mrs. Soldani." Elsie offered her hand.

"We don't shake hands," she said bluntly, opening her arms for a hug.

There was something so warm and motherly about it that Elsie didn't want to let go. When she did, Mrs. Soldani smiled and patted her cheek, then became all business. "Gabe, you can take Elizabeth's things up to Angela's room."

"Mom, I just thought we'd—"

"If the next words out of your mouth are going to be 'sleep in my old room,' don't even bother. Joseph is spending the night, so the two of you will be in the guest room and Nick can sleep on one of the extra beds in Luke's room."

"Mom, I'm a grown man and a doctor."

"And not married to her."

Gabe looked to Joe for support.

Joe barked a laugh. "You must be joking. First, I'm a grown man and a priest, and she tells me when to cut my hair, so I'm not sure why this would surprise you. Second, I'm a priest, and I'm duty bound to agree with her."

A joyful laugh built deep within Elsie and came bubbling forth. Times might have changed, but evidently not that much. "Gabe, this is not a battle you can win, my love. Show me where Angela's room is."

When Luke and Angie got home from school, Angie immediately latched onto Elizabeth. She asked a never-ending stream of questions, finally declaring, "You can't remember anything but Gabe. I think that is soooo romantic."

"Angie, *sta 'zitta*."

"I'm just being friendly."

"Friendly? Before she has one question answered, you ask two more. Give the girl a chance to breathe."

Angie huffed and then brightened immediately. "Hey, I need to go to the store. You wanna come with me?"

Elsie smiled. "I'd love to."

"Be sure to fasten your seatbelt, Elizabeth," warned Luke.

"Shut up. I'm a good driver."

"Tell that to the mirror you knocked off when you hit the recycling bin," said Joe.

"That was over a year ago when I was just learning, and Dad kept saying I was too close to the middle of the road."

Gabe shook his head. "Stop it, guys. She's a good driver."

"Thank you, Gabe. At least I have one nice brother." She wrinkled up her nose and stuck out her tongue at Joe and Luke.

"You're welcome." Gabe winked at Elsie. "But do fasten your seatbelt, sweetheart."

Angie frowned. "*Gabe.*"

"What? It's the law."

"Stop teasing your sister," said their mother, who took a set of keys from her purse and gave them to Angie. "You can take the minivan and pick Nick up on your way back. His train gets in at 5:30. Don't be late. We are having dinner at six, right after your dad gets home."

"Okay, Mom."

Angie drove Elsie to a place she called *the mall.* It wasn't tall, like buildings in New York, but it covered a huge area and was surrounded by a *parking lot.* Inside were many stores of varying sizes.

"I just wanted to go to the card store to get Gabe a birthday card. I made his gift."

"What is a birthday card?"

"Oh, I'm sorry, I forgot you don't remember some things. It's a card that...it's easier to show you than tell you."

When they reached the card store, Elsie understood. There were cards for every imaginable occasion, expressing a variety of sentiments.

"The guys always get jokey cards, like *Happy Birthday to the World's Okayest Brother*. But I like nice cards. Do you have a card for him? The boyfriend birthday cards are there." She pointed to another rack.

Elsie nodded and went to look at them. She figured out *Happy Birthday* because it was on nearly every card. That was about the limit of her reading skills, and she didn't want to ask Angie to read them to her. Having Gabe's sister help pick out a *boyfriend* card for Elsie to give him didn't feel right. But as Elsie looked, she found some beautiful cards that only had Happy Birthday on the front and were blank inside. She could manage to write a few words. The picture on one was a bird in a nest. She smiled to herself. Only she knew what it meant, but that was the card she bought.

As they left the store, Elsie remembered something. "Angie, you said you made Gabe a gift. Is it customary to give someone a gift on their birthday?"

"Man, you really have forgotten everything. Yeah, people get gifts on their birthday. I made him a collage of photos from when we were younger. He had his guitar or mandolin in almost every picture I found, so I wrote *Music is the voice of the soul* on the matting."

Elsie frowned. "I don't have anything to give him."

Angie looked thoughtful for a moment. "I'm sure he doesn't expect anything from you, but I know something little that you could give him. Something he really likes. But we have to drive to a different store." She glanced at her watch. "We have just enough time."

Angie took her to a huge store that seemed to sell everything. "You have your choice. He really likes these chocolates called Baci—that means kiss in Italian." Angie grinned, and Elsie blushed.

She took Elsie to another aisle. "He also likes these shortbread cookies. Mom doesn't buy them very often because they're a little pricey compared to other cookies, but they are really good."

Elsie took Elizabeth's wallet from her purse. "I hate to ask this, but I'm not good with money yet. Do I have enough to buy both?"

Angie looked in the wallet, laughed, and said, "Yeah. You have way more than enough."

After paying for the treats, Angie drove to the train station. "I'm taking the back way. Traffic on Route One will be crazy now and Mom will kill me if we're late."

They weren't at the train station yet when Angie said, "Darn. It's 5:30 now, and we're about five minutes away. Here's hoping the train is late."

When they pulled into Hamilton Station about five minutes later, Nick was waiting in front. Angie stopped the van, pushed a button, and the side door opened.

Nick shook his head. "Hi, Elizabeth. Angie, I should've known you'd be the one picking me up when no one was here." He put his overnight bag in the back, pushed a button inside the van to close the side door and walked around to Angie's door. "I'll drive."

"No. I'm driving."

"Get in the back, Angie. Elizabeth may have a death-wish, but I don't."

"I'm driving, Nick. Mom said I could."

He stared at her, arching one eyebrow. "I can stand here all evening."

Angie's chin began to tremble. "I'm a good driver."

"Come on, Angie. Don't cry."

She continued to sit there, her eyes filling with tears.

Nick huffed. "Fine. You can drive."

As he closed her door and walked around to get in the back, Angie cast a sly look at Elsie and winked. It was all Elsie could do to contain her laughter. *Wrapped around her little finger indeed.*

Chapter 19

Gabe always enjoyed time with his family, but this birthday had been one of the best in years. There was no mystery as to why. Elizabeth being there and fitting in so smoothly with his family was what made it most memorable.

Nick left at the crack of dawn to make it to his office by eight, but Gabe and Elizabeth took a late morning train to avoid the rush-hour crowds. It was a blustery, cold day, and with a large bag of leftovers and other homemade delicacies as well as several bulky birthday presents, Gabe decided to take a cab back to the apartment.

Once they were inside, he'd barely put down his things before he pulled Elizabeth into his arms and kissed her until she was flustered and breathless. "I've wanted to do that for ages."

She laughed. "Ages? We haven't been gone a full day."

"But I have gotten quite used to having you in my arms. I'm sorry Mom made you sleep in Angie's room"

She swatted at his chest. "Gabe, did you really think your mother would do anything else?"

He shrugged. "Nothing ventured, nothing gained. I guess I'm going to have to ask you to marry me soon." *Christ almighty, did those words just come out of my mouth?* He hadn't considered marriage to anyone, since...well, years. "I mean...uh...not immediately...but soon."

She rested her head against his chest and said, "I'm sure you'll know when the time is right."

Wow. She didn't jump on his declaration or slam on the brakes. "At the moment, the time is right to take you to the edge of bliss and let you teeter on the precipice until you beg me to send you over."

"No, at the moment, the time is right to put away the delicious food your mother sent with us." She ducked under his arm and made to grab the bag he had dropped on the floor.

He looped an arm around her waist, pulling her back against him. He kissed her neck and then sucked her earlobe before nipping it lightly. "*You* are the most delicious thing I brought home."

She laughed. "Five minutes."

He growled. "Fine. Five minutes."

His gaze followed her into the kitchen. He'd intended to help her, but the sight of her exquisite ass in snug jeans mesmerized him. He imagined one round cheek in each hand as he buried himself in her. To him, she was flawless—soft and round where she should be, amazingly responsive, and surprisingly uninhibited. He'd been her first, and there hadn't been many before her in his life. They had been, for the lack of a better term, *friendly fucks*, intended to make everyone feel good, but with no deep emotional attachment. He believed Elizabeth was the first and perhaps only girl he had ever *made love* to. Even so, the connection between them now was beyond anything he'd experienced with her before.

She shut the refrigerator door and turned to face him. "What are you doing?

"Looking at perhaps the most perfect ass God has ever made."

"Stop teasing."

"I am absolutely serious. In fact, there is only one thing wrong with it."

"What's that?"

"It isn't naked."

"Oh, well, as much as I strive for perfection, I find it a little difficult sometimes with this." She waved her casted arm. "Perhaps you'd like to help?"

He groaned and grew even harder. "I think I'd like that very much."

She took a step toward the bedroom, looked over her shoulder with a sly grin, and twitched her hips.

He arched an eyebrow. "And just where do you think you're going?"

"Into the bedroom in the pursuit of perfection."

"Oh, no you don't. Stay right where you are."

He stepped toward her from behind, reaching around her waist to unbutton her jeans and unzip them slowly.

"You don't mean to undress me here?" she squeaked. "In the kitchen?"

"That's exactly what I mean to do." He hooked his thumbs in the waistbands of her jeans and panties, easing them over her hips and down to her knees. "Lean over onto the counter."

"Gabe, I…"

"This is all in the pursuit of perfection." He cupped the cheeks of her luscious ass in his hands and nuzzled the back of her neck. "Do it," he whispered in her ear.

She leaned forward until her stomach was against the edge of the counter, her hands resting on the surface.

"Good girl." He went down on one knee and lifted her left foot from the floor. He untied the laces of her boot, pulling it from her foot. He removed her sock and then stroked his thumb up the center of her foot.

She squealed and jerked her foot, but her jeans trapped her legs. "You're wicked."

He laughed, nipping one cheek and causing her to squeal again. He placed her bare left foot onto the floor and repeated everything with the right foot.

She started to straighten up and remove her jeans the rest of the way.

Gabe stood, grabbed her arms gently, and placed them back onto the counter. "Not yet, precious." His hands returned to her creamy thighs, massaging them and moving ever higher. He brushed his fingers ever so lightly over her mound, gratified to hear her sharp intake of breath. He continued his slow exploration, stroking her center lightly, coming ever nearer but never quite reaching the spot.

She squirmed, trying to push against his hand.

He took his hand away. "Not yet." He reached around her, unbuttoning her blouse and allowing his hands to roam over her bra. He slipped his fingers under the edge of the lacy garment and lightly squeezed her nipples, eliciting a moan of pleasure. "These are nearly perfect, too. Shall we add them to our pursuit?"

"Yes," she said breathlessly, and that was all he needed.

He unhooked her bra and then pulled her away from the counter. "Raise your arms."

She did, and he pulled her blouse and bra off, dropping them on the floor. He pushed gently on the small of her back until she was leaning on the counter again.

"Almost," he whispered.

She gave a mewling moan.

"And so needy. I'll see what I can do to fix that."

He slid her jeans to her ankles and removed them, spreading her legs wider when they were free of constraint.

"So very beautiful." He massaged her ass and then her breasts. "Perfection." His right hand slid down her belly and cupped her mound. "Absolute perfection," he whispered as his finger slipped between her legs and circled her apex.

She drew in a ragged breath, trembling with desire. Just as she was about to climax, he took his hand away and stepped back.

"Gabe," she practically wailed.

"Don't move."

He kicked his shoes off and removed his shirt before moving close again. A shiver ran through her body.

"Let me see if I can warm you up." Again, he let his hands slide over her body until he reached her clit.

She panted and arched her head back. So close.

He moved his hand away, stepping back one more time.

"No…please." She started to turn.

"Stay as you are. Don't move. We're almost there."

He pulled off his jeans and briefs, pausing long enough to sheath himself in a condom from his wallet.

He turned her around and lifted her onto the counter. He wouldn't tease her any longer. He lowered his mouth to her, licking and sucking on the swollen nub until she was at the edge once more. He straightened and entered her in one hard stroke. She cried out as her orgasm overcame her. Locking her legs around him as he thrust into her, she rode the waves of her climax even as another built.

He was perilously close to his own orgasm when he whispered, "Come for me now."

She threw her head back and soared into ecstasy with another cry, taking him with her.

He wasn't sure how long they stood like that, completely spent, but when his brain began to function again, he lifted her into his arms and carried her to their bed. Still in a haze of post-orgasmic bliss, he disposed of the condom and climbed into bed beside her.

"Absolute perfection," he whispered, pulling her close.

"Mmm. Perfection," she purred.

Chapter 20

Saturday dawned cold but sunny. Knowing Gabe had to work that night, Elsie intended to let him sleep as long as possible, so she padded into the kitchen to make a much needed pot of coffee. As it brewed, she glanced into the living room and grinned. Her small suitcase, Gabe's backpack, and the shopping bag containing his birthday gifts still lay where he dropped them by the door.

After they recovered from the incredible kitchen counter sex, they revived long enough to eat his mother's homemade clam chowder while curled up on the couch in front of the television. Then they had another round of soul shattering sex and slept in each other's arms for the rest of the night.

Once fortified with coffee and a banana—oh, how she wished bananas grew in Scotland—she tidied up. She put the toiletries away in the bathroom, added the dirty clothes to the hamper, and started a load of laundry. Then, she unpacked the bag containing Gabe's presents. His mom and dad had given him a new pair of trousers, a nice shirt, and a sweater. She would hang them in the bedroom closet after he woke.

Angie's collage was beautiful. It was a wonderful thing to be able to take photographs and hold on to memories in such a tangible way. She thought about her parents. She couldn't remember what her father had originally looked like, and she only had fading memories of her mother. She knew with certainty that when she returned, her memories of what Jo and Aldous looked like would also eventually wane.

And Gabe? With memories of him making love to her so vivid, she didn't want to believe that someday she would

Ceci Giltenan

be unable to remember his face, his smile, the sparkle of his eyes. But if these emotions she felt were Elizabeth's, perhaps those memories would be even more fleeting.

She looked at the words written so beautifully around the pictures.

Music is the voice of the soul.

Her thoughts turned to Geordie and the night she had met him. He had said something about how much he loved to see the pleasure his music gave people. *When the tune leaves my fingers and reaches the hearts of those listening, it gives me joy. When it stirs their feet and they dance, becoming one with the melody, we are connected in an extraordinary way. It feeds my soul.*

Gabe's guitar stood in a stand in a corner of the living room, but she had never heard him play it. She would like to hear him play at least once before she had to leave.

She sighed, laying the collage aside and pulling out the cookies and chocolates. She chuckled when she looked at them. She hadn't realized it when she purchased them, but the cookies had been made in Scotland and the chocolates in Italy. It was really kind of perfect, but just like the card with the drawing of the bird in the nest, she was the only one who would ever know what it meant.

She retrieved the card from the bag and opened it. She didn't know many words, but she had very carefully copied the words *Happy Birthday* on the inside of the card and added *Love, Elizabeth.* There was so much more she wanted to say. Thank you for taking care of me. Thank you for teaching me letters and numbers. Thank you for the day at the flower market. Thank you for pizza and pasta and bagels and bananas and peanut butter. Thank you for letting me glimpse this incredible love you have for Elizabeth.

She tucked the card back in the envelope and put all of his birthday cards in a stack for him on the table.

The last gift she removed was Luke's. He liked woodworking, and like Angie, he had made Gabe's present.

185

It was a wall clock, the back of which he'd fashioned using old, weathered wood. It was rustic and very beautiful. The rough wooden background reminded her of the knot representing the pocket watch, carved into the tree of life on the Sinclair's doors. A tear slipped down her cheek as she looked at the clock. Time was passing. She couldn't stop it, and this was the first time she had allowed herself to admit that she didn't want to go back.

Ever.

She didn't want to leave her parents. And she didn't want to leave Gabe.

But it isn't you he loves, Elsie.

At that thought, she couldn't hold back. She put her face in her hands and gave into sorrow. She fought desperately not to sob, fearing that it would wake Gabe.

Eventually, she managed to regain control and stop the flow of tears. She washed her face, poured another cup of coffee, and put the laundry in the dryer.

By the time Gabe awoke, all evidence of her breakdown was gone.

Chapter 21

Elsie decided immediately that she didn't like it when Gabe worked nights. He had been gone for less than an hour based on Luke's clock, which Gabe had hung in the living room that afternoon.

She tried doing some work in her workbooks, but couldn't concentrate.

She tried watching television, but without Gabe to explain things, she didn't understand a lot.

Eventually, she went to bed, but without his comforting presence, she didn't sleep well. After waking nearly every hour throughout the night, she gave up just before dawn and got out of bed. She started the coffee brewing, wrapped her cast as best she could, and took a shower.

A little before eight in the morning, keys rattled in the lock as Gabe let himself in. He looked at her and frowned. "You look like you got less rest than I did. It was a quiet night, and I was able to get two short powernaps. Did you sleep at all?"

"Honestly, not much. I knew it would be hard not having you here, but it was worse than I thought."

"I'd say you could take a little nap with me today, but that might make it even harder for you to sleep tonight."

Her heart fell. All she wanted was to crawl back into bed next to him now that he was home.

"Let's go to Mass, and then maybe you should call the Sinclairs. You could go for a swim and have some stimulation, then meet me back here for an early dinner before I go to work."

She didn't want to be away from him all day, but he was probably right, so when they returned from Mass, she did just that.

Dixon arrived by half past ten. She kissed Gabe goodbye and left him to get what sleep he could in the darkened apartment. She enjoyed the day with the Sinclairs, and she had the opportunity to have a long talk with her mother about love and time travel.

Dixon had her home by five, just as Gabe was just waking up. They ate the leftovers from his birthday dinner. After he left, she cleaned up the dishes and stared at the empty apartment. Just as it had the night before, her anxiety rose as darkness fell. She finally forced herself to do some pages in her workbooks.

At about eight, she nearly jumped out of her skin when the phone rang. She answered it tentatively. "Hello?"

"Hello, darling, it's Mom."

"Uh...hi."

"Are you all right?"

"Yeah, fine, it's just Gabe isn't here. He's working nights and I...uh..."

"Aren't used to being alone?"

"I guess not."

"Actually, that is why I called. I figured he was working nights this week, and I wanted to check on you."

That completely surprised Elsie. "Thanks. I appreciate that."

"Are you okay alone?"

"I didn't sleep well last night, but I'm really tired tonight. I think I'll be okay."

"Well if you need someone to talk to, just call. I don't care what time it is."

"I don't want to bother you. I'm sure I'll be fine."

"Darling, I do actually understand what you are going through. Your dad is a surgeon, remember? When he was on call, he often had to go to the hospital in the middle of the night. I hated it. I called my mother, of course."

Elsie laughed. "Okay. I will call if I need you."

Ceci Giltenan

"Good. Now, I also figure that with Gabe needing to sleep during the day, it might be good for you to get out. I've cleared my schedule tomorrow. There's a wonderful spa here in the Fitzwilliam. We can have the works."

"I don't know exactly what *a spa* or *the works* are."

"You'll love it. We'll have facials, salt scrubs, a full body massage, and top it off with manicures and pedicures."

Pedicures? Elsie didn't know what the other stuff was, but Gabe had mentioned that his mom and sister loved pedicures. "Okay, that sounds great. Can I be home by five?"

"You can be, but then you will be sitting alone in an empty apartment for hours. Maybe we could have dinner together in my suite, and I'll see you home by bedtime."

"I don't know…"

"Whatever you want is fine, but see what Gabe thinks before you say no."

By all that's holy. Charlotte seems to be adapting. "Okay, I will."

"Good. I'll send a car for you at nine."

"Perfect."

"Then I'll say goodnight, and I'll see you tomorrow. But, darling, I mean it. Call if you need me."

"I will. Goodnight."

The phone rang again just after ten.

"Hello?"

"Hi, sweetheart."

"Gabe." Her voice was heavy with relief. "I couldn't imagine who was calling this late."

"I had a few minutes, so I thought I'd call to check on you."

"I'm glad you did."

"Are you okay?"

"I still wish you were here. I don't like being alone, but I'm okay."

189

"I wish I was there too. I think it will get easier with time."

Time. There it is again. "I'm sure it will. My mother called a little while ago."

"Did she? Why?" Gabe tried not to let it show, but it was clear to Elsie that the tense relationship with her parents bothered him.

"Actually, she called to commiserate with me. She said she figured you were working and that I might be missing you."

"She did?"

Elsie smiled at his incredulous tone. "Yeah, she did. She said she remembered what it was like when my father was called into the hospital at night. She liked it no better than I do."

"Wow. I forgot that once upon a time, renowned thoracic surgeon James Quinn served call duty just like we ordinary mortals."

Elsie giggled. "Does it make him seem more human?"

"A little."

"My mom also said she cleared her schedule for tomorrow so we can go to the spa for the works."

"That's great, just what you need. But be sure to tell the massage therapist that you have broken ribs."

"That sounds ominous."

"No, really, you'll love it. They just have to be very gentle when massaging over your broken ribs."

"Okay, I'll tell them. I told my mother I wanted to be back by five, but she suggested that I have dinner with her so I have less time alone."

"As much as I would love to see you before I go to work, I think she is right. I suspect the long evening alone is what makes you more anxious than anything else."

"So you're okay with that?"

"Absolutely."

"Okay."

"Look, sweetheart, I have to go. Sleep tight, and I'll see you in the morning. I love you."

"I love you too."

~ * ~

After the day she spent with Charlotte, Elsie was forced to add one more thing to her list of remarkable twenty-first century things.

Spa days.

Elizabeth's mother and Gabe had been right: she had loved every minute of it.

It was nearly half past five when she returned to Charlotte's suite that evening feeling relaxed and pampered. Realizing that Gabe would be up and getting ready to leave for work soon, Elsie asked, "Would you mind if I gave Gabe a quick call?"

"Not at all, darling. I'll just step out onto the balcony and enjoy the evening skyline."

It was kind of Charlotte to give her privacy, but it was cold out, so Elsie didn't talk long. Gabe promised to try and call her after she was home.

Elsie opened the sliding door to the balcony, thinking to join Charlotte for a minute, but as soon as she had taken the first step, she was gripped with a horrible fear of falling. Instinctively, she took a step back into the room.

Charlotte turned toward her and smiled. "It looks like you haven't forgotten your fear of heights."

That was clearly another of Elizabeth's memories pushing through because Elsie had never been afraid of high places.

"Don't worry, darling. I'm coming in. It's too cold to stay out here long anyway, and our dinner should be arriving soon. I hope you don't mind, but I took the liberty of ordering for both of us. The chef prepares some excellent middle-eastern dishes, and you've always been partial to exotic food."

Elsie smiled. Well, she couldn't expect Charlotte to give up all control at once. "I'm sure it will be great."

And it was. She thought nothing could be better than Italian food, and while she wouldn't admit it to Gabe, this came close.

Charlotte also took the liberty of ordering drinks called lemon-drop martinis. By everything that was good and holy, Elsie thought it might be the most wonderful drink she'd ever tasted.

Charlotte raised her glass to Elsie. "Here's to spectacular mother-daughter spa days and even more spectacular lemon-drop martinis."

Elsie tapped her glass against her mother's. "I'll drink to that." She'd heard someone say that on television and was chuffed to be able to use it.

Charlotte frowned. "Why have we never done this before?"

"Maybe we were always too busy?"

"I suppose so, but we should do it more often."

"I agree. I'm sure Elizabeth would love it." The words were out of her mouth before she could stop them. *Keep talking, maybe she didn't notice.* "Did you call this hummus? I really do like it. Do you know how to make it?"

"What did you just say?"

"Do you know how to make hummus?"

"Before that."

"Well, just that I like the hummus."

"No. You said *Elizabeth would love it.*"

"Did I?"

"You know you did. What did you mean?"

"I suppose…it feels like Elizabeth is a different person. And when her memories—uh, that is, my memories—come back…well, I'll be Elizabeth again."

"Elizabeth, look at me."

Elsie, who had been looking anywhere but at Charlotte, finally made eye contact with her.

Charlotte continued. "I am a lawyer. Over the years, I have learned how to recognize lies, especially when the person telling them isn't accustomed to lying. Now tell me again, what did you mean by *Elizabeth would love it?*"

Elsie didn't want to tell Elizabeth's mother about the pocket watch. She tried again. "It's just as I said, it feels like Elizabeth is a different person."

"I'm sure it does. But feeling that way and actually internalizing it to the point that you refer to yourself as a separate individual are two completely different things. Fugue states are one symptom of dissociative identity disorder. I don't think believing that Elizabeth is a different person is a good sign. Have you expressed this to Dr. Rose? If not, we need to see him immediately." She pulled her phone from her pocket and started pushing the buttons.

Elsie put a hand on Charlotte's arm to stop her. "No, we don't. Dr. Rose is aware of why I think of Elizabeth is a different person. He understands it, and it isn't part of any disorder."

"How is that possible?"

Elsie sighed. "What I am about to tell you is going to be hard to believe. After I'm done, you will probably want to call Dr. Rose, and you can do that. But let me tell you first."

Charlotte eyed her warily. "All right. I'm listening."

"Promise that you'll let me finish the story before jumping to the conclusion that I've lost my mind."

"Elizabeth, darling, maybe it's better if we just call Dr. Rose."

"Please, I'm just asking you to suspend disbelief for a few minutes."

"Fine. I'll listen and try not to judge."

Elsie nodded resolutely and launched into the story of the pocket watch, soul exchange, and time travel.

For her part, Charlotte listened until Elsie reached the end of the story before saying anything. "That's what you want me to believe? The soul of a twenty-one year-old peasant from thirteenth-century Scotland has taken up residence in my daughter's body? And vice versa?"

"That is what happened."

"And Dr. Rose believes this? If that's the case, I'm filing a malpractice suit and finding you another psychiatrist."

Elsie sighed. "Dr. Rose believes it because he has met Gertrude and used the pocket watch himself. Over the years, he has been called upon to counsel other time travelers."

"And you believe you are on a mission to bring Elizabeth and Dr. Soldani together? And by the way, if he is involved with this in any fashion, I will include him in the suit."

"Gabe is not involved. He doesn't know anything about this. He believes I am Elizabeth, and he loves her with his whole heart. And while I believe the primary mission was to put Elizabeth where she could help Lady MacKenzie, I also think Gabe and Elizabeth are meant to be together." Elsie thought it better not to mention that the rift between Elizabeth and her parents needed to be mended as well.

"I don't believe any of this."

"Then perhaps you should call Dr. Rose now."

"After you told me he believes this nonsense? Not a chance. I need to get you out of that quack's clutches."

Fear rose in Elsie like hot bile. Telling Elizabeth's mother had been a huge mistake. "Please, you must believe me. What would it take to prove it to you? There are other people who have used the pocket watch. I would need their permission first, but perhaps talking to one of them would help."

"Talking to similarly deluded people will not change my mind. Nothing short of, what did you call the old woman?"

"Gertrude."

"Well, nothing short of Gertrude stepping in off that balcony and offering me the pocket watch will convince me that this isn't a well-developed delusion."

Before Elsie could respond, a tap came at the balcony door. She glanced that direction, but the drapes were drawn.

"How did you do that?" Charlotte demanded.

"I didn't do anything."

The tap came again.

"There is no access to that balcony from anywhere but those doors. You must be doing something. Stop it this instant."

"I swear, I'm not..."

The balcony door slid open, and Charlotte jumped to her feet just as Gertrude pulled the draperies aside and stepped into the room. "I am not in the habit of entering without an invitation, but I fear ye'd have left me standing out in the cold all night. Besides, ye did say the only way you would be convinced that Elsie is telling ye the truth would be if I stepped in off the balcony and offered ye the pocket watch. I'll accept that as an invitation."

"Who are you, and how did you get out there?"

"I'm Gertrude."

"How long have you been hiding out there?"

"Ye know I wasn't hiding out there. Ye stepped out to look at the skyline right before ye drew the curtains and ye haven't left since then."

"You could only know that if you had been hiding out there."

"Where would I hide, lass? I'm a rather conspicuous size."

"This is impossible. People can't just appear from nowhere." She rounded on Elizabeth. "How did you set this up? How did you know I'd—I'd—,"

"Say ye'd believe her if I stepped in off the balcony?

She didn't. And people can't just appear from nowhere. However, I can. I am one of the ancients, just as Elsie told you."

"And why are you calling her Elsie? I haven't called her that since she was a little girl."

"I call her Elsie because that's the name she goes by. She is not your daughter Elizabeth."

Charlotte sat down, looking bewildered. Elsie moved to sit beside, placing an arm around her shoulders.

Charlotte looked her in the eye. "Elizabeth, why are you doing this? Why is it so important to draw me into this delusion? You need help, my darling."

"I'm so sorry to have caused you this distress. Truly, I am. But it isn't a delusion. Elizabeth accepted the watch and...well, here we are." What else could she say?

"Do ye mind if I sit down?" asked Gertrude.

Charlotte nodded her head absently.

Gertrude settled herself in the chair across from them. She reached in her pocket and pulled out the pocket watch. Opening it, she held it so Charlotte could see its single hand pointing to six. "Elsie has been here for thirty days. There are thirty days left to switch places again before the exchange becomes permanent."

"You expect me to just believe that? Did you hypnotize Elizabeth? Is that why she is in the fugue?"

Gertrude sighed. "There are some people who simply refuse to take anything on faith. Charlotte, we actually met years ago."

"I think not. I certainly would remember being offered a time-traveling pocket watch." Her voice was thick with disdain.

Gertrude smiled indulgently. "I'm sure ye would have, if I had offered it to ye then. But I didn't."

"I don't remember ever meeting you."

"Perhaps I can help ye a bit. Do ye remember going to the New York World's Fair in 1964?"

Charlotte canted her head. "Yes."

"Ye were eighteen at the time. And you had gone with some friends who had managed to get tickets to *Les Poupées de Paris*."

Charlotte smiled for the first time. "The *adult* puppet show with the naked puppets. It was scandalous, and everyone wanted to see it. I'd forgotten all about that."

"But ye didn't see it."

"No."

"Because you had seen the boy you were dating waiting in a line with another girl. If I recall correctly, he was *practically eating her*."

Charlotte blushed but chuckled. "Well, he was. I'd never seen anyone kissing like that before. Now that I think back, his technique was *awful*."

"But at the time, yer heart was in tatters. Ye ran away in tears and didn't go to the show. I found ye sitting on a bench, crying."

"That couldn't have been you. It was forty years ago and that woman would have to be well over a hundred. She looked to be about the age you are now." Charlotte looked at Gertrude as if really seeing her for the first time. "It can't be…"

"I sat with ye and listened as ye poured yer heart out to me. We chatted for a bit and ye had decided ye were well shot of him before long. Then we walked around the fair, marveling about all of the futuristic ideas being presented."

"It was you."

Gertrude nodded. "Yes, it was. And at one point, I asked ye if ye could, would ye take a trip to the future."

"I remember that. Dear God, you were serious?"

"I was indeed. But ye said nay, ye'd rather meet each day as it came. 'Twas a very good answer and an excellent philosophy. So ye didn't need the watch."

Charlotte looked from Gertrude to Elsie. "But you came to the future."

"Not exactly by choice, as I told you."

"Elizabeth is as discontent a soul as I have encountered in ages. She longed to practice medicine as it once was. And yet, she never slowed down enough to look around and experience *each day as it came*. She was always charging forward, planning three moves ahead. She was never happy."

Charlotte looked away for a moment, her eyes becoming bright with tears. "I guess I stopped living by the philosophy of my eighteen-year-old self at some point. By the time we had Elizabeth, James and I were building our careers. She learned her perpetual forward motion from us."

"Yes, she did."

Charlotte looked wryly at her. "You don't sugar-coat anything, do you?"

"Why would I do that? The fact is many people create the circumstances in which they find themselves. To let them believe otherwise accomplishes nothing."

"But Elizabeth is well?"

"Extremely well. The pace of her life has slowed down, and she is finding exactly what she sought."

Charlotte turned her attention to Elsie, taking her hand. "I'm so sorry I didn't believe you. This has to have been beyond frightening, especially since you didn't choose this path. And we certainly made it no easier for you."

"It was scary at first, but I am getting used to it. Dr. Rose has been a huge help."

"Does Dr. Soldani know?"

Elsie shook her head.

"And you believe he and Elizabeth are meant to be together?"

"I don't know why I would feel so strongly about him otherwise. From the first moment I saw him, I felt it. It had to be one of her memories influencing that."

"What do you think, Gertrude?"

Ceci Giltenan

"I think the universe is unfolding as it should."

Chapter 22

Once Charlotte finally believed Elsie was not delusional, she'd been full of questions. She fired them off at Elsie, one after another in rapid succession. Elsie was reminded of when Mrs. Soldani scolded Angela for doing much the same thing.

Eventually, Gertrude put up a hand. "Charlotte, I know the lawyer in you wants to know all the details, but you can't learn it all in one night, and it's getting late. I must be going."

Charlotte took Elsie's hand. "I'm sorry, Elsie. I'll hold my other questions for now."

Elsie smiled and nodded. "I understand. Really, I do. I don't mind answering your questions, but I am tired."

They said goodbye to Gertrude, and Charlotte called for a driver. She rode with Elsie and saw her all the way to the apartment. She frowned when she saw the interior. "Oh dear, this is tiny."

Elsie nodded. "But I like it. It's cozy."

Charlotte smiled. "I'm sure it is. Well, I should be getting to bed myself. Tomorrow is an insanely busy day. I'm glad you told me everything."

"I know it was hard to believe. *Really* hard to believe. But I'm glad you know." Elsie frowned. She didn't want to cause any hurt feelings, but she really needed to say something.

Charlotte picked up on Elsie's hesitation. "I can tell you want to say something."

"I'm sorry, but I am a little worried about something."

"What is it?"

"It was so very hard for you to accept my story that you believed I had a serious psychological problem and were prepared to sue Dr. Rose…and Gabe. It took an appearance from Gertrude for you to believe it."

"I'm sorry, darling. It's my nature to question things."

"I know. And I think it will be even harder to convince Elizabeth's father. In fact, I don't think he could be convinced even if Gertrude materialized out of thin air directly in front of him."

"Ah, I see where you are going, and you are right. As much as I hate to keep this from him, we must."

"I think that's best. I suppose you should also keep calling me Elizabeth."

"I'm going to let you in on a little secret. Your father and I called you Elsie for years. When you started school and the teacher used your given name, you insisted on being called Elizabeth and wouldn't answer if we called you anything else. I like calling you Elsie. It actually makes me feel closer to Elizabeth. At least to the Elizabeth I knew before we all went our separate paths. Everyone will understand if I call you Elsie."

"Okay. Honestly, I'd like it, too."

"Good. And another thing, Elsie, I would like to continue spending time with you. Gertrude was right. Elizabeth has grown very distant from us, and it is our fault. I had to make more time in my life for her because of all of this. I don't want that time to fill up again before she returns."

Elsie smiled. "I'd like that."

"Excellent. Perhaps we could spend Wednesday afternoon together again. Lunch, Dr. Rose, and shopping?"

"That sounds perfect."

To Elsie's surprise, Charlotte gave her a kiss on the cheek. "Good night, Elsie."

~ * ~

The rest of the week seemed to drag by. As planned, Elsie spent Wednesday afternoon with Charlotte and

Tuesday and Thursday with her own mother.

But Friday belonged to Gabe. He'd explained that he would normally have to work one more night, but he had made some changes to be off for Joe's birthday.

"I'll be working days Saturday, Sunday, and Monday and then an extra Friday night in a few weeks. I'm just going to sleep a little now. Otherwise, I won't sleep tonight and I'll be trashed tomorrow."

Even with Charlotte and Jo keeping her busy during the day, Elsie still hadn't slept all that well. She longed to curl up next to him for a while, so she told him so.

"Sweetheart, if you come to bed with me, we won't sleep—and it was a crazy night. I need a little rest. When I get up, we'll go do something touristy."

She sighed heavily. "All right."

He chuckled and gave her a kiss. "Don't let me sleep for more than three hours."

She nodded. "Okay."

"I mean it, Elizabeth. No matter what I say, absolutely no more than three hours. Don't take no for an answer. Promise me."

"I promise."

She thought the warning and the promise he forced from her were silly until three hours later when he groaned and rolled over. "I'm exhausted. Wake me in another hour."

"You said not to take no for an answer."

"I know I did, but one more hour will be okay."

"You made me promise."

"I know I did, but I really need another hour. It will be fine."

"*Gabe.*"

"It's just an hour, Elizabeth. Let me sleep for another hour."

His tone was a little sharp, so she decided to give him the hour he requested. Then his words came back to her. *No matter what I say, absolutely no more than three hours.*

She smiled to herself. Challenge accepted. Wardrobe change required.

She stripped off her clothes and slipped into the bedroom. She watched him sleeping for a minute. With his face completely relaxed and his curly black hair tousled on the pillow, he looked almost boyish.

I hope you remember that you asked for this.

She padded over to the bed and climbed on next to him. She began stroking his body softly. Clearly enjoying her touch even in his semi-conscious state, he rolled toward her. She rose up on her knees, replacing her hands with her lips, sprinkling kisses across his chest and down his stomach.

He gave a contented sigh, but didn't open his eyes.

Her touch became more insistent. She stroked and kissed his chiseled muscles, pulling the covers back and moving lower. When she reached his manhood, she wrapped a hand around it, stroking it tentatively at first and then with increasing confidence.

He opened one eye and emitted a low, rumbling growl.

"Don't worry. You've had your three hours of sleep, but if you don't wish to wake, you needn't." Even as she said it, she crawled on top, straddling him. "Still, ye might regret sleeping through this."

His eyes flew open. The shocked look on his face brought on a fit of laughter.

After a moment, he began to chuckle. "I did say not to take no for an answer."

"You did."

"Well then, do your worst."

She took his rigid length in her hand, guiding it toward her opening and lowering herself onto him. He filled her, stretched her, completed her. She rose up on her knees and slowly sunk down again. She moved her hips in a small circle, and the sensation was exquisite. She repeated the action again and again, finding a rhythm that suited her. As she rode him, she was vaguely aware of how much control she had: her movements, her speed, her pleasure. Based on his moans of bliss, her pleasure was clearly his, too.

He cupped his hands around her breasts, massaging and teasing the firm peaks.

As her need built, she was no longer satisfied with the steady pace she'd set. She increased it, rising higher, falling faster, and burying him even deeper within her. The feeling was sublime, and she reached her climax almost without warning. The world shimmered around her, and she was lost in pure sensation. She was barely aware of Gabe's primal groan and the heat that filled her as she floated back to consciousness. She collapsed on his chest, panting and sated.

He wrapped his arms around her, gently moving her to his side. He kissed the top of her head. "That is, hands down, the best wake-up call I've ever received."

She chuckled. "You said not to take no for an answer."

"And I meant it. I'd say I'm sorry that I didn't wake when you first tried, but honestly, since I so enjoyed your creative solution, I am not sorry in the least." He kissed her again. "Let's have a shower and go explore the city."

He climbed out of bed and froze. "Elizabeth, you didn't use a condom."

She frowned. "What's a condom?"

"Sweetheart, it's the sheath I cover myself with every time we have sex—so you don't become pregnant."

She knew that he did that, but didn't know what it was for. "I'm sorry. I didn't know."

"Oh God. I should have explained it. I just assumed. Damn it."

"Gabe, I'm sorry."

He put two fingers to his forehead. "It's not your fault. Sometimes, it's hard to remember that you aren't exactly Dr. Elizabeth Quinn at the moment." He shook his head and smiled. "Don't worry. It happened, and the universe unfolds as it should."

~ * ~

Gabe had suffered a moment of panic when he realized that they'd had sex without protection. He had never done that before, and it weighed heavily on him for several hours. But as he spent the day with lighthearted, adventurous Elizabeth, his worries dissolved.

It didn't matter. He loved her. He intended to marry her and have lots of children with her. If they had just started one, then it was God's will. If they hadn't, that too was ordained. Just as Gabe had told Elizabeth in the moment, *the universe unfolds as it should.*

That night, he slept with her spooned against him. This was right. This was perfect. He never wanted to be without her again.

Work over the next three days sped by, punctuated at the end of the day with mind-numbing sex and a sound night's sleep with the woman he loved.

Before Elizabeth landed in his life, he'd planned to escape the city for the whole week of Joe's birthday. He could catch a late train home when he got off Monday evening, and he wouldn't have to return until the next Monday evening because he didn't have to be a work again until the following Tuesday.

However, he massaged those plans a bit. He enjoyed the feel of her in his arms as he slept at night—and her absolute abandon when he made love to her—much too much to tolerate the forced separation imposed by his mother.

He might have considered going down on Saturday night and back on Monday morning, but Friday was Saint Patrick's Day and the city would be crazier than usual. He settled on going down early Thursday afternoon—before the evening rush hour but after he'd spent the morning in carnal pursuits with his beloved.

When they arrived at the Hamilton train station, Angie was there to pick them up.

"We're going to drop you off, Gabe, and then I'm taking Elizabeth to shop for prom dresses."

"Angie, can't that wait? Prom is months away."

"Wait? Months? You are totally clueless. Do you think a girl just goes out the week before and picks something? Jesus, almost all the other girls have theirs already. I just waited this long because I wanted Elizabeth to go with me. Mom's already seen the ones I'm considering. I've narrowed it down to four, but I want another opinion."

Gabe smiled at Elizabeth. "Do you mind?"

Elizabeth laughed. "I'm not sure I completely understand, but I think Angie needs a dress for something important, so she has picked out several and wants my opinion of them."

He nodded. "That's the gist of it."

"No, I don't mind."

Elizabeth and Angie came in the house long enough to say hello to his mother and for Angie to get the shoes she intended to wear to prom.

Once the girls were gone, Gabe and Luke sat at the kitchen table to chat with their mother as she made ravioli.

"Is that what's for dinner?" Gabe asked hopefully.

"No, it's for Joe's birthday dinner on Sunday. We're having patches tonight."

Gabe grinned. Patches were the leftover pieces of pasta dough that his mom cooked and served with meatballs. "I love patches."

"I know you do. That's why I made the pasta today instead of yesterday."

"Thanks, Mom. You're the best. Do you need any help?"

"No, I'm almost done with this, but then I need you."

For the next few minutes, Luke entertained them with

stories of high school from a teacher's point of view.

When his mom was finished and had washed the flour off her hands, she said, "Okay, you can come with me now. It won't take long. I've been sorting out closets and things trying to get rid of stuff that we will never use. I have boxes for each of you to go through. Luke and Angela have already taken care of theirs, and I was hoping you, Nick, and Tony can sort yours this weekend. Since Angela is entertaining Elizabeth at the moment, can you come upstairs with me and take a look at yours?"

"Sure, Mom. I'd be happy to."

This was perfect. Gabe wanted to speak with his mother alone.

When they got upstairs to her bedroom, there were three boxes against one wall. His mother put one on the bed and sat on her vanity stool while he explored the contents. It was mostly full of old clothes and a few participation trophies. "Mom, I don't think I need to keep any of this."

"That's what I thought, but I wanted to make sure. I also wondered if you still wanted your grandfather's mandolin. You haven't played it in years. If you don't want it, I thought one of your cousins might like it."

"I'd forgotten about it. Yeah, I'd like to have that. I'll take it back with me this time."

"If you do, I want to hear you play it once in a while. There is no sense letting it gather dust."

He laughed. "I will, Mom. I promise."

She canted her head to one side.

"Really, I will."

"Okay. That's all I have for you to sort."

"Uh, Mom, since we have a minute, I want to ask you something."

His mother's eyes narrowed. "You can always ask me anything as long as you are willing to hear the answer."

He smiled. "I know, Mom, and you are just like Mary Poppins—"

"—practically perfect in every way. So what is it you want to ask?"

"I really love Elizabeth. I want to ask her to marry me—not immediately, but soon. You always said grandma's engagement ring would be for my bride. I'd like to have it for when I'm ready."

She frowned, looking very serious, but opened a drawer in her dresser and took the faded velvet box from where it was hidden among her socks. She walked to the bed and sat down beside him. "We need to talk for a few minutes."

Gabe sighed. This wasn't going to be easy. "Sure, Mom."

"Gabriel, this ring is yours and I will give it to you. However, I am going to ask you to think long and hard before you ask that girl to marry you."

"Mom, I love her. I've loved her for years."

"And she broke your heart once. Which, quite frankly, makes me not like her so much."

"It was a misunderstanding."

"That's right. Because she is from a different world. She isn't like us."

"But that's just it: she wants to be like us. I think she has always wanted to belong to a family like ours. Her parents...I've been closer to some teachers than they are to their daughter. After the accident, she didn't want to go to Baltimore, but her dad tried to have her declared incompetent so he could force her. Her mom is coming around a little. I think the accident scared her."

"As it should have."

"I agree. They've lived separate lives for years. Do you remember how I thought what Elizabeth said that day—about not believing they'd come to her graduation—was a pathetic lie?"

"Yes, I do. And I agreed with you."

"Well, I found out from an old friend of hers that it

wasn't a lie. Her parents hadn't attended her high school or college graduation, and she'd been valedictorian at both of them. She had no reason to think they would be there."

His mother pursed her lips in disapproval.

"I know, right?"

"Be that as it may, you are ignoring something very important here. She's lost all her memories."

"That's just it, Mom. The one memory that she hasn't lost is loving me. I was the one who walked out before, not her."

His mother smiled. "Exactly. Maybe she did love you. Maybe she harbors some love for you still that she latched onto at a time when it was all that was familiar to her. But what happens when her memory returns? What if she doesn't love you? What if she was as hurt by the breakup as you were and she wants nothing to do with you?"

"I don't think that will happen. This thing between us, I can't describe it."

"Hormones?"

"*Mom.*"

"I'm teasing, but I really don't think you should jump into marriage with her just yet. Give it some time. Maybe wait until she gets her memories back."

"I won't jump into anything. I promise."

She arched an eyebrow at him. "But you still want the ring."

He smiled. "I still want the ring."

She shook her head and put the box into his hand.

Chapter 23

Gabe sat in on the couch, idly tuning the old mandolin he'd brought back. He hadn't played it in years. The long weekend in New Jersey had been fun, as it always was. Returning home and making love to Elizabeth after several days of enforced chastity was even more fun. This time, they made it out of the kitchen.

Did it get any better? Great afternoon sex, a delicious dinner, and a quiet evening with the woman he loved. He wanted more of this.

"Do you like living in New York?" he asked Elizabeth, who sat at the table working in one of her books.

She looked up and smiled. "I like living wherever you are."

He chuckled. "I like that answer. But if you had the choice, would you rather live here in the city or in a more suburban place...like central New Jersey?"

"There are things I like about the city. I like Dr. Rose and the Sinclairs. But there are other nice things about not being in the city that I like, too. Why do you ask?"

"Just curious."

But it was more than curiosity. Gabe was considering looking for a job in a pediatric practice in the area where his family lived. Maybe buy a house and start a family.

Maybe.

If he wasn't a hospitalist, he would have more regular hours. Sure, he'd be on call once in a while, but that was nothing compared to working seven nights in a row and barely crossing paths with Elizabeth.

He started idly plucking a tune on the mandolin. It had been years, but the melodies came back. His fingers remembered the strings.

Elizabeth stopped writing to watch him, closing her eyes for a moment as if she were absorbing the melody. She picked up the tune quickly, humming as he played. "That's lovely. I love music. I love to dance." She stood and started swaying and dancing as he continued to play.

In that moment, they were enfolded in a cocoon of music and the indescribable connection between musician and dancer. She was breathtaking to watch. Her right hand was extended over her head as she moved gracefully in the classic, slow-quick-quick, slow-quick-quick combination of steps common to folk and country dances from all over the world.

But even as she enthralled him, something nagged at him. Why had they never done this before? He had played for her years ago, but she had never enjoyed it so much or danced while he played.

Then realization dawned. *Elizabeth doesn't dance. Ever.*

And she doesn't pray in Latin.

All of the incongruous images from the last few weeks bombarded him in rapid succession. Elizabeth in the ICU cowering from an ophthalmoscope. Unable to read. Gripping his hand in terror as they rode in the elevator. Delighted by how the toilet worked. Wanting to walk home from the hospital instead of getting into a car.

Bras and panties had been foreign to her. She hadn't known how to use a phone. She didn't recognize a lot of ordinary foods.

She had vehemently insisted that she was Catholic, but hadn't understood the concept of other Christian denominations—and she had no idea what a rosary was.

Suddenly overwhelmed, he stopped playing.

The first night he stayed with her in the hospital, when she'd been drowsy with pain medication, she had said, "I want to remember it all when I go back."

Was this possible? Could this woman in front of him

who was confused and sometimes terrified by the world around her, who had a deep faith that Elizabeth didn't share, and who danced so beautifully be another soul from another time? Could souls come forward? He'd always assumed they only went backwards.

Dear God, that's it. She's a time traveler. She had remembered him and believed she loved him, but that must have been one of Elizabeth's memories. The fact that Elizabeth did love him only comforted him for a moment. If this girl had used the pocket watch, it meant Elizabeth's life was over.

I've lost her. The realization gutted him.

"What's the matter, Gabe?"

He looked at her for a moment, trying to convince himself he was wrong, but he knew with certainty he was right. "You aren't Elizabeth."

"I...I..."

"You aren't. Someone gave you the pocket watch."

"How do you know about it?"

"Because someone—an old woman named Gertrude—gave it to me once a long time ago."

"Gertrude didn't give it to *me*."

"Well, someone did."

"No, Gabe. Gertrude gave *Elizabeth* the pocket watch."

"That isn't possible. The person with the watch is only gone for sixty seconds at the most. If she were given the watch, she'd be back—or dead."

"It didn't work that way this time. Elizabeth was needed for something, but I hadn't done the thing yet that would end in my death. She went back when she lost consciousness during the accident, but she dropped the watch. It stayed here, so time is equal. When the time comes, we'll be able to change back."

"Then Elizabeth can return?"

She nodded.

"And she loves me?"

"I think she does. I don't know how to explain how I feel if she doesn't."

That should have given him hope, but if anything, he felt worse. Why would he feel worse? The woman he loved was returning to him. That was when the horrible truth sunk in: he didn't know if it was Elizabeth who he loved or this soul from the past. "But you aren't Elizabeth, and you let me love *you*."

She looked stunned, as if he had slapped her. "I...yes...I..."

"Never mind. I'm going out for a while. I'm sorry, but I need some space to think. I can't do that here. I don't know if I can stay here with you. I-I-I'm sorry." He grabbed his jacket and left.

~ * ~

Elsie watched him leave, and it felt as if her heart had been torn to bits and thrown at her feet. She sunk to her knees, sobbing. Why did this hurt so badly? She had been doing this for Elizabeth, hadn't she? Elsie had wanted to give her back a lost love, and she wanted to return to her own love. But the answer stared her in the face.

Because you don't want to return to your own love, and you don't want to give Elizabeth's love back to her. And now you know for certain, you must.

The truth completely shattered her.

She sobbed on the floor until she had nothing left. Pulling herself together, she stood to look around at the little home she had grown to love. But it wasn't home without Gabe.

His words echoed in the empty apartment. *I don't know if I can stay here with you.*

Right. She found Aldous Sinclair's card and picked up the phone. She dialed the cell phone number he'd told her to use in an emergency.

He answered immediately. "Elsie? Is something wrong?"

The sound of his voice started tears flowing again. "Da?"

"Elsie, what's happened?"

"Gabe knows about the pocket watch. He left."

"What? I'm sending a car for you. Dixon will be there soon. Tell me what happened."

"I'm not sure I know. We had a wonderful weekend with his family. He brought back his mandolin and was playing for me. It was beautiful, and I started to dance. Then he just started looking at me so strangely and said that someone must have given me the pocket watch."

"How did he know about it?"

"He said Gertrude gave it to him a long time ago. I explained what happened with Elizabeth and the watch and time being equal. I told him she can return. He wanted to know if Elizabeth loves him. I told him I didn't know how to explain how I feel if she didn't love him."

"Then why did he leave?"

"I'm not certain. He seemed angry that I wasn't her, but that I had let him…well…I'd let him love me. He said he needed to think, grabbed his jacket, and left."

"Oh, my sweet girl. I'm so sorry."

The lump rose in her throat. She didn't want to cry again. "Thanks, Da. I'll just gather my things so I'm ready to go when Dixon gets here."

As she packed, she tried to tell herself that this had always been about Elizabeth, but she knew better. At some point, she—not Elizabeth—had fallen in love with Gabe.

She left Elizabeth's computer in the closet where it had been since the day she left the hospital. It would give them a reason to get together when Elizabeth returned. Elsie knew she should not feel so abandoned. But she did.

When Dixon arrived, she made another call. She wanted to tell Gabe where she was going. She wanted to apologize. She wanted to say goodbye.

He didn't answer.

"This is Gabe. Leave a message."

"Gabe...I'm sorry. I didn't mean to make you so angry. Thank you for everything you've done for me. I don't want to put you out any longer. I'm going to stay with the Sinclairs until...well...it shouldn't be much longer until...uh," she glanced at Dixon, "...until I'm my old self again. Goodbye. I'll never forget all you've done." She hung up the phone.

"Are you ready, Dr. Quinn?"

"Yes, thank you, Dixon."

He picked up her suitcase and a shopping bag containing the overflow and then held the door for her. "After you, ma'am."

She fished the key Gabe had given her from her purse and locked the door. She couldn't stop another tear from slipping down her cheek. She wiped it away hastily and left with Dixon.

~ * ~

Gabe walked to a local pub. It was a Friday night, and there was a good crowd at the bar, but he spied an empty booth in the back. He ordered a drink and sat there, trying to get his head around what had happened. He loved Elizabeth. He had for years. But when this girl entered his life, his feelings were more intense than they had ever been before. He hadn't quite understood how that was possible. He thought maybe he had pushed away his true feelings for so long that they came bursting forth more powerful than ever.

But she wasn't Elizabeth.

Elizabeth loved him. The girl couldn't have felt the way she claimed to feel otherwise.

The problem was that he was no longer sure if it was Elizabeth he loved or the soul from the past.

It really didn't matter. She was going back. He was losing her.

No, Elizabeth was returning. Why would he think of it as losing this woman he didn't know?

Because you do know her. You knew she was different from the start.

Damn.

He took a drink.

"Do ye mind if I sit with ye?"

Gabe looked up to see Gertrude standing by his table. She hadn't changed a bit since he last saw her over twelve years ago. "Be my guest."

She sat and arched an eyebrow at the sight of the drink in his hand. "You once told me ye'd never be a sick, drunk doctor."

"And this is just one drink. I have no intention of becoming drunk or sick."

"So what has ye upset enough to make ye drink alone tonight?"

"Don't try to tell me you don't know."

"I have no idea what's in yer head, lad."

"But you know about Elizabeth."

"Yes, of course I know that."

"Then you know I've spent the last five weeks falling in love with someone I can't have. Again."

"What are you talking about?"

"The girl, the soul that is in Elizabeth's body. I think I love her."

"Well, that's very nice indeed."

"No, Gertrude, it isn't *nice*. It isn't nice at all. She's only here until Elizabeth returns. She'll leave, and my heart will be broken once again."

"Now that's the second time you've said that. What do you mean?"

He sighed, shaking his head. "Years ago, when I went back, I fell in love with a girl there." He put his head in his hands. "Dear God, Gertrude, nothing has ever hurt so much as that."

"Falling in love?"

"Having to leave her."

"Ye could have stayed."

"Believe me, I considered it. I considered leaving my family and my education, everything, just to be with her."

"Why didn't ye?"

"My only skill there was as a musician, which meant traveling as a minstrel. And yet, I had every intention of asking her to go with me."

"What changed?"

"Several things. I would have been taking her away from her life and the things she loved. I also realized how very fragile life was and what a gift I had been given. In the future, I would have the ability to go to medical school and learn how to keep people well and save lives. In the past, I had no such opportunity. Suddenly, the musician's life didn't look so good to me." He cast her a sidelong glance. "Which is what I suspected you intended for me to learn from the start."

Gertrude smiled. "I've said before, ye're a good lad. But ye could have stayed anyway. The choice was always yers."

"I could have, and I had almost decided to, but…"

"But what?"

"She disappeared. I tried to find her, but before I could, someone killed me. I whispered the return word just as I lost consciousness and then woke in my own bed. I'd hoped to see you again, to return the watch. I wanted to find out what happened to her. I wanted to know she was safe."

"And we haven't had a chance to chat."

He nearly rolled his eyes. *We haven't had a chance to chat?* It had been over eleven years, but he wouldn't point that out. "No, we haven't."

"Do ye remember what I told ye when ye arrived in the thirteenth century?"

"You said a lot of things."

She chuckled. "I might have. But ye asked me if there was anything else ye needed to know."

"And you said, *Love is a marathon, not a sprint.*"

"That's right."

"I'm not sure I understand how that applies here."

"Do ye not? Well that's a shame."

"Not terribly comforting when I am on the verge of losing yet another woman I love."

"Well, now, let's think about that. Why do ye think ye're on the verge of losing her?"

"Because she has to trade places again with Elizabeth."

"But ye love Elizabeth."

"I do. At least I thought I did. I'm confused. I think I might love the girl who's here."

"It seems to me ye ought to figure that out. If it's Elizabeth ye love, 'tis Elizabeth who'll return to ye."

He shook his head. "I might have loved Elizabeth, but I'm fairly certain what I feel now is for the girl who's here."

"The answer seems clear. If ye love her and she loves ye, perhaps she should stay."

"You mean that the girl, whoever she is, might want to stay?"

"Have ye asked her?"

"No."

"Did ye tell her ye wanted her to stay?"

"No."

"Then how on earth would she know, lad? It seems to me the sorts of things one would find out when learning who she really was and what led her here."

"What about Elizabeth?"

"Elizabeth has decisions of her own to make."

"But why would she choose to stay in the thirteenth

century?"

"I imagine for the same reason that ye would have."

"She's fallen in love?"

"It's possible. Perhaps ye shouldn't worry about Elizabeth's choices until ye know yer own heart and that of the lass who ye think ye love. Fix today, lad."

"Gertrude, I...Jesus, I have to get back to her. I was upset. I didn't ask her any of those things. I left to try to get my head around what I was feeling."

"Then ye're definitely in the wrong place."

Gabe stood to leave, but Gertrude stopped him. "Will ye accept a bit of advice from someone who has been around a while?"

He smiled. "Love is a marathon, not a sprint?"

She chuckled. "While that is true, I was thinking of something a bit more concrete this time."

"I've clearly fouled this up, so I'll take any advice you have to offer."

"Don't hold back. If ye love this lass, tell her. Tell here ye're sure it is her and not Elizabeth that ye love."

"But what if she doesn't love me? What if she's married or has a family?"

"Ye have to take that risk. But I suspect she believes ye love Elizabeth, not her, and that it would be wrong to steal ye away. She has a decision to make, and even if she is married or has a family, she deserves to know all of the facts before making it."

"Everything? Even about falling in love before?"

"Everything, Gabe. Tell her about your experience with the watch and that you were willing to leave everything else you held dear behind for the lass you loved, but the decision was taken from ye. Tell her how it caused yer heart to ache. Tell her that ye've fallen in love again, but now ye're certain it isn't with Elizabeth but her, and you fear losing her will be worse than the first time. Ask her to stay."

"I will. I'll go tell her now. Thanks, Gertrude." He kissed the old woman's cheek before leaving.

Gabe practically ran the few blocks back to his building. When he entered the apartment, it was dark. He slipped silently into the bedroom. If she was asleep, he wouldn't wake her. He stopped short and flipped on the light when he saw the empty bed.

"Elizabeth?" he called, knowing there would be no answer. He would have seen if she were in the bathroom or kitchen. He opened the closet door. His heart fell. Everything but Elizabeth's laptop bag was missing. Where would she go?

He pulled his phone out of his pocket, not sure who he intended to call, but saw that he had a voicemail message. He dialed and listened.

"Gabe...I'm sorry. I didn't mean to make you so angry. Thank you for everything you've done for me. I don't want to put you out any longer. I'm going to stay with the Sinclairs until...well...it shouldn't be much longer until...uh...until I'm my old self again. Goodbye. I'll never forget all you've done."

"No. I can't lose you." He heard the despair in his voice as it pierced the stillness of the deserted apartment.

The only Sinclair whose number he had was David's. He glanced at his watch; it was nearly eleven. He only hesitated a moment before calling.

"Hello?"

"David, it's Gabe Soldani."

"What's wrong? Has something happened to Elizabeth?"

"No, not exactly."

"What does that mean?"

"It means we had a misunderstanding. I went out for a little while. I needed to think." Gabe felt smaller than a cockroach. "I just got back, and she's not here."

"God damn it. How the hell could you let this happen?

She's alone in New York somewhere? How long has she been gone?"

"She isn't alone in New York. The message she left was that she was going to stay with your parents."

"How did she get there? Or did she even get there?"

"I don't know, David, that's why I'm calling you. I don't know how to contact your parents."

"I'll call you back." David hung up on him.

It was less than fifteen minutes before David called, but it felt like an eternity.

"She's safe. My dad sent Dixon and a driver for her. Soldani, I don't know what you did, but you've fucked this up royally."

"I don't need you to tell me that. I think I can fix it, but I need to talk to her."

"Well, that's not happening. Not tonight anyway, and frankly, tomorrow isn't looking good either. My dad couldn't be angrier if Elizabeth were one of my sisters."

"Christ, David, you don't understand. No one understands. Please, I just need a few minutes."

"You heard me. Not tonight. You work days tomorrow?"

"Yes."

"Dad said he'd call you tomorrow evening after he's had a chance to cool down."

"Damn it, David, this won't wait until tomorrow."

"It's going to have to."

"Then can you at least give her a message?"

"I'm not promising anything, but what's the message?"

"I was not angry. I was confused, but I'm not now. I love her, and more than anything, I want her to *stay*."

Gabe hoped she would understand what he meant by that.

Chapter 24

Just as David had said he would, Aldous Sinclair called Gabe on Tuesday night.

"I'm sorry, sir. Please, may I speak with Elizabeth?"

"You are out of your mind, young man, if you think I'll let you do that before we've had a serious discussion. And that cannot happen over the phone. I will meet you at your apartment tomorrow after you are off work. Call this number when you are leaving the hospital."

Gabe agreed. He called Mr. Sinclair and then hailed a cab. He had barely reached his apartment when the buzzer from the main doors sounded.

When the knock came, Gabe checked the peephole. Aldous Sinclair—a very angry Aldous Sinclair—stood at his door with his bodyguard, Dixon, behind him.

He opened the door. "Good evening, sir. Thank you for seeing me. There has been a terrible misunderstanding."

"I don't want to hear anything from you until we are in your apartment."

"Yes, sir."

Gabe stepped back to let them in. Mr. Sinclair nodded to Dixon, who took up a post in the hall. Mr. Sinclair strode past Gabe into the apartment.

"Please, sit down. Can I get you something to drink?"

"This isn't a social call."

"I know. Like I said, there has been a terrible misunderstanding."

"Maybe, but you have *a lot* of explaining to do before I'll be convinced of that."

"I'm sorry—really I am—but there are some things, lots of things that I can't explain to you. I need to speak to Elizabeth."

"Perhaps you don't understand what's happening here. The girl you crushed is my daughter. You will make things right with me before you ever come within a mile of her."

Gabe nodded. "David said you feel very protective of her."

"Dr. Soldani, David has no idea what the real truth is. He doesn't know about the pocket watch. But I do, so you can, in fact, explain everything to me. And you are going to. Now."

Gabe was beyond shocked. "You know about the pocket watch?"

"I just told you I did. Stop stalling."

Gabe sighed and nodded. "Then you understand how it works. I went back years ago. I was twenty. I thought it was a lark, only I fell in love." Gabe looked down. "I fell so desperately in love. I was willing to leave everything I knew. *Everything*, sir. My family, my education, my future."

"Then why didn't you stay?"

"I was killed. I whispered my return word as the young man's body I had entered lay there dying. She was lost to me forever."

"I'm sorry about that." Mr. Sinclair's expression softened ever so slightly.

"Ironically, going to the past helped me see my destiny. I returned with a broken heart, but completely committed to becoming a doctor. I always believed that was what Gertrude had intended, but it came at a steep price."

Sinclair sighed. "It often does, son."

"I didn't risk my heart again for years. Initially, it was self-protection, but eventually I realized it was more than that. It wasn't that I didn't want to love again, I simply never met anyone else with whom I had that kind of spark. Elizabeth was the first woman I ever dated seriously and that was almost five years later. It wasn't exactly the same with her, but I guess I saw things in her that reminded me of my lost love."

"And yet, you let her go."

"Yes, sir, I did. I found out on the day we graduated that I didn't really know her. Although I'd asked her about her family numerous times, she always evaded the question. I found out that she was the daughter of Charlotte Matheson and James Quinn when the medical school faculty and the entire graduating class did. I didn't understand why she had hidden this from me. When she told me why later that night, I didn't believe her. I couldn't believe her. How could anyone want to distance themselves from family? Dear God, I know now. Her parents...well, you know."

"Matheson & Matheson have represented me for years. Charlotte and her father are brilliant attorneys. They've always been available for whatever any of my companies needed. But I understand better why now. So you found love and lost it again."

"Yes, sir. Then suddenly, the night of the blizzard, Elizabeth was back in my life, and I was the only person she remembered. I guess I might have wondered about the pocket watch if it hadn't been for that."

"But you knew how it worked. Some memories push through."

"I'd forgotten. I also thought souls only went backwards. So, I believed Elizabeth was mine again, and I suspect I didn't want to see the inconsistencies for what they were."

"Odd. It was obvious to the rest of us."

"It was obvious to the *rest of you*?"

"Gabriel, I was offered the pocket watch years ago."

"You went back in time, too? When you said you knew about it, I just thought you meant Elizabeth told you."

"No, I have first-hand knowledge, but I didn't go back. I came forward—and stayed. Gerald Rose went back and returned."

"Dr. Rose? Wait, Elizabeth said your wife suffered a permanent memory loss. Is she from the past, too?"

Sinclair nodded.

"And I'm the only idiot who didn't see it?"

"To be fair, Gertrude sends travelers to see Gerald from time to time. As you can understand, sometimes a traveler returns who needs a little help dealing with the difficult choices they may have been forced to make. After he sees them, he often sends them to me, so we have encountered many more time travelers over the years than you. Maybe the signs are more obvious to us."

"Why does he send them to you?"

"I was a very young man when I came, and I landed in the body of a foolish boy who had every possible advantage at his fingertips, but valued none of it. The opportunity for education was more of a temptation than I could resist. I stayed. But I left a wife and child in the past."

Gabe couldn't hide his shock.

"I know. It was the selfish choice a young man with no future."

"Sir, it's not my place..."

"To judge? You couldn't possibly be harder on me than I've been on myself over the years."

"And your wife? Did she leave a family behind?"

"She left a child. Our child. She was my wife in the past. She would never have stayed, but Gertrude gave her the watch on her deathbed. Jo would have died within hours of returning, leaving our child an orphan anyway. Even so, our greatest regret was not knowing what became of the child we loved. That's why Gerald has sent travelers to me. I had always hoped to meet someone who'd been to my time, to my clan. I hoped to learn what happened to our daughter, but I never did. At least not until Elizabeth."

"She knew what happened to your daughter?"

"Gabriel, I've already told you. She *is* my daughter."

"You mean...I thought you meant she was *like* a daughter. You can't be serious."

"I am. So it should be absolutely obvious that the very last thing in the world that I want is for her to return to her own time. I thought she was falling in love with you. Perhaps it was selfish of me, but I had hoped she would love you enough to want to stay." Sinclair's voice hardened. "But you've made a complete mess of this. She won't stay because she thinks you love Elizabeth."

"But I don't. I mean I do...or I did, but that isn't why I was upset. I realized it was her I'd fallen in love with. I've finally found the kind of love I had only experienced once before, and the thought of losing her..." Gabe swallowed hard, trying to hold back tears. "I can't lose her, sir. I can't. I want her to stay more than I want my next breath. And if she truly can't stay, if Elizabeth must return, I will beg Gertrude to let me go with the girl who holds my heart."

Aldous Sinclair stared at him as if considering him for a few moments. "I want her to stay, and if you can convince her to, I will be eternally grateful. But I know Elizabeth's choice may be what drives everything. I don't want my little one to go back alone. I was prepared to ask Gertrude the same thing."

"I saw Gertrude the night I figured it out. She said to fix today and that Elizabeth has her own decisions to make."

"Then maybe there's a chance she'll choose to stay in the past?"

"It is my fervent prayer. Please, sir, may I see your daughter now?"

"I'll allow you to speak with her and explain all of this, but not tonight. This is not a conversation to have when you are exhausted and have to return to work in mere hours."

"Mr. Sinclair, it's Wednesday. I have two more days to work. This can't wait. There isn't much time."

"I know that. Twenty three days at the most. So I am

going to interfere. I have money and pull. Go to work tomorrow, and I will see that you are sent home and given Friday off too."

"I can't ask you—"

"First, you didn't ask me. And second, I suspect you want the new pediatric wing as much as everyone else at NYUHC does. I am about to fully fund that endeavor in exchange for a few days of your time. Would you refuse that offer if you were the chief of pediatrics?"

"No, sir."

"Then I'm fairly certain you will be sent home before your next shift is over. Then I want you at my house with flowers and ring in hand. Do you understand me?"

"Yes, sir. Flowers and ring. I'll be there."

~ * ~

Just as Aldous Sinclair promised, early the next afternoon, Gabe was paged to Dr. Sweeny's office.

"I'm not sure what you did, Gabe, but the obscenely wealthy Aldous Sinclair has just donated *millions* of dollars to NYUHC—every last remaining penny we needed to build the pediatric center. And his only stipulation was for *you* to be given the rest of today and tomorrow off."

"Will that be a problem?"

"A problem? Is that a trick question? Sign your patients out to me. I'll finish this shift for you and get coverage tomorrow or do it myself."

Gabe gave Sweeny a quick rundown of his patients.

"Okay, just let the unit staff know and then get the hell out of here. *Millions*, Gabe, in one fat check. Thank you for whatever it was you did to put this bug up his ass."

Gabe smiled wryly and shrugged. *I broke his daughter's heart* didn't seem like an explanation Dr. Sweeny would appreciate.

On his way home from the hospital, he stopped to buy the requisite flowers. It would have been simple to be traditional and pick up a dozen red roses, but he remembered the morning they had strolled through the flower markets. She had taken such pleasure in seeing the extraordinary variety of blooms, but she had fallen in love with the delicate blue irises. The old woman told her they represented faith and hope.

No, roses wouldn't do. He wanted it to mean more. Elizabeth knew flowers had meanings. The old woman agreed. *Flowers speak a language of their own.* As he looked at the vast array of blossoms, he wanted his choices to mean something, but he didn't speak the language.

A woman about his mother's age wearing a florist's apron approached him. "You look confused."

"I am confused. I want a bouquet of flowers for the woman I love. I'm going to ask her to marry me." Saying the words aloud brought a broad smile to his face.

"I see. Most fellas just go for the red roses."

"I know, but I want something unique. I want the flowers to mean more."

"Let's see what we can find. You will want at least a few red roses—they are the symbol of passionate love."

He grinned. "Yes, I suppose I do."

"Do you know what she likes?"

"She loves irises, and I know they represent faith and hope."

"That is an excellent choice. What else?"

"My heritage is Italian. Is there a national flower or something for Italy?"

She chuckled. "Some say red roses because of the passionate nature of Italians, but lilies are generally considered symbols of Italy. White lilies are pretty and they represent purity. Of course, they also represent a secret, but I trust she knows you love her."

A secret? Well some of those were about to be revealed, so it seemed perfect. "Okay, white lilies it is."

"You said you are Italian. What is her heritage?"

He looked at her blankly for a moment. He had never asked Mr. Sinclair from where or when they came, but he remembered something Aldous had said. *I had always hoped to meet someone who had been to my time, to my clan.* "She's Scottish."

"Well, some thistle would be perfect. We will finish it off with orange blossoms. You must have those, of course."

"What do they represent?"

She tsked. "Young people today know nothing. Orange blossoms are the symbol of eternal love, marriage and," she wiggled her eyebrows, "fruitfulness."

He laughed. "Yes, I must have some of those."

Gabe purchased the flowers and practically ran home. He changed his clothes and then retrieved his grandmother's ring from his sock drawer. With the ring in his pocket and the carefully wrapped bouquet in his arms, he took a cab to the Sinclairs' posh SoHo address.

He gave his name to the security guard on duty at the building.

"Good afternoon, Dr. Soldani. Mr. Sinclair is expecting you. Go through to the private elevator and the security guard there will let the Sinclairs know you're here."

Aldous was waiting as Gabe got off the elevator.

"I see you took me seriously about the flowers. Well done. Thistle? That's a nice touch. Do you have a ring?"

"Yes, sir. I had it before we talked." He pulled the box from his pocket. "It was my grandmother's."

Aldous nodded approvingly. "There is nothing more valuable than love that's passed down through generations. My daughter is in the library with her mother. Follow me." Eventually, he stopped outside a room with double wooden doors. Aldous gave him a stern look. "You probably only have one chance at this. Don't foul it up."

"Yes, sir."

Gabe followed him into the enormous room. Elizabeth

and Jo Sinclair were sitting at a table. Elizabeth's back was to the door. "Jo, my darling, someone is here to see our girl."

Jo looked up. "Gabe, how lovely to see you."

Elizabeth's back went rigid, and she didn't turn to look at him.

"Yes, it's very nice to see you again, Mrs. Sinclair. How are you?"

"Very well, thank you. I trust you've been keeping well?"

"Yes, ma'am."

"Well, I suspect you aren't here to chat with me. Aldous, shall we give them privacy?"

"Yes, my love."

Jo rose gracefully and left the room with her husband, closing the door behind them.

Elizabeth still hadn't turned around, so Gabe crossed to her. "Do you mind if I sit?"

"No, that's fine." She didn't make eye contact.

"I brought you these." He handed her the bouquet.

She accepted the flowers from him, a slow smile spreading across her face. She traced the petals of one of the irises with a finger. "Faith and hope...they are so beautiful."

"And the red roses represent love. That's why I'm here, Elizabeth. I love you. I mean, the real you, the girl I've spent the last few weeks with. That's why I became so upset. I knew it was you who I loved, and the idea of you going back, of losing you forever, nearly killed me."

"No Gabe, it isn't me. It can't be me. You were intended for Elizabeth."

"I don't believe that. I think I was intended for you."

"But that can't happen. Elizabeth will be coming back."

"For the next few minutes, let's not think about Elizabeth."

"Fine. But why are you so sure you love me and not her?"

"Because I've only experienced the feelings I have for you once before in my life."

"With Elizabeth?"

"No. It was for a girl I met several years before I met Elizabeth. A girl I could not have. But for the first time since then, I feel the same profound love. There is a connection between us that I can't explain, but you can't deny it. I know you feel it."

"Yes, I do. But if you felt this before, why did you let it go?"

"It wasn't my choice. It was when I used the watch. I met a girl in the past who I adored. I had decided to give up everything I held dear to stay with her forever. She meant more to me than my family, my education, my very life."

"But you didn't stay?"

"I couldn't. I was stabbed in the belly. I knew I was dying, so I said the return word. Leaving her was the hardest, most painful thing I have ever done, but I fear losing you will be even worse. More than I have ever wanted anything, I want you to stay and be my wife. If you don't want to stay or you can't stay, I will beg Gertrude to let me go back with you."

She caressed his cheek. "Oh, Gabe, I love you too." His heart leapt for a moment before she uttered the words he had most feared. "But there is someone in my own time who I think I was beginning to love. And Elizabeth...what she did was so wonderful. If she wants to return, I have to agree."

"Tell me what it is Elizabeth has done."

"According to Gertrude, a neighboring clan needed a skilled midwife. The laird's wife had miscarried four babies and was pregnant again. Her husband hoped a different midwife might know what to do. My Aunt Dolina was the midwife they were seeking, but Laird Macrae had no intention of sending her. Figuring that no one could help, he intended to send me instead, but I was just an apprentice. He thought to gain MacKenzie as an ally simply by appearing to *try* to help."

Gabe could barely believe what he was hearing.

"I would not have agreed to that deception and, according to Gertrude, I would have been whipped and ultimately died from my injuries. Perhaps because of the accident, the soul exchange happened earlier than it should have. Elizabeth went back when she lost consciousness and arrived before I ever had the chance to refuse my laird's command."

"And she wouldn't refuse because she has more skills even than your aunt."

"That's what Gertrude said. So you see, she helped the poor woman and saved my life. I can't refuse to let her return."

"My darling girl, I have a story to tell you that I think you will find very interesting."

"About your experience with the pocket watch?"

He smiled confidently. "Yes. And when I'm done, I think you'll agree we belong together. It happened a little over eleven years ago…"

Chapter 25

Gabe was finally on his way home for Christmas. He had finished with classes the previous week, but had stayed over the weekend to get a few more shifts at work. People tended to be a little more generous with tips around the holidays, and he needed every cent he could earn. His car was packed before he started his shift, and he left as soon as the restaurant closed. The old Ford Escort he drove didn't have a CD player, but he'd driven the route enough in the last two and a half years to know where the good radio stations were along the way. With that knowledge and a large to-go cup of coffee, he was armed for the three-hour drive to his family's home in New Jersey.

Route 13 was fairly deserted this late on a Tuesday night. He hadn't been on the road long when he saw a car pulled over on the shoulder. An elderly woman stood beside a very old sedan and waved to him. This was a rural stretch of road with little late-night traffic and no services within walking distance. It could be ages before someone else helped her. He slowed down and pulled off the road behind her.

He got out, but left the engine running and the lights on. Zipping his jacket, he walked to her. "Is everything okay? Do you need help?"

"Oh, thank ye for stopping, lad. Aye, I do need help. I have a puncture." She had some sort of accent—maybe English, but he wasn't sure.

"A puncture?" He looked at the car and saw the problem. "Oh, a flat tire."

"Aye, a very flat tire."

"I can change it for you. Is your spare in the trunk?"

"I suppose it is. Let's look, shall we?" She opened the trunk and stepped aside. "Ah, there it is. Thank ye so very much. I don't know what I'd have done if ye hadn't stopped."

"It's no problem at all." He removed the jack and put it together.

"What's yer name, lad?"

"Gabriel Soldani, but you can call me Gabe."

"Lovely to meet ye, Gabe. My name's Gertrude."

Gabe lifted the spare out of the trunk, but as soon as the light from his headlights hit it, he knew they had a problem. "Uh, Gertrude, how old is this tire?"

"It came with the car."

"And how old's the car?"

"I don't pay much attention to those things, but it's got to be twenty years old, maybe more. Why?"

"The spare doesn't have enough air in it, and I think it's dry-rotted."

"Oh dear."

"It's usually a good idea to have the spare checked every time you have it serviced."

"Serviced?"

"Yeah. You know, changing the oil, checking the fluids, rotating and balancing the tires."

"Oh, those things. I've been meaning to have those things done. I guess I shall have to now," she said cheerily.

"Yeah, that's probably a good idea." The car must be new to her. It wouldn't still be on the road otherwise. "Listen, there's no point in putting on a dry-rotted tire. How about I put everything back, you get your things, and lock the car. I'll drive you to where you can get a tow truck. There'll surely be something open in Dover."

"That's a fine idea, lad."

By the time he'd put the tire and jack back and closed

the trunk, she stood waiting with her handbag. He walked to the passenger side of his car and opened the door for her. As he walked around to the driver's side, he remembered the urban legends of ax murderers disguised as little old ladies. He smiled to himself. He wasn't sure of many things, but he was confident Gertrude was not an ax murderer.

"I certainly do appreciate this," she said as he pulled into the road. "Several cars passed me and didn't even slow down. You'd think I was an ax murderer or something."

What the hell? God, please don't let her be an ax murderer.

"So, Gabe, where are ye heading so late at night?"

"I'm on my way home from college for Christmas."

"College, ye say. What college?"

"Salisbury University in Maryland."

"And what are ye studying there?"

"I'm majoring in biology. I'm in my third year."

"That's fascinating. And what do biology majors do when they graduate?"

"I had planned to go to medical school."

"Had planned?"

"I guess I still plan to. It's just...well, I really like music. I play the guitar and piano, and I've fooled around a bit with a mandolin."

"A mandolin? That's not very common these days."

"My family is Italian. There is an old one at the house that belonged to one of my grandfathers."

"I see. So ye like music. Ye can still be a doctor and like music," she teased.

"I suppose I can. But right after I went to college, some friends and I formed a band. We are getting really good, and sometimes we get paid gigs. They're talking about going to California after we graduate and trying to, you know, break into the music industry. I think it would be great."

"Ah, there's a 'but' hovering at the end of that sentence."

Gabe nodded. "But my family—my parents—won't understand. My dad's an electrician and my mom's a housewife. Neither one of them went to college. They are set on me becoming a doctor."

"You don't want to be a doctor?"

"That's just it, I do. But I want to be a musician, too. I'd like to just try it. I want to see what that kind of life would be like. If it didn't work out, I could go to medical school then."

"But yer parents won't understand."

"No. When I mentioned it at Thanksgiving, I thought my mother was going to have a heart attack. You would have thought I'd suggested dealing drugs or something."

Gertrude chuckled. "Surely, it wasn't that bad."

"Oh, trust me, it was that bad. She was calling on every saint in the book. Dad's reaction might have been worse."

"What did yer dad do?"

"Nothing. He said nothing. He did nothing. He just looked so disappointed. It was terrible. So I assured them it was just a crazy idea and that *of course* I intended to go to medical school."

"Ah, that is quite a dilemma."

"I just want to try it. I feel like I'll always regret it if I don't."

"Hmm. What if I had a way that ye could try the musician's life and it wouldn't interfere with any of yer plans?"

"I'd say sign me up."

"I'm serious, lad."

"So am I. What do you have in mind?"

"I can give ye sixty days as a musician."

"I don't have sixty days. I don't have to go back to school until February, but I'm supposed to take an MCAT prep course in January."

"Ye needn't worry about those things. I'll explain, but ye must promise to set aside yer disbelief and listen to the whole story before ye say anything."

"Okay, sure." He wasn't sure where this was going, but it was entertaining.

"I have the ability to let ye time travel."

He cast a sideways glance at her. "Are you serious?"

"Remember, suspend disbelief and listen before ye comment."

"Okay. Sorry."

She opened her purse and pulled out what looked like a pocket watch on a chain. "This pocket watch is a conduit through time. It allows yer soul to trade places with someone else's. Ye put it around yer neck or in yer pocket before ye go to sleep. When ye wake up, ye will be in someone else's body in another time. Ye'll have all of yer memories. Ye'll be able to speak whatever language that person speaks—it will sound just like English to ye. A few other memories belonging to that person may leak through as well."

Gabe could barely believe what he was hearing. The woman was nuts. She really believed what she was saying.

"Ye have sixty days." She opened the watch. Glancing at it, he noticed it only had one hand that seemed to be stopped at twelve. "Each day that ye're in the past, the hand will advance one second. Before ye go to sleep, ye must pick a word—one ye wouldn't use accidentally—and ye tell the watch. It is yer return word. Anytime ye say it within those sixty days, ye'll be brought back to yer own body immediately. Ye don't even need to have the watch on ye."

"But I don't have sixty days." *Gabe, why are you engaging a crazy woman?*

"I am not crazy, and ye don't need sixty days. I told ye that. Only sixty seconds will pass here."

"How? Whose body will I be in and where will they be?"

"Ye will pop into the body of a professional musician. He will have done something that will ultimately result in his death, and you will do something the instant ye arrive to stop that."

"I'll save his life?"

"Not exactly. His life was over. You extend it only by the amount of time ye stay there. When ye leave, he will die. His soul will go on, and ye will return to yer own body mere seconds after ye left it."

Gabe's mind whirled. She didn't seem crazy. What she said was impossible to believe. *But, wow, if it did work, how cool would that be?* "All I have to do is put the watch around my neck, tell it a word, and go to sleep. I'll be in someone else's body for sixty days. Does it automatically bring me back then?"

"Nay, ye must choose to say the word. If ye don't, ye'll stay there forever."

"If I stay there, what happens to my body here?"

"It will die, and the other person's soul goes on as it should."

What harm was there in trying? *The worst thing is that I wake up in the morning with the watch around my neck feeling silly.*

"Gabe, ye said that ye feared ye'd always regret it if ye didn't give the musician's life a try. I'm giving ye the opportunity to live the life of a professional musician for sixty days. The pocket watch will take sixty seconds or less of yer time. Don't ye think ye'd regret not at least trying it?"

It was so tempting. If he could just try it, just taste life as a musician, he'd know what to do with his life. There was no risk with this. "Okay. I'll try it."

"Good. I hope ye have a wonderful time and learn a bit about yerself in the process." She handed him the watch.

Ceci Giltenan

He put it in his pocket. "Thank you, Gertrude."

"Ye're welcome."

"How will I get it back to you?"

"Oh, the watch always manages to be where it needs to be. It'll find me. Ah, now look there, ahead at the next exit. There is a service station. I expect I can get a tow truck there."

Sure enough, there was a sign in the station window: Carl's 24-hour Towing. Gabe pulled in. He started to get out of the car, intending to help her out and make certain she could get a tow, but she stopped him.

"There's no need to get out, lad. I'm sure Carl will be able to help me. Ye've got a couple hours left to drive, and I don't want to keep ye any longer. Drive carefully. Watch out for drunks."

She was already out of the car, so he leaned across and rolled down the window. "Bye, Gertrude. Thanks again."

It was after two in the morning when Gabe parked in front of his home. The outside Christmas lights were still on. Mom must have left them on for him. He grabbed his backpack and locked the car. He would unload tomorrow.

He slipped in the house as quietly as he could. Their dog, Chase, met him at the door. That was odd because Chase usually slept with Angela. It only took him a moment to realize why. Angela was curled up on the sitting room couch, asleep.

"She snuck downstairs, did she, boy?"

Chase whined.

"Don't worry. I've got this." He put his backpack down and lifted his sleeping baby sister off the couch.

She roused a little. "I was waiting up for you."

He chuckled. "I see. But Chase wants to go to bed now."

"Okay." She yawned and closed her eyes again.

He carried her upstairs and tucked her in. Chase jumped onto the bed, curling up beside her.

"Sleep tight, princess."

He made his way back downstairs to the bedroom on the main floor that he shared with Joey and Nick when he was home. He kicked off his shoes and shrugged out of his jacket, dropping it on the floor by the bed. It hit with a dull thud.

The pocket watch. He fished it out and laid it on the bed while he finished undressing. Climbing under the covers in his tee-shirt and boxers, he held the pocket watch in his hand for a moment. Well, here goes nothing. "*Angela Rose*," he whispered to the watch before slipping the chain around his neck and going to sleep.

~ * ~

It felt as if Gabe had just barely closed his eyes when he awakened to find himself on the back of a pony on a dirt road in a forest.

Holy shit. A frickin' pony?

He was supposed to be in a musician's body. He looked down. What in the hell was he wearing? Was this some kind of joke? Was he some sort of Renaissance Faire performer? That couldn't be right because it was bitter cold and spitting snow. They weren't usually held in winter.

He looked up again, and the world spun. For some reason, he found it very funny and started giggling.

Giggling?

"Christ, what's the matter with me?" His speech sounded so strange.

"Ye're drunk," said a familiar voice.

"Gertrude?"

She stepped out of the forest. The well-dressed, refined woman he had helped on the side of the road in Delaware wore a voluminous cloak over clothing as old-fashioned as his own. "Aye, lad. So ye tried the pocket watch. Well done."

"I don't understand." His head swam, and he broke out

in a cold sweat. "Damn. I think I'm going to puke." He started to get off the pony.

"Don't climb down, lad. He's not that big, but ye might not be able to get back up and ye'll freeze to death. Just hang on to the beast's neck and try to miss yer clothes."

Gabe barely had time to throw his arms around his noble steed's neck before he vomited spectacularly. After he heaved several times, he groaned. "Oh, God. This is awful."

"Ye've never been drunk before?"

"Nay." The mere thought of it combined with the sour taste of alcohol caused him to spew more of the contents of his stomach. He inhaled several deep breaths of the fresh air, trying to regain control. "And I sure as hell never will be again."

"There now, that's already one good lesson ye've learned. Just more proof that the universe unfolds as it should." She stepped onto the path a few paces in front of the pony and clicked to it. "Come on to Gertrude now, there's a good lad. I'd rather keep my shoes clean."

The pony took several steps away from the mess on the ground.

The old woman pulled what looked like a pottery flask in a leather case from her cloak. "Here is a costrel of water. Rinse yer mouth with it. Ye'll feel better."

He followed her instructions and handed the *costrel* back to her.

"Nay, lad, keep it. Ye can give me that wine skin hanging over yer shoulder though. Ye'll not want to drink any more of that sour wine anyway."

He handed it to her. "It's yers. I'll never drink again."

Gertrude chuckled. "All things in moderation. You will want to try the ale here. What's served most of the time is very low in alcohol and may be better for ye than water, all things considered. Even the little children drink it. Just be careful not to over-imbibe the stronger stuff."

"Exactly where is *here*? Ye said I'd get to try a professional musician's life."

"And that is exactly what ye are. Ye're a professional, traveling minstrel in the Scottish Highlands. It is Tuesday, the twentieth day of December."

"The day I left?

"Aye, except over seven centuries earlier. 'Tis the year of our Lord, twelve-hundred and seventy-eight, a Tuesday."

"The thirteenth century? Are ye jesting?"

She chuckled again. "I am most certainly not *jesting*."

"This isn't what I thought…I mean ye never said…"

"I said ye'd go back in time."

"I know ye did, but I thought maybe to the sixties."

"Did I imply that?"

Gabe thought hard. With the wine-befuddled body he was in, it took great effort. "Nay, I suppose ye didn't."

"Did ye ask?"

"Nay, ye know I didn't."

"Then whose fault is it?"

"I know it's my own, but I never imagined ye'd send me to the dark ages. And why does my voice sound so odd?"

"Ye're voice sounds odd to ye because it isn't yer voice. 'Tis the voice of the minstrel yer soul currently resides in. And don't be so quick to judge. There is much to be learned and enjoyed here in the *dark ages*."

"Ye could have fooled me."

She laughed outright. "Poor lad. All of the misery of the morning after without the frivolity of the night before."

Gabe groaned. "I think I'll just go home."

"That's up to ye, but it's as I said to ye before: ye'll regret it if you don't give it a try."

"Ye also said I'd do something to stop this man from dying. What do I have to do?"

"Ye've already done it. Ye gave me the wineskin. The

miserable sot into whose body you landed would have just kept drinking it until it killed him."

"How?"

She shrugged. "One of several things. He would've fallen from his mount. That alone could have done him in if he'd landed on his fool head. It's also blue cold out this evening. While it's commonly believed alcohol warms ye, it really doesn't. It causes the blood vessels in yer skin to open, making ye feel warm. If ye're out in the cold, that actually allows ye to lose body heat rapidly. He could have frozen to death. Then again, as ye're painfully aware, he was drunk enough to be sick. He could have aspirated—"

"Ew, don't say it. I get the picture."

"And ye're going to be a doctor?"

"I'll never be a sick, drunk doctor. I'll swear that to ye. Don't make things worse now."

She smiled broadly at him. It was peculiar, but she looked almost proud. "I won't. Ye're a good lad, Gabriel Soldani. These sixty days are a gift that ye'll treasure if ye give it the chance."

He nodded. "But what do I do now?"

"If ye stick to this road, it will bring ye to a village surrounding a castle. Go to the castle and tell them ye're a minstrel. The Christmas season is upon us, and extra minstrels are nearly always welcome for major feasts. Ye'll find that lute slung over yer back is much like a mandolin. Ye'll have no trouble playing it. Both of ye are very talented. If ye allow it, his melodies will guide yer fingers."

"All right. I'll try it."

"Ye remember yer return word?"

"Aye."

"I believe ye'll find the watch 'round yer neck under yer clothes. Don't let anyone see it. Watches haven't been invented yet."

"How do I explain not having any memory?"

"You won't need to. He's alone in the world. His

entire family died by the time he was ten and five. No one here knows him. He is essentially a man without a past. Absolutely perfect for a time traveler." She pulled a silver coin from her pocket. "On the way into town, stop at the inn to stable yer pony. Give this coin to the innkeeper for the pony's care."

"Maybe I should just give the innkeeper the pony. After all, I won't be needing it again."

"That's not necessarily true. Ye just never know. Besides, it would raise suspicion. No minstrel would give away a mount if he had one."

"All right. Is there anything else I need to know?"

Gertrude nodded sagely. "Ye must remember: love is a marathon, not a sprint."

He laughed. "Wise words, I'm sure, but is there anything I need to know to get by here?"

"I can't think of anything else."

"Off to the castle I go. Will I see ye again?"

"Only time will tell, lad."

"Then I'll say farewell, Gertrude." Gabe started to ride away slowly.

Gertrude called to him. "Now that I think on it, there is one more thing ye should know."

"What's that?"

"Yer name, lad. Ye're called Geordie."

Chapter 26

Gabe had done exactly what Gertrude told him to do. He rode toward the castle and into the village, left his mount with the innkeeper, and presented himself at the castle as a minstrel. He was given entry. The evening meal was being cleared, but he didn't think he could stomach much anyway.

A pretty, young serving girl smiled, offering him what appeared to be round, flat bread. "Ye're a bit late for the meal, but here's a bannock. I could maybe find ye some cheese or cold meat if ye want it."

He smiled back at her. "Nay, thank ye. This will be fine." He ate a few bites of it. It was a bit like a dense biscuit. It sat well enough on his unsettled stomach.

"The minstrels usually sleep over there." She motioned to a corner of the hall, where there did indeed appear to be a number of people with a variety of instruments.

He ambled toward them, eating the rest of the bannock, not exactly sure what to do.

A man with dark hair and a wooden recorder watched Gabe approach. "Look, Paul, a newcomer with a lute. Just the thing we need."

Another man sitting nearby with a large drum next to him nodded. "Aye, there's a lot of wind amongst the musicians here, a few drums and the odd harper, but he's the first lute to arrive."

"I'm…Geordie."

"Come join us, young Geordie."

"Thank ye." Gabe sat with them.

"I'm Robin. This is Paul and the lovely lass beside him is his wife, Jean. We travel together."

"It's nice to meet ye."

"Care to show us what ye can do with that lute?" asked Paul.

"Uh...sure." Gabe took the lute from his back. It looked very much like a mandolin, with strings in pairs. His mandolin had twelve strings arranged in six pairs. He had seen lutes with many more sets of strings, but this one had eleven strings: five pairs plus a single string for the highest pitches. He plucked the strings to check the tuning. The lute seemed to be tuned in fifths, as was his modern mandolin. Instinctively, he adjusted the pegs. He played a few bars of an Italian folk song. He could do this. Gertrude's words came to him. *If ye allow it, his melodies will guide yer fingers.* He relaxed and let the medieval minstrel take over.

As he started to play, Paul picked up his drum and added a driving rhythm. A broad smile spread across Robin's face as he joined in with his recorder to play a counter melody. Jean added her sweet, lilting voice to the mix, joined by Paul on the refrain.

Gabe could only describe it as magical. He had never heard the tune before, but just as Gertrude promised, it flowed from within him. When they had finished the song, there was silence in the hall for a moment before it erupted into applause and hoots of appreciation.

Robin glanced at Paul, raising an eyebrow as if communicating an unspoken question. Paul nodded. "Geordie, that was truly excellent. Would ye like to perform with us?"

"Aye, I'd like that. As long as I'm here, that is. I may not be staying long."

Paul laughed. "None of us will be staying long. We're minstrels, lad, or had ye failed to notice? Robin is askin' if ye want to join up with us. Stay together, ye ken? Travel with us?"

Travel with them? This could be fun. As long as he remained in the thirteenth century, he should experience what he could. *What can go wrong? I can leave at any moment.*

~ * ~

Over the next few days Gabe jammed with his medieval friends. It wasn't long before his own musical abilities blended with Geordie's. Gabe knew he added a slightly twentieth-century edge to their combined sound, making them unique. That and the fact that they had a woman singing with them garnered no small amount of attention.

When he thought about it, Gabe had to laugh. He was a member of the most popular band around. It hadn't been what he'd expected when he put the watch chain around his neck, but he was having a blast. On Christmas Eve, he sat near one of the hearths plucking at his lute and watching as the hall was prepared for the Christmas feast.

He noticed a little girl standing shyly off to one side and watching him play. He smiled at her. She reminded him of Angela. "Good evening, lass. What's yer name?"

"Kyna."

"How old are ye, Kyna?"

"Almost six."

He smiled. Angela's birthday was Christmas Eve and she had been *almost six* since about August. "When will you be six?"

She smiled. "I was born on the Epiphany."

"The twelfth day of Christmas. My sister was born on Christmas Eve." It was out of his mouth before he realized it.

"Ye have a sister? How old is she? Where does she live?"

"My sister...well, my whole family..." What could he say? Geordie's family had all passed away. But his family hadn't even been born yet. "My family is in heaven with the angels."

"All of them? I'm sorry."

"It's all right, Kyna. I have friends here, and someday I'll see my family again."

"I like the music ye play."

"Thank ye."

"Did your sister like yer music?"

"Aye, she did."

"Would ye play me a song that she liked?"

Gabe thought for a moment before plucking the melody to a lullaby he had sung Angela many times about asking guardian angels to keep her all through the night.

When he finished and looked up, the little girl smiled. "I like that song. Do you know any other angel songs?"

Gabe smiled. Billy Joel had an angel lullaby on the album he had released last year. Gabe loved the song and had wanted his band to do a cover of it, but had been voted down. He learned it anyway, to the delight of his baby sister. He played it for the little medieval girl, who closed her eyes as she listened and only opened them as the last notes faded away.

"I like that song too. Will ye play another one? I like angels." She sat down in front of him, looking expectant.

Gabe laughed, reminded again of Angela. "I know a few more." He switched to Christmas carols—there were angels aplenty to be found there. As he played and sang, a vague sense of homesickness grew within him. He had never been anywhere but home with his family on Christmas Eve. *Stop being an idiot, Gabe. You'll be home for Christmas.*

After he had sung a few more, he heard someone calling her name. "Is that ye they're calling or some other wee lass named Kyna?"

She sighed. "That's my nursemaid. I have to go." She hopped up. "Thank ye for singing to me. I liked it." She ran toward the woman who called her.

"That was brilliant." Robin walked toward him and sat

248

down.

"What was brilliant about it?"

"Do ye know who ye were serenading?"

"She told me her name was Kyna. Is there more to know?"

"She's Kyna Macrae, *Laird* Macrae's oldest child."

Gabe frowned. "Did I do something wrong?"

"Nay, far from it. She seemed enthralled. That could serve us very well."

"I don't understand."

"Geordie, ye're a great musician, but it's a wonder ye don't starve to death. After the Epiphany, when the feasts are over, Laird Macrae will not allow all of the minstrels here to stay. He won't want to feed that many extra mouths. But most noble houses have a few minstrels in residence all of the time. Our goal, the goal of every minstrel here, is to be asked to stay through the winter months."

"I didn't know that." Gabe would only stay until the middle of February anyway.

"Like I said, it's a wonder ye haven't starved. But now ye know, I expect ye can see why having admirers in the laird's family could give us an advantage."

"I suppose so."

Gabe became instantly aware that this wasn't simply a lark for Robin. As carefree and easy as the minstrel's life seemed, those who were here—all of them—were just trying to keep body and soul together for one more day. Being popular in the thirteenth century didn't mean screaming groupies, it meant having a roof to sleep under and food to eat.

Although being asked to stay at Castle Macrae for the rest of the winter didn't matter much to Gabe, he wanted to do everything he could to see that Jean, Paul, and Robin got to stay.

~ * ~

To Gabe's surprise, three separate Christmas Masses were celebrated: The Angels' Mass at midnight, the Shepherds' Mass at dawn, and the Mass of the Divine Word later in the morning. While the great hall had been decorated with greenery, there was no Christmas tree and no gifts exchanged. However, when the feasting started in the early afternoon, it was lavish and went on for hours.

At some point after the meal was over and the dancing was in full swing, Gabe's eyes were drawn to a girl. She whirled and danced as if she were one with the music. She was beautiful, and Gabe felt a connection to her through the music like nothing he had ever experienced before.

When he was finally free, he searched the crowd for her, finally spotted her sitting on the floor with her back against the wall and a tankard of ale in her hand. She looked just as absorbed by the music as she had been while she was dancing.

She looked at him, catching him watching her. He'd better make a move or wind up looking goofy, just staring at her.

He walked toward her. "Do ye mind if I sit here with ye?"

"Nay, it's fine."

He sat next to her. "My name's Geordie."

"I'm Elsie. Ye and yer friends were wonderful."

"Thank ye."

"I love music."

He smiled broadly. "I do too. But what I love most is seeing the pleasure people take from music. When the tune leaves my fingers and reaches the hearts of those listening, it gives me joy. When it stirs their feet and they dance, becoming one with the melody, we are connected in an extraordinary way. It feeds my soul."

She stared at him with a slightly awed expression. "Aye, it's just so for me. I mean, I can't make music, but dancing, letting the music flow through me...there is nothing else like it."

"I have to confess, I've watched ye dancing all night. I've barely been able to take my eyes off ye. Ye're lovely, and when ye dance… I don't think I've ever seen anything more beautiful. I dreaded the last note of every song because it severed that momentary connection between us." He caressed her cheek with his fingertips. "So beautiful. If only…" *I could stay with ye* was on the tip of his tongue. Where had that come from?

She blushed. "If only what?" Her voice was breathy.

He smiled sadly. "'Tis nothing."

Elsie glanced around. "I—I suppose I should be going home. It's late."

"Will ye be here again tomorrow?"

She nodded. "Aye, I will."

He stood and offered her a hand. "I'll look forward to it."

She took his hand, allowing him to help her stand. "So will I. I always do."

"Until tomorrow then." For some unknown reason, he kissed the back of her hand. He had never in his life done anything like that. Maybe that was one of Geordie's memories, but it had evidently been the right thing to do.

She nodded, her blush growing deeper. "Until tomorrow."

She turned to leave. He couldn't let her leave without asking her for a date, but how did one do that here? "Elsie, I was just thinking. We won't be playing until after the feast. Will ye sit with me?"

"Sit with ye?"

"Aye. During the feast."

She smiled. "Aye, I'd like that. I'll look for ye."

Chapter 27

Elsie could scarcely believe what she was hearing. "It was you. You were Geordie?"

"Yes."

"And you would have left your family forever to stay with me?"

"Yes. Even though the only skill I had was as a minstrel, I would have stayed."

She laughed. "I had decided that if you asked, I would go with you."

"Although I'd initially intended to ask just that, I realized it would have been a mistake. You clearly loved learning to be a midwife. Not only was it a skill that would make you valuable to the clan, it gave you a sense of purpose. I understood that, and I didn't want to take it away from you. I still would have stayed, even if it meant being a laborer. The morning you found me in the church, I was praying for guidance. You were so very sad. I wanted to offer you comfort. I wanted to be there for you always."

"The baby was dying. It happens often enough, but it is always heart-rending."

"I remember. You said her lips and fingers were blue and that it got worse when she cried. Even then, I knew she wasn't getting enough oxygen in her blood."

"Could you have helped her now?"

"I expect so. It could have been any number of things, all of which could be treated here. It made me think long and hard about my future. Even that didn't change my mind. I planned to tell you who I was and that I intended to stay if you would marry me. But I knew you'd been up all night and needed rest first. I was heading to see you that afternoon when one of Laird Macrae's guardsmen dragged you past me into the keep."

"I was already gone then. The change happened while Drummond was hauling me through the village."

"Oh, my God, the person I saw was Elizabeth?"

"Yes."

"I tried to help, but the guard told me to mind my own business. I was worried, so I slipped inside to see what was going on. There were men waiting in the hall."

"They must have been the MacKenzies."

"That's what one of the serving maids told me. I waited to see what was happening. After a little while, I heard people on the stairs and hid. The laird emerged from the stairs with you—or Elizabeth, it would seem—and the big guardsman. I couldn't hear what was going on. She didn't seem upset and went with them without a single farewell. Now I know why. At first, I was crushed. But then the laird told your aunt and the whole clan what had happened. He said the MacKenzies came seeking a midwife, but after he had sent them away, you lied to them about your skills in order to get them to take you along."

"I would never have done that," she said vehemently.

"I knew you wouldn't have, and your aunt didn't believe him, either. Except for the guardsmen, I may have been the only one to see you—or her—being dragged to the keep and handed over to them. I didn't understand why Laird Macrae was lying, and I started asking questions, but I got nowhere. I even tried to talk my friends into going with me to the MacKenzie's. I was worried about you. But Robin said haring after them in the dead of winter was foolhardy. He said if you hadn't been returned by Easter, they'd go with me to the MacKenzie holding then. But, as you know, my time was limited—I just had a week left on the pocket watch. I intended to stay if you wanted to marry me, but if you didn't… I had to find out."

"So ye went after her?"

Gabe nodded. "I guess my asking questions hadn't gone unnoticed. I was followed and attacked. The big guardsman who had dragged her to the keep was one of my attackers. He stabbed me in the gut. I whispered the return word just as I lost consciousness and woke seconds later in my own bed. I believed I had lost you forever." Gabe's voice sounded bereft. "I had hoped Gertrude would find me again. I wanted another chance. At the very least, I wanted to know what had happened to you. I wanted to know you were safe."

She smiled and took his hand. "I'm sorry it has taken eleven years for you to find out, but I'm safe. And I do love you. That must be why my feelings for you were so strong. Elizabeth's brain might have recognized Gabriel Soldani, but my heart recognized Geordie."

"I'm certain you're right. The way this feels is intense and different. You are the first woman I ever loved. It was you and not Elizabeth who loved me."

"Elizabeth might have, too. I don't know. But I'm certain my feelings are my own."

"Elsie, this should be proof enough that we are meant to be together. We are soulmates. Like your parents, our souls have been pulled through time twice to ensure we are together." Gabe got down on one knee. "Please, Elsie, marry me."

"I want to marry you and spend the rest of my days here with you as my husband. My parents also desperately want me to stay." Tears sprung to Elsie's eyes. "But what about Elizabeth?"

"My darling, I can only believe that her soul is where it belongs as well."

"How can you be so sure?"

"She hasn't come back yet."

"But she was meant to help Lady MacKenzie."

"Yes, she was. But based on what you've told me, I suspect Lady MacKenzie has a condition known as an incompetent cervix that prevents her from carrying a child to term. Elizabeth would have been able to diagnose her and tell her what she needed to do immediately. After that, there's nothing else that could be done, so she could have returned weeks ago. But she hasn't. Something is holding her there as surely as our love holds you here."

Could it be? Could she actually stay here forever? It was what she wanted more than anything. Somehow, she knew the first step was declaring her intention. "Yes, Gabe, I'll marry you."

He pulled the box from his pocket and slipped the ring on her finger.

"Gabe, this is beautiful. What is it for?"

He grinned. "In this time, when a woman agrees to marry a man, he gives her a ring. It's called an engagement ring. She wears it as a sign of the promise to marry him. This ring is the one my grandfather gave to my grandmother when they were engaged."

"It's beautiful."

He gathered her in his arms and kissed her.

When he broke the kiss, he rested his forehead on hers. "I swear to you, I will always love you and care for you. Time will not part us."

There was a tap at the library door a moment before it opened. Gertrude stepped into the room positively beaming. "I see you've sorted things out nicely."

Fear coursed through Elsie, and she tightened her grip on Gabe. "Gertrude, please, I want to stay."

"And that is just what ye were intended to do, lass. Souls are rearranged for a multitude of reasons. The two of ye were truly destined for each other, but Gabriel was equally destined to be a doctor. "

"And Elizabeth wasn't?" Elsie asked hesitantly.

"Aye, she was—just not here. Her skills were needed

in another time and place—and her heart belonged there, too." Gertrude grinned slyly. "She fell in love ages ago and made the decision to stay. You just needed a little extra time to discover your heart's desire."

"My parents will be excited. I suspect they were worried you'd come to tell me it was time to trade souls again."

"Sweetling, they don't know I'm here. You are well aware that I have a way of coming and going unnoticed. Still, I have no doubt they will be thrilled. Their greatest regret has always been leaving you. And yet, this is where your father belonged. He had a hunger for knowledge that was unmatched, and he could never have been satisfied in yer own time. But more than that, he has a compassionate heart. His businesses are not only sound and profitable, but his employees are treated well and compensated fairly. His wealth supports medical research, global clean water initiatives, famine relief, and charities intended to promote the safety and advancement of women around the world." She winked at Gabe. "I even understand he is the major contributor to a new pediatric wing at NYUHC."

Gabe smiled. "Funny, I heard the same thing."

Gertrude caressed Elsie's cheek with one hand. "I know your life until now has been difficult, made harder still by losing your parents when you were so very young. But I cannot apologize for that. Unlike your parents, I have no regrets. I provide the means for gifts to be used to their fullest advantage in the place where they will have the greatest benefit. Even so, each person makes their own choices. The fact is that Alder Macrae was born with tremendous potential and absolutely no way to achieve it. Aldous Sinclair was born completely blind to the advantages and potential with which he had been gifted. But young Aldous, with full knowledge of the risks he took—he had been injured before when climbing over the fence—made his choice. When presented with opportunity,

Alder Macrae made his as well."

"But Gabe wasn't able to stay with me in the past."

"That wasn't where his gifts were needed, pet. His potential here was yet to be achieved. I gave him the opportunity to learn some valuable lessons from you first."

"What could I teach him?"

Gabe smiled. "You helped me recognize the gift I had already been given—an opportunity for education. You embraced the ability to learn midwifery, a skill that would be infinitely valuable to your clan. You found a sense of purpose in that. I had the opportunity to become a doctor and had been willing to throw it away to live a musician's life. When you told me about the baby who was dying, I was reminded of what I could achieve in the future, versus my complete lack of real skills in the past."

"But you said you were prepared to stay with me anyway."

"I was, but the man who murdered me took that decision from me. I suppose that was for the best. However, I had been wrestling with my career choice before I used the pocket watch. When I came back, the things I had learned from you and the love and respect I had for you made my choice clear." He cocked his head and looked at Gertrude. "Of course, I fully believed that I had found my true love only to lose her forever."

Gertrude smiled indulgently. "Once love is found, it is never truly lost. It may evolve. Loved ones may be separated for a while by time and space. But love exists forever. Thus, loving someone is a marathon—"

"—not a sprint. Yes, a wise woman once told me that."

Gertrude chuckled. "Ye understand it now, do ye?"

"I think I do. But what would have happened if Elizabeth had returned?"

"We'll never know for certain, but she actually did have strong feelings for ye. When Elsie recognized ye, part of it *was* Elizabeth's memories at work. If Elizabeth had elected to return, the two of ye would have rediscovered the affection ye held for each other. Ye and Elizabeth are compatible and would have had a loving marriage. And a MacKenzie guardsman would have been Elsie's solace after losing Geordie. Each of you would have loved your partner, but it would never have been as it is between the two of ye. It's as ye said, Gabe, Elsie is your true soulmate."

Gabe kissed the top of Elsie's head. "I couldn't agree more."

Gertrude smiled indulgently for a moment. "Part of the job is done now, but ye've still got a few things to sort out."

Elsie nodded, but Gabe's brows drew together. "What still has to be sorted out?"

"Elizabeth's parents," said Elsie.

"But they've accepted the diagnosis of fugue."

"That's not the whole of it. Charlotte knows I'm not Elizabeth."

"You told her and not me?"

"It was an accident when I told her. I slipped and referred to Elizabeth as another person. Charlotte was all over that and ready to have me committed. It took a visit from Gertrude to convince her. And I thought I was intended to help you fall in love with Elizabeth. Telling you would have ruined that."

"But there is more to it than that," said Gertrude. "A rift had formed between Elizabeth and her parents long before she took the pocket watch. That rift can be mended."

"But Elsie isn't their daughter Elizabeth, and now she never will be."

Gertrude shook her head. "Of course she is their daughter. You're a doctor. Do I need to explain biology to you?"

Gabe shook his head. "No, but that's not what I meant. The Elizabeth they know is gone."

"Not completely. Gabe, you know what it is like to be in another's body. You have a bit of them with you. You were able to play medieval music on a lute, were you not?"

He nodded.

"So, they have lost part of the old Elizabeth—who they had nearly lost anyway. But it would be wrong to allow that rift to grow. Elsie is right—Elizabeth's parents must be told."

"I agree that we need to tell Charlotte," said Elsie. "She has accepted things as they are because she believes Elizabeth is coming back. This will be a blow to her. But I haven't spoken to Dr. Quinn since that day in the hospital. He hasn't contacted me or even attempted a visit. There is nothing to tell him."

"Tell me, Elsie, did you contact or visit him?"

As soon as Gertrude said it, Elsie felt like a prime idiot. She shook her head. "No, I didn't."

Gertrude patted her on the arm. "Don't be too hard on yourself. Simply becoming accustomed to life here was a monumental task. If Elizabeth were coming back, connecting with her mother in the short-term would have been sufficient. But now that you have elected to stay, you must reach out to him as well."

Gabe stiffened. "You don't mean to tell him about the pocket watch? He will be convinced that we are all crazy."

Gertrude laughed merrily. "Nay, of course not. But ye must help him face the fact that Elizabeth's memories, other than her love for Gabe, have not returned and may never return. Only after he accepts that will he be ready to be a father to *Elizabeth* as she is now."

"I'm not sure he can be convinced," said Gabe. "Fugues nearly always resolve."

"The operative word being *nearly*," said Gertrude. "The fact is fugues don't always resolve, and while both Dr. Rose and Dr. Levi have agreed on a diagnosis of fugue, in the absence of a documentable physical cause, they also both agree Elizabeth's condition is extremely atypical. James is a doctor, so use science. Jo may be an asset there."

Gabe nodded. "That could work."

"There is one last thing. Do you remember the return word? The word I told you not to say when you woke in the hospital?"

"The return word?" asked Elsie. "I'm sorry, I don't think so. It was a terribly odd word. Why do I need to know it now? We've both decided to stay."

"Yes, and while I am certain neither of ye will change yer mind, ye continue to have freewill, so ye could theoretically still change places for the next twenty-two days while the return word remains active."

The color drained from Gabe's face. "Dear God, I hadn't thought of that."

"There isn't much cause for worry. As Elsie said, it's an odd word, and she was never likely to say it accidentally, but we cannot risk it. So, Elsie, the word ye must not say is *nintendocore*."

Elsie nodded. "I didn't ask before, but just out of curiosity, what is it?"

"It's a music genre," said Gertrude.

Gabe shook his head. "I've never heard of it. How on earth did Elizabeth decide on that as the return word?"

"That's another story altogether. The important thing is that Elsie must not say it in the next twenty-two days."

"My lips are sealed."

"And with that, my work here is done. However, I will offer ye one last bit of advice. I've said it before, but it bears repeating: love is a marathon, not a sprint. Ye are soulmates, but that doesn't mean yer life will always be perfect. Ye will hit rough patches as everyone does. Be steadfast. Remember yer love for each other and aim for that finish line many miles down the road, not the fast, easy solution." She smiled broadly at them both and opened her arms. "Now, give me a hug. I must be going."

They hugged her, and Elsie said, "Won't you stay long enough to see my parents? I know they'd love it."

"And they might, but they have no *need* to see me. I am needed elsewhere."

With that, she dissolved into mist.

Elsie looked at Gabe. "I wonder if we'll ever *need* to see her again."

"Part of me hopes not. I think in this case, no news is good news. Speaking of good news, let's go tell your parents."

The Sinclairs were as overjoyed as they were relieved.

Elsie's mother took her hand. "When I found out you had come forward, I was ecstatic. It was a miracle I'd never dared hope for. When I learned you would probably have to leave again, I vowed to make the most of our time together. And yet, I knew it would never be enough. I prayed fervently that Elizabeth would elect to stay in the past."

"But I was the one who would have to say the word."

"Oh my precious child, I know you. You would not have said the word until Elizabeth completed her task, and I doubted you could be convinced to force her to stay in the past if she wanted to come back."

"I fear I'd almost decided to do that just before Gertrude told us it wasn't necessary."

Her mother hugged her. "You are a good woman, and thanks be to God that you didn't have to make that choice."

Her father put his arms around them both, kissing Elsie's head. "Our little lost bird is returned."

Chapter 28

Charlotte Quinn stood staring out her office window. She was not one to given to tears. Ever. Not even as a child. She couldn't remember the last time she cried, but tears slipped silently down her cheeks now.

Her daughter was gone.

Elsie had called a little while ago. "Hi. Would you have a little time later? I need to talk with you."

"I'm a bit busy today. Maybe we can have dinner tomorrow?"

There was a pregnant pause before Elsie said, "I'd love to have dinner with you tomorrow, but this can't wait."

"We could have a late dinner this evening."

"It would be better if we had privacy."

Charlotte's hopes had soared. If Elsie needed to talk privately and the issue couldn't wait, perhaps it meant she and Elizabeth would be switching places soon. "All right. Come to my office. The address is on the card I gave you. I'll make time for you when you get here."

Elsie arrived accompanied by Gabriel Soldani within the hour. Charlotte finished the telephone conference she was on before her assistant showed them in.

But Elsie had not brought news of when Elizabeth would be returning because Elizabeth would never be returning.

Charlotte had wanted to rail at Elsie and Gabe. She wanted this to be their fault. Elizabeth had made the independent decision to stay in the past. Yes, Elsie and Gabe were happy about it, but it seemed Elizabeth hadn't known that when she elected to stay.

Elsie had said something about wanting to stay in Charlotte's life.

Charlotte hadn't really processed it. "Yes, I'm sure we'll see each other again. Now, I'm terribly sorry to rush you out, but as I mentioned on the phone, my schedule is overbooked this afternoon. I'll have my assistant call and set up some time to chat next week."

"But—"

"I said I'm busy. We'll discuss this some other time."

The words had appeared to crush Elsie, but Charlotte was feeling too crushed herself to say any more.

Gabriel Soldani stood and took Elsie's hand. "Come, Elsie. There will be time."

When they were gone, Charlotte called her assistant. "Clear my schedule. I'm not feeling well."

Charlotte wasn't sure how long ago that was. She was still trying to process the fact that her daughter was lost to her forever when her intercom buzzed.

"I'm sorry, Mrs. Quinn. There is a woman here insisting on seeing you. I've told her there's no time in your schedule, but she is adamant that you will see her. She says her name is Gertrude."

Charlotte swiped the tears from her cheeks and took a deep breath, trying to regain control. "Yes, I'll see her. Send her in."

"Good afternoon, Charlotte. I hope I'm not disrupting yer afternoon overmuch. Thank ye for squeezing me in."

"I'm fairly certain you are aware that I cleared my schedule. But if I hadn't, I certainly would have made time to see the woman who lured my daughter away from me." Charlotte found it nearly impossible to keep the bitterness from her tone.

Gertrude tsked as she sat in one of the visitors' chairs without being invited. "I did nothing of the sort. I offered Elizabeth an opportunity. The choice was completely hers—as was the choice to stay in the thirteenth century."

"Are you saying my daughter, my only child, chose to leave us forever?"

"Charlotte, leaving ye was not the choice. It was only a consequence. She discovered her true destiny and chose to follow it."

"That doesn't change the fact that Elizabeth is lost to me forever." Charlotte's heart ached unbearably.

"I see. Ye spent a lot of time with Elizabeth? The two of ye were very close?"

"Yes, we were close. Well, not terribly close, I guess. We both have careers."

"But ye were close when she was younger?"

"She has always been a bright, driven young woman, focused on her future."

"So ye were there at her side, cheering her on?"

"She didn't need that. She was self-motivated."

"Self-motivated? My, that sounds impressive. But I suspect the truth is more that ye and yer husband were absentee parents."

Gertrude's words hit hard. "How dare you suggest that? Elizabeth had the absolute best of everything."

"I didn't suggest ye were *negligent*. I said ye were *absent*. Those are two very different things, and if ye're truly honest with yerself, ye'll agree. Ye and Dr. Quinn were very busy. Nannies, housekeepers, and teachers cared for Elizabeth. She did have the absolute best of everything...except her parents' time."

Charlotte opened her mouth to defend her choices, but she simply couldn't when she looked into Gertrude's eyes. She looked away. "I know it's true."

"The fact is, as I told ye when we first met, Elizabeth had been unhappy and floundering for some time. Ask David Sinclair if ye don't believe me. She was searching for purpose in her life and has not only found it, but she has also found the love she craved."

"Could you talk to her for me? Could you tell her I love her and I want her to come home? She still has time to come home, doesn't she?"

"Mrs. Quinn, ye're not listening. I know ye love yer daughter but until she took the pocket watch, ye barely had a relationship with her. I have just told ye that not only has she found her destiny, but she's blissfully happy. Do ye really want her to return to a life where she felt adrift? Do ye want her to turn away from a love that completes her? Shall I tell ye what will happen if she does?"

Charlotte didn't want to hear this, but she didn't stop Gertrude.

"If she comes home, she will return to her life as a doctor. She might rekindle her affection for Gabe or find someone else, but any relationship in the future will pale in comparison to the love she knows now. For the most part, yer lives will all return to the way they were, and ye'll forget ye almost lost her eventually. Other things will become more important once again. 'Twas already beginning to happen. When Elsie called earlier, ye intended to put her off until tomorrow. And as for Elizabeth, after a glimpse of pure happiness, life here will become a sad, mundane existence. Is that what ye want?"

"No, but I don't want to lose my daughter."

"Choices like this are seldom easy. But for every sad consequence, there are multiple blessings. There's still more to this story. The skills Elizabeth passed on with such joy ensured that the MacKenzie women delivered healthier children for generations. In fact, ye're here today because of her. In the fourteenth century, one of Elizabeth's heirs married the leader of Clan Matheson—from whom ye're descended."

"Are you saying that my daughter is my great, great, however-many-times-great-grandmother?"

"Nay, of course I'm not saying that. Yer daughter's physical body and DNA are still here in Manhattan. A Macrae lass named Elsie was yer great, great, however-many-times-great-grandmother. But yer daughter's heart and mind and soul brought knowledge and skills to the clan from whom yer forbearers came. Had it not been for Elizabeth's legacy, her youngest great-granddaughter would probably never have been born. That sweet lass married Laird Matheson, becoming yer ancestor. But there are other blessings. Blessings here for ye."

"What possible blessing could come from losing my daughter?"

"Elsie is a fine lass with a gentle heart. It was because of Elsie's goodness and sense of honor that she's here and Elizabeth's body didn't die. Her noble choice changed the way things usually work. She, like Elizabeth, has found her soul mate. Elsie and Gabriel Soldani were meant to be together. And don't forget that she resides in your daughter's body. Her children will be yer grandchildren, and if ye allow her to, she'll embrace ye and ensure that they are a part of yer life. What's more, as painful as it may occasionally be, she'll be a living, loving reminder of what should always come first."

Charlotte nodded sadly. "You're right. The night the police arrived to tell us about the accident, I realized how very close we'd come to losing her, but we had already all but lost her." She looked at Gertrude again. "My husband was furious that it took so long to inform us, but the officers said she hadn't listed us as emergency contacts. They only found us as quickly as they did because someone at the hospital recognized her."

"Gabriel."

Charlotte nodded. "It's a terrible thing to realize you have grown so distant from your child. When we arrived, she seemed so fragile and afraid, but she clung to Gabe instead of turning to us. James meant well—he just wanted to ensure she had the very best possible care—but he only made things worse."

A lump rose in her throat, and she swallowed hard against it. "When I learned about Elsie, it somehow made Elizabeth's rejection sting less. After all, it wasn't really her who refused to go home with us. But now Elizabeth has turned from us again, only this time it's forever."

"Charlotte, ye're missing the point. She didn't turn away from ye. She turned toward her true purpose, toward the life she longed for. Would ye want anything less for her?"

"No, of course not."

"Then rejoice in her happiness, and accept the gift that Elsie will be in your life. Love her. Let her love ye in return. Celebrate the grandchildren she'll give ye. Can ye do that?"

Charlotte considered Gertrude's words. The truth in them was undeniable. Eventually, she nodded. "I can."

"And don't lose sight of the fact that part of Elizabeth lives on in her, just as part of her remains with Elizabeth. They are, essentially, two sides of the same coin."

Charlotte considered that for a moment. "I guess you're saying that my daughter has changed, but she is still my daughter."

"Exactly."

Remorse filled Charlotte. "I sent her away. She came to talk to me, and in my grief, I sent her away."

Gertrude smiled. "She is a loving, forgiving woman. Reach out and she'll return."

Chapter 29

Elsie was thrilled when, after recovering from her initial shock, Charlotte reached out to her that evening.

"I'm sorry I hurt you this afternoon, darling. It was hard news to hear. But she is living a life she chose with a man she loves. I could not wish more for her than that." Charlotte sighed. "Is living? I guess I should say lived. Her life ended centuries ago."

"I don't think of it that way," said Elsie. "If I've learned nothing else, it's that time is not linear. After all, Gertrude can pop back and forth between us. Maybe it's easier to think of her as just being somewhere else."

She and Gabe had dinner with Charlotte the next evening to discuss the best way to handle Elizabeth's father.

"Maybe we should all go to Baltimore this weekend," said Charlotte.

Gabe's brows drew together. "We could, but I think if we hope to have him accept that Elizabeth may never recover her memories, perhaps he should come here. That way, we can set up a meeting with Dr. Rose and perhaps Mrs. Sinclair."

"A meeting with Jo Sinclair? Why?"

While Aldous Sinclair preferred that no one ever knew he had used the pocket watch, they agreed that if necessary, Elsie could tell Charlotte that Jo had. The fact that Jo was Elsie's mother would remain a secret—at least for now.

"Were you aware that Mrs. Sinclair once suffered profound retrograde amnesia?"

Charlotte nodded absently. "Vaguely. But that was from a head injury not a fugue. I understand that fugues generally resolve. I think James would see these as two entirely different situations."

Elsie looked at her pointedly.

"You don't mean…are you saying Jo Sinclair…?"

Her point made, Elsie smiled. "I'm saying she once suffered profound retrograde amnesia *from which she never recovered.*"

Gabe nodded. "If the goal is to help Dr. Quinn accept that Elizabeth's memories will not return, we may have an easier time of it with both Dr. Rose and Mrs. Sinclair available. I fear the harder part will be telling him Elsie and I are engaged."

Charlotte nodded. "You're right on both counts, but it must be done. I'll call him this evening."

Elsie took a deep breath. "I think I should call him."

"Are you sure, darling?"

"I'm sure…Mom." Elsie had avoided ever calling Charlotte *Mom*, but she and Gabe had discussed it and agreed that had to change. In private, the Sinclairs were Mama and Da. Elsie needed to begin thinking of Charlotte and James Quinn as Mom and Dad.

Charlotte took her hand and simply said, "Thank you."

When Elsie and Gabe returned to the apartment, Elsie sat at the table staring at the phone trying to gather her courage.

"Elsie, you can't just sit there. The phone isn't going to dial itself."

"I know." Still, she didn't reach for it.

"Charlotte said she would call him."

"I know, but it's better if I do."

"Then you have to put on your big girl panties and do it."

"My *big girl panties*?"

"It means to find your courage and do the mature, adult thing. Call your dad."

"Okay," Elsie said resolutely.

"Good," he said, before leaning down to her ear and

whispering, "And when you're done, I'll take off your panties and do another mature, adult thing."

"That's certainly incentive."

Elsie picked up the phone and dialed.

"Hello?"

"Hi, Dad."

"Elizabeth. Is something wrong, darling?"

"No. I just wanted to talk to you."

There was a brief pause. "I...I'm sorry I upset you when you were in the hospital. I...I would have been happier if you'd agreed to come here, but I handled it badly."

"It's okay, Dad. I was so confused that day. The only thing that felt real to me was Gabe. I needed him. I probably needed you too, but he was my lifeline and I thought you wanted rid of him."

"I did."

"Dad, I love him. I did years ago, I did that day, and I do now."

"I know, darling. Your mom has been keeping me updated."

"So you're okay with it?"

There was another longer pause.

"Dad?"

"Elizabeth, I'm not sure any father immediately believes the man his daughter loves is worthy of her. But I cannot deny he stepped up to the plate and chose to take care of you when I turned my back."

"So you're okay with it?"

"No...but I expect I will be someday."

Elsie smiled. "Would you come up to New York this weekend?"

"You don't want to come home and see if it jogs any memories?"

"Nothing has jogged any memories, Dad. That's one reason I want you to come up here, so we can talk to Dr.

Rose."

"Dr. Rose. I did a little research on him."

Elsie was worried about what was coming next, but she didn't interrupt.

"It turns out that he is one of the world's leading experts on non-traumatic memory loss."

"I didn't know that, but it doesn't surprise me. He has been really helpful."

"Okay. I'll come up in the morning. See if Dr. Rose is available sometime after noon."

She smiled at the curt order. "Sure."

"If I'm flying up there tomorrow, I have things I need to do. Goodnight, Elizabeth."

"Goodnight, Dad."

She hung up the phone.

Gabe smiled at her. "That wasn't too bad, was it?"

"No. However, you should know, he doesn't think you're worthy of me."

Gabe shrugged. "I'm probably not, so I suppose it's fair."

"What do you mean?"

"Well, my dad adores you, and he has from the moment he met you. But Italian mothers rarely believe any woman is worthy of their son. My mom will take more convincing."

She nodded sagely. "I expect I should start on that right away."

"That's a good idea. We should go down sometime this week anyway to tell them about the engagement."

"We should, but we don't have to wait until then."

"What do you mean?"

"Your mom would be much happier if we don't sleep together until we are married."

He laughed. "No, I don't think we want her that happy."

She raised an eyebrow. "You're sure?"

"Positive."

"Then I guess we can get to the taking-my-panties-off part of the evening.

"With pleasure." He scooped her up in his arms and carried her to the bedroom.

Epilogue

Elsie had trouble taking her eyes off the window even though there was nothing to see. "I can't believe I'm actually flying."

Gabe chuckled. "So you've said. Many times."

Elsie blushed. "I know. I'm sorry. It is just so hard to believe."

Gabe kissed her. "Sweetheart, you can say it as many times as you wish. One of the things that has delighted me from the moment we reconnected is the unbridled enthusiasm you show for things you enjoy."

She grinned slyly. "You mean like this?" Putting a hand behind his neck, she pulled him down to her lips for a deep, passionate kiss. He ran a hand over the delicate fabric of her blouse, stopping to caress one breast and tease it to a firm peak even under her bra. She arched into his hand, reveling in his touch.

When she broke the kiss, he smiled and tucked a stray lock of hair behind her ear. "Just like that. But I should probably warn you, engaging in this sort of behavior on an airplane would normally be frowned upon."

"Will you admit that letting my da give us the use of his private jet for our honeymoon was a good idea?"

"Yes, I'll admit that. I know you are not like either set of your parents where money is concerned, but it does make me a little uncomfortable from time to time."

"A *little* uncomfortable?" When they first started discussing wedding plans, Gabe balked at the lavish affair Charlotte and James wanted to hold at the Engineer's Club in Baltimore. Elsie feared all-out war would ensue between Gabe and her dad. Jo Sinclair, Elsie's matron of honor, provided gentle support, convincing the Quinns to hold the reception at an equally wonderful, but perhaps less ostentatious, venue near Gabe's parents' home. The sculpture garden was perfect.

"We understand your concerns," Jo had assured them privately.

"You don't want to appear to be showing off or creating a situation that might make your friends and family feel uncomfortable," added Aldous.

"I hate to sound shallow or ungrateful, but you're right," said Gabe.

Aldous nodded. "I've learned that subtlety is often a wiser approach. The natural setting of the sculpture garden feels simpler and isn't an obvious show of wealth."

"I'm glad you understand."

Elsie smiled at this memory. What neither of them knew at the time—and Gabe still didn't know—was that the sculpture garden had been booked by another couple ages in advance. The Sinclairs bought out the wedding party by completely paying for their weddings at another fabulous venue after all parties signed non-disclosure agreements, of course. The other bride simply couldn't contain herself, broke the agreement, contacted Elsie, and gushed about how wonderful the Sinclairs were. Elsie thought it better to pretend she didn't know.

Once Gabe had been confident that the Sinclairs understood his position, he said, "It isn't that I don't appreciate their desire to give us a wonderful wedding."

"Of course not," agreed Jo.

"And yet you want Elsie to have a memorable wedding. This solution gives you that," said Aldous.

"Exactly," said Gabe.

With a confident smile, Aldous had moved in for the kill. "That's exactly why Jo and I are keeping things very low-key. Our wedding gift to you is the use of our private jet to fly to your honeymoon."

Gabe had been flabbergasted. "You can't be serious. You think a private jet is *low-key*?"

"Of course it is. Your friends and family won't have any idea how you are getting to Italy. For all they know, you'll be flying coach on a commercial airline."

"I'm sorry, sir, that's just...no, we can't accept it, but thank you."

"Gabe, you just agreed you wanted the experience to be memorable without appearing too grandiose."

"Yes, sir, I did, but—"

"There is no but. A private jet is both memorable and, as the name suggests, private." Before Gabe could offer another argument, Aldous added. "Don't forget, this isn't about you and your wants. It's about our desire to have a hand in the wedding of a daughter who we can't publically acknowledge. Do you realize how my heart will ache when James Quinn escorts *my daughter* down the aisle? Would you deny me this small opportunity to do something wonderful for her because of *your* pride?"

"No, sir."

"Then to ensure a spectacular honeymoon for the woman you love, you'll accept our private gifts with grace."

"I...yes. Thank you."

Her da was very good at this. Elsie was fully cognizant of the "s" at the end of the word *gifts*, but was certain Gabe had missed it at the time. She had no idea what else her parents might have done, but she was certain it didn't stop with the use of the jet. At the moment, she was simply glad Gabe had given in.

"Okay, I was more than a little uncomfortable at first."

Elsie became serious. "I know that. But you must know, neither set of my parents do what they do because they think less of you. Dad finally came around after he spent time with you. He loves that you are a doctor," she gave him a sidelong glance, "even if you're not a surgeon. The Sinclairs will always be grateful because you convinced me to stay."

"You're right."

"Of course I'm right. All you have to do to keep both sets of my parents happy is to allow them to indulge me once in a while. I have a much harder road ahead of me with your mom."

"You're kidding, right? My mom adores you."

"No, she doesn't."

"Yeah, she does. You became Catholic."

"I was already Catholic."

"But not on paper."

"God doesn't care about paper."

"But my mother does. We've been through this."

"Yes we have, and all I can say is that it's a good thing Joe is a priest and he believed us when we told him about the pocket watch. Otherwise, I wouldn't have gotten the paperwork until next Easter. Still, my becoming Catholic on paper didn't suddenly make her love me."

"It started the ball rolling. Asking her to teach you how to cook went a long way, too."

"Who wouldn't want to learn to cook like that?"

Gabe chuckled. "How could my mother not love an attitude like that?"

"Well, she seems awfully critical for someone who you think likes me."

"She criticizes all of us. Do you not pay any attention? That's her way of saying *I love you*. If she didn't love you, she'd treat you like a guest."

He shifted into an imitation of his mother's voice. "Joseph, how many times do I have to tell you, get a haircut? Luke, you're a slob. At least get your clothes *near* the hamper. Tony, what, you can't come home once in a while for Sunday dinner? Angela, you want a good man

Ceci Giltenan

like your father, you've gotta be able to feed him. *Elizabeth* is already a much better cook than you and she's not even Italian. Dominic, when are you gonna stop dating every floozy with a tight skirt and fake boobs that crosses your path and settle down with a nice girl like *Elizabeth*? You better treat her like a princess Gabriel, or I'll have to knock some sense into you."

Elsie stared at him for a moment. "She said those things?"

"Yeah, she did. You have a big heart, and you're hard not to like."

Elsie smiled.

"So, *principessa*, were you happy with the way the wedding turned out?"

"I loved it." She chuckled, remembering how one of the altar servers, a thirteen-year-old neighbor of the Soldanis, absolutely gushed. "Didn't you hear? *It was perfect, absolutely perfect. Perfect in every way: the weather was perfect, the flowers were perfect, the blue dresses were perfect. It was just perfect.*"

Gabe chuckled too. "Yeah, Maggie Mitchell mentioned that to me once or twice or fifteen times."

"I have to agree. It was perfect in every way." Elsie sighed and turned to look out the window again. "I still can't believe I'm flying. How high in the air are we?"

"I understand private jets cruise at 41,000 feet or higher."

"How far is that?"

"It's over seven miles, close to eight."

"You're kidding."

"I'm not kidding. But that does remind me of something. We have the perfect opportunity to join the *mile-high club*."

"What's that?"

"Oh, my innocent little wife, one joins the *mile-high club* by having sex in an airplane."

She grinned. "I think I definitely want to be a member of that club."

~ * ~

The Grand Canal, Venice
July 9, 2006

Their honeymoon was supposed to be a quick trip to Italy, but about a month before the wedding, Gabe had been offered a position in a suburban pediatric practice. He negotiated a late August start date so that he and Elsie could have time to find a place to live, move, get married, and take an extended holiday. They flew to Rome and spent two weeks touring Italy, winding up in Venice. They would soon be boarding a ship for a fourteen-day cruise of the Adriatic. When they returned, the Sinclairs' private jet would take them to Scotland for another eight days before they flew home.

At every planned stop, their hotel rooms had been upgraded to the best available, and he suspected it would be no different on the cruise ship. These upgrades had Aldous Sinclair's hand all over them, but Gabe didn't complain. Beside the fact that it would do no good, his medieval wife, who, before she awoke in NYUHC, had never ventured farther than the village in which she was born, was having a marvelous time, which meant he was having marvelous time. Her enthusiasm was infectious.

As they rode the water-taxi to the cruise terminal, her joyful face watched the sights of the Grand Canal go by. Enthralled with his beautiful wife, Gabe took in fewer of the sights around him. He noticed instantly when her brows drew together as they neared the Rialto Bridge.

"Elsie, what is it?" he asked as his head turned in the direction she was looking.

"There near the bridge. Is that…it can't be."

"What, sweetheart?"

"That looks like Gertrude, there on the steps."

He caught a brief glimpse of a sharply dressed older woman who could have been Gertrude, but a group of people stepped in front of her, blocking his view. He craned his head to try to get a better look at the woman before the taxi went under the bridge. At the last minute, the people moved and he saw her.

"It is Gertrude," Elsie exclaimed.

She looked directly at them, waved, blew them a kiss, and in true Gertrude style, simply disappeared.

About The Author

Ceci started her career as an oncology nurse at a leading research hospital, and eventually became a successful medical writer. In 1991 she married a young Irish carpenter who she met when his brother married her dear friend. They raised their family in central New Jersey but now live with their dogs and birds in paradise, also known as southwest Florida. After a rewarding career in the pharmaceutical industry, she is thrilled to simply put her feet up and write "happily ever afters."

Her bestselling, Duncurra series, Highland Solution, Highland Courage, and Highland Intrigue are available as e-books, audiobooks, and paperbacks. There are also inspirational versions of each of these which close the bedroom door. Ceci will be continuing this series in the near future.

The Fated Hearts series begins with Ceci's novella Highland Revenge (originally appearing in Highland Winds, The Scrolls of Cridhe – Volume 1) and continues with Highland Echoes and Highland Angels.

The Pocket Watch Chronicles were actually born in the early eighties, when Ceci was in college when she first wrote *The Pocket Watch*. The series now includes *The Midwife*, *Once Found*, and *The Christmas Present*. The fifth book in the collection, *The Choice* will be released early in 2017.

The Pocket Watch Chronicles

If you enjoyed Once Found,
read Elizabeth's side of the story in:

The Midwife: The Pocket Watch Chronicles

Can a twenty-first century independent woman find her
true destiny, in thirteenth century Scotland?

At his father's bidding, Cade MacKenzie begs a favor from
Laird Macrae—Lady MacKenzie desperately needs the
renowned Macrae midwife. Laird Macrae has no intention
of sending his clan's best, instead he passes off Elsie, a
young woman with little experience, as the midwife they
seek.

But fate—in the form of a mysterious older woman and an
extraordinary pocket watch—steps in.

Elizabeth Quinn, a disillusioned obstetrician, is transported
to the thirteenth century. She switched souls with Elsie as
the old woman said she would but other things don't go
quite as expected. Perhaps most unexpected was falling in
love.

Once Found

More Pocket Watch Chronicles:

The Pocket Watch:

When Maggie Mitchell, is transported to the thirteenth century Highlands will Laird Logan Carr help mend her broken heart or put it in more danger than before?

Generous, kind, and loving, Maggie nearly always puts the needs of others first. So when a mysterious elderly woman gives her an extraordinary pocket watch, telling her it's a conduit to the past, Maggie agrees to give the watch a try, if only to disprove the woman's delusion.

But it works.

Maggie finds herself in the thirteenth century Scottish Highlands, with a handsome warrior who clearly despises her. Her tender soul is caught between her own desire and the disaster she could cause for others. Will she find a way to resolve the trouble and return home within the allotted sixty days? Or will someone worthy earn her heart forever?

The Christmas Present

Faced with an empty nest, and heartbroken, Anita Lewis is given the chance to experience Christmas in another time with the help of a mysterious old woman and a pocket watch.

The gift she receives is priceless as she rediscovers the magic of Christmas in the past.

More from Ceci Giltenan

The Fated Hearts Series

Highland Revenge

Does he hate her clan enough to visit his vengeance on her? Or will he listen to her secret and his own heart's yearning?

Hatred lives and breathes between medieval clans who often don't remember why feuds began in the shadowed past.

But Eoin MacKay remembers.

He will never forget how he was treated by Bhaltair MacNicol—the acting head of Clan MacNicol. He was lucky to escape alive, and vows to have revenge.

Years later, as laird of Clan MacKay, he gets his chance when he captures Lady Fiona MacNicol. His desire for revenge is strong but he is beguiled by his captive.

Can he forget his stubborn hatred long enough to listen to the secret she has kept for so long? And once he knows the truth, can he show her she is not alone and forsaken? In the end, is he strong enough to fight the combined hostilities and age-old grudges that demand he give her up?

Highland Echoes

Love echoes.

Grace Breive is strong and independent because she has to be. She has a wee daughter to care for and, having lost her parents and husband, has no one else on whom she can rely. Driven from the only home she has ever known, she travels to Castle Sutherland to find a grandmother she never knew she had.

As Laird Sutherland's heir, Bram Sutherland understands his obligation to enter into a political marriage for the good of the clan, but he is captivated by the beautiful and resilient young mother.

Will Bram and Grace follow the dictates of their hearts, or will echoes from the past force them apart?

Highland Angels

Anna MacKay fears the MacLeods. Andrew MacLeod fears love.

Anna, angry with her brother, took a walk to cool her temper. She had no intention of venturing so close to MacLeod territory—until she saw a wee lad fall through the ice.

Andrew becomes enraged when it appears the MacKay lass has abducted his son, his last precious connection to the wife he lost—until he learns the truth. Anna, risked her life to save his beloved child.

Now there is a chance to end the generations old hate and fear between their clans.

Fate connects them. The desire for peace binds them. Will a rival tear them apart?

Highland Solution

Laird Niall MacIan needs Lady Katherine Ruthven's dowry to relieve his clan's crushing debt but he has no intention of giving her his heart in the bargain.

Niall MacIan, a Highland laird, desperately needs funds to save his impoverished clan. Lady Katherine Ruthven, a lowland heiress, is rumored to be "unmarriageable" and her uncle hopes to be granted her title and lands when the king sends her to a convent.

King David II anxious to strengthen his alliances sees a solution that will give Ruthven the title he wants, and MacIan the money he needs. Laird MacIan will receive Lady Katherine's hand along with her substantial dowry and her uncle will receive her lands and title.

Lady Katherine must forfeit everything in exchange for a husband who does not want to be married and believes all women to be self-centered and deceitful.

Can the lovely and gentle Katherine mend his heart and build a life with him or will he allow the treachery of others to destroy them?

Highland Courage

Her parents want a betrothal, but Mairead MacKenzie can't get married without revealing her secret and no man will wed her once he knows.

Plain in comparison to her siblings and extremely reserved, Mairead has been called "MacKenzie's Mouse" since she was a child. No one knows the reason for her timidity and she would just as soon keep it that way. When her parents arrange a betrothal to Laird Tadhg Matheson she is horrified. She only sees one way to prevent an old secret from becoming a new scandal.

Tadhg Matheson admires and respects the MacKenzies. While an alliance with them through marriage to Mairead would be in his clan's best interest, he knows Laird MacKenzie seeks a closer alliance with another clan. When Tadhg learns of her terrible shyness and her youngest brother's fears about her, Tadhg offers for her anyway.

Secrets always have a way of revealing themselves. With Tadhg's unconditional love, can Mairead find the strength and courage she needs to handle the consequences when they do?

Highland Intrigue

Lady Gillian MacLennan's clan needs a leader, but the last person on earth she wants as their laird is Fingal Maclan.

She can neither forgive nor forget that his mother killed her father, and, by doing so, created Clan MacLennan's current desperate circumstances.

King David knows a weak clan, without a laird, can change quickly from a simple annoyance to a dangerous liability, and he cannot ignore the turmoil. The MacIan's owe him a great debt, so when he makes Fingal MacIan laird of clan MacLennan and requires that he marry Lady Gillian, Fingal is in no position to refuse.

In spite of the challenge, Fingal is confident he can rebuild her clan, ease her heartache and win her affection. However, just as love awakens, the power struggle takes a deadly turn. Can he protect her from the unknown long enough to uncover the plot against them? Or will all be lost, destroying the happiness they seek in each other's arms?

Other Titles from Duncurra

New York Times Bestselling Author
Kathryn Lynn Davis

Highland Awakening

Can the transforming power of magic help two people on a perilous journey create a miracle—even when one of them doesn't believe?

Since she lost her brother and nearly her father, Esmé Rose fears the world beyond her family and her garden. But one year when winter clings overlong, a dream begins to haunt her, forcing her to take a journey and face a challenge more difficult than she could ever imagine.

Magnus MacLeod is a skilled healer, always curious to know more. He, too, is called by a dream he doesn't quite believe in, despite its physical effects on him. He and Esmé travel a treacherous road that takes them to a magical place. There they must put aside their feelings for one another— and their difference in beliefs—long enough to make a miracle.

Sing to Me of Dreams

One woman's journey of discovery...through all the mysteries of the human heart.

As a child, Saylah held the magic and wisdom of her Salish Indian people. But when tragedy ravages the Salish, she must leave them for the world of the Ivys – an English/Scottish family whose traditions are as strange to her as her spirit world is to them. The Ivys have come to fertile British Columbia in search of paradise, but the secrets and mysteries surrounding them are overwhelming – until Saylah comes to help them understand the darkness holding them back.

Frustrated Julian Ivy, in whom sophistication and fury entwine, is drawn to Saylah's healing strength and disquieting beauty. Through sorrow and elation, the two discover the fullness of love...but no one can resolve for her the contradictions of her birthright. Following the songs of her heritage, she will finally make the most wrenching choice of all...

Internationally bestselling author:
Lily Baldwin

Jack: A Scottish Outlaw

Freedom is not won...it is stolen

Jack MacVie and his brother are thieves, robbing English nobles on the road north into Scotland. They're about to attack the Redesdale carriage when another band of villains, after more than Lady Redesdale's coin, sweeps down and steals their prize. Despite his hatred for the English, Jack's conscience forces him to kidnap the lady to save her life.

In the aftermath of the Berwick massacre, Lady Isabella Redesdale's world is shattered. Her mother is dead, her father lost to grief, and she's risking it all, journeying north into war-torn Scotland to be with her sister.

Although they come from different worlds, Jack and Isabella are more alike than they first realize. They both crave freedom from war and despair, but in a world where kings reign and birth dictates one's station, freedom is not won, it is stolen.

Quinn: A Scottish Outlaw

He is an outlaw...And the only man she can trust.

Quinn MacVie is in pursuit of a prize, but it is unlike any plunder he has stolen before. He seeks neither gold nor jewels, but something infinitely more valuable—Lady Catarina Ravensworth. Sent by the lady's sister, who fears Catarina is in danger, Quinn's mission is to steal the lady away from Ravensworth castle. But nothing there is as Quinn expected.

Lady Catarina has been accused of a horrific crime and is forced to run or face a fate worse than death.

But she is not alone.

Thief and Scottish rebel, Quinn MacVie, is at her side. With a price on her head, they must disappear into the wilds of the Scottish Highlands where the only thing greater than the danger following at their heels is the desire burning in their hearts.

Rory: A Scottish Outlaw

Lady Alexandria MacKenzie is one of Abbot Matthew's network of rebels, fighting for Scottish independence. When her father dies, leaving their clan without a laird, she asks the abbot for aid in finding a husband. He sends her a selection of three noblemen from which to choose. Accompanying them is secret agent and reputed rake, Rory MacVie, who must assist Alexandria with a perilous mission for Scotland. But the abbot makes one point very clear--Rory is not a potential suitor.

This is a passionate story of honor, rebellion, and forbidden love.

Stephanie Joyce Cole

Compass North

Can you ever run away from your own life?

Reeling from the shock of a suddenly shattered marriage, Meredith flees as far from her home in Florida as she can get without a passport: to Alaska.

After a freak accident leaves her presumed dead, she stumbles into a new identity and a new life in a quirky small town. Her friendship with a fiery and temperamental artist and her growing worry for her elderly, cranky landlady pull at the fabric of her carefully guarded secret. When a romance with a local fisherman unexpectedly blossoms, Meredith struggles to find a way to meld her past and present so that she can move into the future she craves. But someone is looking for her, someone who will threaten Meredith's dream of a reinvented life.

MJ Platt

Somewhere Montana

Can Callum "Mac" Maclain make Sage Burnett believe in his love for her and save her from her stalker?

Escaping from a stalker, Sage Burnett crashes her plane on a mountain, part of the ranch owned by the man who rejected her eight years ago. She still loves him and prays he isn't around because she dreads facing him to only have him reject her again.

Callum "Mac" MacLain, the ranch owner, a Marine home on medical leave rescues her from the mountain. He persuades her to stay until she heals. He realizes he is still in love with her. Can he save her from her stalker and convince her his love is real?

Ford Murphy

Taking the Town

Lissadown, Ireland 1986.

A ruthless, violent criminal gang has held the small midlands town in its grip for too long.

Innocents have been maimed, raped, killed.

Law enforcement is paralyzed.

Finn Lane has had enough. A newcomer to Lissadown and an expert MMA fighter, Finn can't be intimidated. Keeping his head down and minding his own business is not an option. The gang may think they own the town and everyone in it but those days are coming to an end.

He will have vengeance...

Look for exciting new titles from Duncurra in 2017!

Made in the USA
Charleston, SC
28 January 2017